ROGUE AVENGER

ROGUE AVENGER

JOHN R. HINDINGER

iUniverse, Inc.
New York Lincoln Shanghai

Rogue Avenger

Copyright © 2007 by John R. Hindinger

All rights reserved. No part of this book may be used or reproduced by any means, graphic, electronic, or mechanical, including photocopying, recording, taping or by any information storage retrieval system without the written permission of the publisher except in the case of brief quotations embodied in critical articles and reviews.

iUniverse books may be ordered through booksellers or by contacting:

iUniverse
2021 Pine Lake Road, Suite 100
Lincoln, NE 68512
www.iuniverse.com
1-800-Authors (1-800-288-4677)

Because of the dynamic nature of the Internet, any Web addresses or links contained in this book may have changed since publication and may no longer be valid.

This is a work of fiction. All of the characters, names, incidents, organizations, and dialogue in this novel are either the products of the author's imagination or are used fictitiously.

ISBN: 978-0-595-47203-1 (pbk)
ISBN: 978-0-595-70887-1 (cloth)
ISBN: 978-0-595-91483-8 (ebk)

Printed in the United States of America

CHAPTER ONE

Olivia leapt from Jean-Claude.

"Aye! I hope you are not that rough with my clients," he said in French.

She rolled off the bed and worked bra straps over her shoulders.

"No," she said. "I treat your clients well. You gave me only the gentlemen."

"I wish I had to share you with no one."

She slid her panty hose up her legs and reached for a blue satin evening gown.

"Consider yourself lucky I sleep with you at all."

"How would it appear if my top lady ignored me?"

"Top lady? You've only known me five weeks."

He strolled to the bathroom. She heard him flush his condom into the Parisian sewer system and splash water from the rushing faucet. He returned and grabbed her waist.

"You are a truly magnificent woman," he said. "Leave the CIA and stay with me. I will triple your salary, whatever it is."

Olivia teased herself with the idea until she could flush the greed from her mind.

"We've got a bad guy to catch," she said.

*

Olivia reached for the sleeve of Jean-Claude's Armani suit and followed him onto the Parisian streets. She had become accustomed to appearing graceful while laboring against four-inch heels but stumbled as she turned from the setting sun.

"Easy," he said as he steadied her.

"I'm fine," she said.

She followed Jean-Claude around a corner, and a black limousine stopped at the curb.

Jean-Claude opened the door and she slid in ahead of the pimp. Her team leader and CIA agent, Gerald Rickets, sat across from her.

Even sitting, Rickets looked large. He filled a gray suit that spanned half the back seat. His deep black eye brows furrowed as he scowled at Jean-Claude.

"You're set for tomorrow?" Rickets asked in English.

"Yes," Jean-Claude said in a Parisian accent. "I will escort Marko to the second floor lounge to close the deal. I told him that his cash is in my safe behind my upstairs bar. He will suspect nothing."

"How many men is he bringing?" Rickets asked.

"How should I know?"

Rickets extended a thick finger at Jean-Claude's nose.

"Don't get flippant with me, pimp."

"I prefer the term 'man of leisure.'"

"You're scum to me," Rickets said, "The only reason I haven't had you shut down is that I need you. After we're done with Marko, if I hear of an American tourist getting so much as a genital wart from one of your whores, I'll become your worst nightmare."

"Marko's been selling his girls across Europe for years," Jean-Claude said. "You didn't find him so offensive until he started shipping to the United States."

"I didn't have jurisdiction until he starting pushing his girls in America. You just follow my plan, and if one hair on her head gets hurt, I'll hang you by your balls."

Jean-Claude looked at Olivia and smiled.

"I would hang myself if I were to let harm come to such a lovely creature."

"You better see that it goes down clean," Rickets said. "If I don't get a takedown signal forty-five minutes after Marko walks through your door, I'm busting in with half of the Parisian police force."

"What of it? You've already threatened to send half of my ladies back to Eastern Europe."

"You bought slaves. Deal with the consequences."

Olivia moved aside as Jean-Claude leaned forward.

"Listen to me, you self-righteous bastard," Jean-Claude said. "I rescued slaves. Any lady who wishes to leave me may do so, but I treat them well, offer them protection, and pay them more than they ever imagined. Those in my employ will laugh in your face if you offer them your version of freedom."

"We'll see how your attitude changes tomorrow."

"My attitude will be better. I will be rid of your constant threat to shut me down, and I will have earned the favor of this lovely woman you sent to tempt me."

Olivia blushed.

"Get out," Rickets said.

Jean-Claude stepped out and slammed the door.

"Why are you so tough on him?" Olivia asked.

"I don't trust pimps," Rickets said.

"He's not a bad guy."

"You're in character too deep," Rickets said. "Rookie mistake. You get a few undercover ops under your belt and you'll know the difference. Until then, watch yourself."

"I'm not scared."

"Rookie mistake number two. Just remember your training and go nail me a slave trafficker."

*

The next day, Olivia held Jean-Claude by the sleeve of a pinstriped Armani suit. She saw a red leather glove grasping his other arm and followed tan skin to the bare shoulder of the pimp's favorite whore, Danielle.

Danielle wore her brunette hair in a bun with curls reaching to either pronounced cheekbone. Olivia thought that in her red satin evening gown, the brunette whore resembled a demon seductress. Danielle met Olivia's glare, exposed capped teeth, and flared her nostrils in a smirk.

Olivia looked away. Her arrival five weeks ago, albeit undercover, had made the brunette whore jealous. Olivia wished Danielle were elsewhere, but Jean-Claude without a lady by either side would arouse suspicion.

Olivia heard a thud from a metal door. One of Jean-Claude's bodyguards stepped to the door, slid a bar aside, and glanced through a peephole. He slid the bar closed, turned to the pimp, and nodded.

"Well," Jean-Claude said in French, "our guests are right on time. Won't you let them in?"

The bodyguard opened the door, and Olivia was disappointed to see only one man—a man too tall to be Marko—march toward the pimp. His boots clapped against the hardwood floor.

The man brushed back shoulder-length blond hair, removed his sunglasses, and slipped them into the breast pocket of his trench coat.

"Pavlo," Jean-Claude said in English. "It is a pleasure to see you again. You are not alone, I trust."

Olivia's disappointment became discomfort as Pavlo let his gaze settle on her.

"I do not remember this whore," Pavlo said in a Ukrainian accent.

"I have suppliers of talent other than your boss. Tell me, is he here? I wish to make his acquaintance."

"Send your bodyguards away."

"Away? Where should I send them?"

"I don't care," Pavlo said. "Send them to the fucking grocery store if you want your new whores. Marko didn't come here to have guns pointed at him."

"Impossible," Jean-Claude said.

"Then we'll distribute our girls elsewhere," Pavlo said and turned away.

Olivia clenched Jean-Claude's sleeve and nodded toward a black marble countertop.

"Drinks?" Jean-Claude asked. "We should drink to failure?"

"No," Olivia said. "Lock their guns in the cabinets below the bar."

"Wait," Jean-Claude said in English. "But where are my manners? I'm sure I could bend my rules for Marko, provided that we lock your firearms behind my bar."

Pavlo raised a wireless phone to his cheek and exchanged words in Ukrainian. He lowered the phone, reached into his pocket, and withdrew a Glock pistol. He extended the handle to the pimp.

"My dear," Jean-Claude said and nodded at Danielle.

Danielle frowned but accepted the pistol and walked towards the bar. She sneered at Olivia as she passed.

"I will return with the guns from my colleagues," Pavlo said, "and give them to you. Then send your guards away, and I will let my colleagues in."

"As you wish," Jean-Claude said.

Pavlo exited and returned with three weapons that he handed to Danielle for storage. The pimp's two bodyguards left the establishment as Pavlo surveyed the room, lifted his phone to his cheek, and spoke again in Ukranian.

A loud thump sounded from the door, Pavlo opened it, and three men walked in. Other than briefcases and darker shades of hair, two of the men were clones of Pavlo, but the third man caught Olivia's eye.

He was shorter and barrel-chested. Combed forward, his coarse gray hair contrasted with the ruddiness of his face. She smelled the sharp, spicy sweet scent of his cologne but wasn't close enough to recognize the brand. The shape of his head reminded Olivia of a melon as he smiled.

"Jean-Claude," he said, "it is good to meet you."

Olivia released the pimp's sleeve as he accepted Marko's hand.

"Marko, I presume?" Jean-Claude said.

"I wanted to finally meet the man who has purchased thirty-four women from me. My top French client."

Olivia glanced at Jean-Claude's breast pocket and trusted that the microphone and transmitter embedded in his wireless phone had relayed Marko's incriminating statement to the surveillance team across the street.

"The honor is mine," Jean-Claude said. "This calls for drinks. What should we serve, my dear? Cabernet? Merlot? Perhaps something stronger?"

Olivia recognized Jean-Claude's question as a veiled request for confirmation of Marko's identification.

The Ukrainian's face matched her memory of the photographs in his dossier. His height appeared correct at five feet, nine inches, and his confident appearance and direct manner of speech matched his psychological profile. The coldness of his eyes suggested a monster lurking beneath his skin. She was certain Marko stood before them.

She signaled Jean-Claude—and the surveillance team listening through the pimp's wireless transmitter—by suggesting the Ukrainian's preferred drink.

"Something stronger," she said while overlaying a Parisian accent on her English to suppress her Connecticut nasal twang. "Perhaps, Finlandia vodka?"

Marko raised an eyebrow.

"Your whores have good taste," he said.

He removed his sunglasses and placed them in the breast pocket of a suit that Olivia suspected was an eastern European imitation of an Italian-cut.

"Your club is a bit dark," Marko said, "but I could get used to it. Pavlo's description did not do it justice."

"Black marble on the dance floor and the bar. Booths of black leather," Jean-Claude said. "As you see, I keep the lighting soft and the décor dark. It creates an air of secrecy my clients appreciate."

Marko grabbed Olivia's chin roughly, but she stayed in character and let him leer.

"Had I known how pretty your whores look in your gentleman's club, I would have come long ago. I will have this one before I leave."

Jean-Claude cleared his throat.

"I have reserved some ladies that you yourself sold to me. I think you'll be impressed how good Parisian food can make a woman more full-bodied, like a fine wine. Or if you wish, I have a nice diversity of ladies available."

"Where?" Marko asked and released Olivia's chin.

"I offer private accommodations on the third floor, and I have closed the club until dinner. The afternoon is yours to enjoy, after business, of course."

"Yes," Marko said. "After business."

*

Olivia poured vodka into shot glasses while Danielle held a tray. The brunette avoided Olivia's gaze. Everyone else had gone upstairs except Pavlo, who watched over the locked weapons.

Jean-Claude's voice echoed from a hardwood staircase.

"Make haste, ladies. Never keep a Ukrainian separated from his vodka."

Olivia poured the final shot, and Danielle raised the tray to her shoulder. She smiled, making Olivia uneasy.

The brunette passed her pimp on the staircase.

Olivia joined Jean-Claude and took his arm. The pimp spoke in French.

"What's in the briefcase?" he asked.

Pavlo shrugged.

"Speak English, pimp," he said. "Or Ukrainian, if you know how."

"The briefcase," Jean-Claude said.

While Pavlo opened it and withdrew a laptop computer, the pimp whispered in French.

"He doesn't understand French."

"Right," Olivia said.

"What are you waiting for?" Jean-Claude asked. "He's already admitted to selling me women."

"Women, yes. But I want him for selling juveniles."

"I don't like this. His men are rough, and rumor has it that they carry more diseases than rats. I don't want him touching any of my ladies."

Olivia glanced at her gold Cartier watch.

"They won't. Takedown happens in thirty minutes. Earlier if I give the signal."

"Give it now," he said. "You have enough evidence."

"Do you know where he's keeping his latest shipment?"

"Not yet."

"Then there are twenty women who want us to find out."

*

Olivia followed Jean-Claude into his second-floor lounge, and Pavlo closed the door behind them. Red lighting around the ceiling trim painted rosewood walls sanguine, but a chandelier illuminated the center of the room in white. Chairs and sofas surrounded a glass coffee table.

Gulping vodka, the Ukrainians encircled the table. Behind the small upstairs bar, Danielle piled clean shot glasses on a tray in preparation for the next round. A mirror spanned the wall behind the brunette whore.

In the mirror, Olivia saw herself as a photographic negative of Danielle. Fiery red curls fell to either of her cheeks, and her black dress complemented her fair skin.

Olivia heard empty glasses clanking on the table and Pavlo setting down the laptop. She worked through the men huddling around the monitor to clear the mess and listened for clues about the location of Marko's slaves.

"Here are your women," Marko said. "They are beautiful, yes?"

On the screen, a video camera panned across women in jeans and tee-shirts huddled in a hotel room.

"You warned me they were young," Jean-Claude said. "But half of these are children. That one can hardly be fourteen years old."

"There are men with fetishes," Marko said.

"Not my clients."

"You wish that I sell them to someone else?"

Olivia glared at Jean-Claude. He understood.

"No," he said. "I will find use for them. I'll take them at the agreed upon price."

"Excellent," Marko said. "More drinks, then."

"Right away," Olivia said.

"No," Marko said. "You stay. Send the other."

Olivia sought Jean-Claude's approval, and he nodded.

She watched Danielle depart. When she turned back, she saw Marko withdrawing a knife from his sock and caught a glimpse of Pavlo's fist before it cracked her jaw.

*

A blast awoke Olivia. Naked, she was lying on a couch. Her jaw ached, and Marko was on top of her, pumping. The stink of his sweat soured the spicy sweet scent of his cologne. During a misplaced thought, she recognized it as Drakkar Noir.

Turning her head, she saw Pavlo knocking away a metal block that had been part of Jean-Claude's safe until blown off by plastic explosives.

Pavlo rattled off words in Ukrainian. The anger in his face revealed that he had blown open a steel box containing no cash.

Pain shot through Olivia's mouth as she turned to Marko. His face was a sick mix of sexual ecstasy and anger. Satiated, he dismounted her.

"So, it is true," he said in English. "It is a setup. Hand me the knife. I will kill the CIA bitch myself."

The door burst open. Wearing body armor, Rickets led a team of Parisian police officers into the room. As Marko raised a bloody blade over Olivia, Rickets sent a bullet through his shoulder.

As police swarmed the Ukrainians, Rickets swept a jacket over Olivia.

"I'm so sorry," he said.

"Jerry," she said.

"Don't talk. Medic's coming."

"Did we get him?" she asked.

"Yeah," he said. "While you were unconscious, they gave enough clues for us to find the girls, and there was plenty of incriminating evidence. You got him."

CHAPTER TWO

Jake Slate stared at a pastel violet dress that cupped rounded breasts and cast oblong shadows under the setting summer sun. He shifted his gaze and watched the lady's bare, sleek arm reach to quiet the infant in the cradle by her foot.

As the crying child fell silent, a blur of black whizzed by. Without breaking stride, a man yanked the cradle upward, and the infant was gone.

Jake leapt and knocked wine bottles from a waiter's hands. Racing after a suited man who balanced the cradle under his arm, he rolled his ankle over a cobblestone, braced himself against a startled tourist, and accelerated.

He sprinted under the awning of a corner restaurant, sidestepped a startled elderly couple, and hurdled their Yorkshire terrier. He gained ground on the suited man and followed him around another corner where three oriental men in identical suits blocked his path.

Behind the threesome, the fleeing man shifted the cradle to his other arm and yelled in Mandarin over his shoulder. The threesome converged on Jake.

What the hell is going on? he thought.

Jake lifted his knee and launched his instep at a head. He missed but twisted and drove his heel into a sternum. A suited man staggered back.

One man threw a punch. Jake deflected the arm, shifted to face the third man, but moved late. A kick knocked him to the ground. He couldn't breathe and his ribs ached. He looked up as an assailant returned his foot to the street and smirked.

Dizzy, Jake struggled to his feet. The trio closed in but stopped as the man with the stolen child yelled another command, and the suited men retreated and fled.

Jake winced as he stood and darted down an alley. A woman carrying baguettes gasped and pressed her back against a cracking plaster wall as he sprinted by.

The oriental men disappeared behind a corner café. Jake pursued them onto a main road and found them encircling a black Mercedes. The kidnapper handed the infant to a thin man in a three-piece suit who placed the cradle on the street and folded back his breast pocket to expose a pistol.

"That's close enough," he said.

In his anger, Jake almost blurted his words in English but remembered to employ his southern Provencal French.

"*Pardonnez moi*," he said.

"I know who you are, Mr. Slate."

He knows my name, Jake thought.

"Give me back the child," he said.

"I am sorry," the thin man said. "I cannot."

"If you hurt him," Jake said, "I will hunt you down."

"I do not wish to harm this child."

"What the hell's this about?"

"Insurance."

"What?" Jake asked.

The thin man raised his eyebrows.

"Do you really not know why I must do this?" he asked.

Jake shrugged his shoulders.

"Renard is sly," the man said, "keeping you ignorant, but you can no longer hide from your past. You are both deeply in my debt, and I will only return Renard's child when he has completed his task. Tell him that our negotiations end here."

Dumbfounded, Jake watched the oriental entourage duck into the car and abscond with his friend's son.

*

Standing beside one of the Renard family's limousines, Jake felt guilty for having let their child be taken. After quick coaching from Pierre Renard, he had just lied to the police about failing to get a good look at his assailants, and the cops departed with minimal questioning.

Pierre doesn't own the Avignon police, Jake thought, *but he can rent them when needed.*

Having lost her child, Marie, Renard's wife, had cried herself into exhaustion. She clung to Renard's shoulder.

"It's okay," Renard said. "Get in the car. Henri will take you back to the estate. I will reunite you and little Jacques soon."

As Marie and the limousine left, Renard lit a Marlboro.

"This is not your fault," he said.

"Who did this?" Jake asked.

"Young Li. The acting Taiwanese Minister of Defense. I just spoke to him to verify."

"You just called the guy who kidnapped your only son?"

"He will not harm Jacques," Renard said. "I would have him killed if he did, even though it would cost me my own life. Li knows this, and I just reminded him."

"That would explain the tirade," Jake said. "I've never heard you swear so much."

"Make no mistake, Jake. Li has played his trump card, and I must honor it, but I will make him answer to it."

Renard stamped out his cigarette.

"In fact," he said, "I arranged to have my wife join my son as detainees on a Taiwanese military installation. Much as Li has aggravated me, Marie and Jacques will be safer under his guard."

"Why?"

"I wasn't going to bring you into it," Renard said.

Jake grabbed and scrunched Renard's shirt collar.

"He knew my fucking name, Pierre! I'm in it."

"And he has my fucking son, if you wish to play one-upmanship. Keep your wits about you and let go of me."

Jake released him.

"He knows everything," Renard said. "Certain men in Taiwan's Defense Ministry know our affairs completely."

"You didn't say there were people watching us. The whole world is supposed to think we're dead."

"Use your head, man," Renard said. "I risked everything when I failed to bring them the weapons. The Taiwanese knew everything about me—my client list, my recruits, my aliases. Li believes that we have unfinished business."

"Oh really?" he asked. "Just because we promised nuclear weapons and didn't deliver? Just because we sank the pride of their fleet and made off with a ton of their cash. Why didn't you tell me they were watching us?"

"What would you have done?"

"I would have looked after myself," Jake said.

"If you had strayed from my side, the Taiwanese would have killed you. Your knowledge of our failed operation is a risk. You're alive because they believe I control you."

"So I'm your puppet?" Jake asked.

"You're my protégé, although I fear I can no longer protect you. Or my family, for that matter."

"Why did they take Jacques?"

"To force me to take command of a submarine."

An array of juxtaposed nightmares passed through Jake's head as he sensed his past overtaking him.

"You're kidding," he said.

"Li wants me to clear out Chinese submarines from the Taiwan Straits, especially the *Kilos*, to help break the Chinese blockade."

"That's it?" Jake asked. "Just take a Taiwanese rust bucket against state of the art Chinese diesels?"

"No, a Pakistani *Agosta* class. Taiwan purchased the fourth *Agosta* 90B hull. For speed and secrecy during construction and delivery, they paid quite a premium for it."

"*Agostas* are tough," Jake said.

"I was hesitant to participate, but it seems I now have no choice. I was fooling myself to believe that I could avoid or delay this."

"Li's threatening you," Jake said. "But he also mentioned negotiations. What's your fee for this one?"

"Nothing. After our failed operation in Taiwan, I am in their debt."

"Then what are you negotiating?" Jake asked.

Renard lit another Marlboro.

"Your freedom."

"I am free," Jake said.

"No," Renard said, "you are miserable. I can see that you grow weary of living in secrecy."

"I'm a traitor on the run," Jake said. "What can a guy in the Taiwanese Defense Ministry do about it?"

"Worse crimes than ours have been excused when extenuating circumstances permit. I want Li to broker clemency with the American Justice Department."

The offer hit Jake like the promise of immortality.

"If I drive front line diesel submarines back to China," Renard said, "Taiwan will regain control of its seas, at least temporarily, and America will escape intervention in an undesirable conflict. I can create enough goodwill for both nations to offset that mess we created by leaving a Trident Missile submarine on the ocean floor."

"Wishful thinking," Jake said, "Li has the upper hand."

"Ah, my friend," he said. "You have much to learn about the art of negotiation. He can threaten my family, but what I do with his submarine is ultimately my business. I'll get what I want from that bastard before this is done."

CHAPTER THREE

EGG-CARTON FOAM COATED SOUNDPROOF walls. Olivia lowered her head and listened to her breathing. Since her rape, she disliked being alone.

As she fiddled with a dimmer switch to distract herself from numbing thoughts, a large black man in a gray suit entered the room and smiled.

He looked more important than she had remembered. Perhaps the demeanor came with the promotion, she thought.

"How are you doing?" Rickets asked.

"Fine," she said.

"I'm sorry for what you went through. We all trusted him, but in the end Jean-Claude was just a pimp."

"Talking about it's not going to help me get it out of my mind. At least the parts I remember."

"Your memory's still sketchy?" he asked.

"I'm starting to reconstruct my memory through reoccurring nightmares. I'm not even sure I want to remember."

Olivia had studied psychology at Yale but had never envisioned looking at herself as a victim through an analytical spyglass.

"I suppose you've discussed it enough in your therapy," he said.

"Yes," she said. "Enough for now. The rest of the healing comes with time. I've been meaning to thank you for spending an entire week by my bedside, by the way."

She felt Rickets' hand on her shoulder. The touch was weighty but gentle.

"I didn't spend the entire week," he said.

"Felt like it."

"I put you in front of those animals," he said. "It's my fault you were hurt."

He walked across the room and sat at a small table.

"Are you ready to get back into the field?" he asked.

She felt unsure but feigned confidence.

"Yes."

"Your new assignment will get your mind off things," Rickets said. "You remember the USS *Colorado*?"

"Of course," Olivia said. "A Trident Missile submarine scuttled at sea after a reactor meltdown."

"This is top secret under all submarine and nuclear compartments," Rickets said. "They're even making up a new compartment for it. The *Colorado* was never scuttled."

That caught her attention. She gazed at a plasma screen that invoked a circle surrounded by darkness.

"Slide one," Rickets said. "The USS *Miami* took a still-life through its periscope of the *Colorado* in the Arctic Ocean, just north of the Pacific."

She saw hatches dangling over the *Colorado's* missile deck and men trotting along the superstructure. Black clouds billowed from the *Colorado's* rear escape hatches.

She squinted at zigzag tiger stripes and noticed that mooring lines held a patrol craft beside the *Colorado*.

"That ship looks Swedish or Norwegian," she said.

"It's actually Taiwanese," Rickets said, "but it's based upon the Swedish *Visby* class corvette, only smaller and even more technically advanced. It's the *Tai Chiang*—or at least it was until the *Miami* took it out. It almost made off with the *Colorado's* warheads."

Rickets clicked his remote. A headshot appeared with features she found rugged and handsome. The image wore an American naval officer's dress whites.

"Lieutenant Jacob Slate stole the *Colorado* with a small team of mutineers," Rickets said. "The *Miami's* torpedo took out the *Colorado*, and we thought Slate was dead until we found him in Avignon last week."

The image of Slate standing beside a shapely woman on a sandstone patio appeared.

"Doctor Marie Broyer," Rickets said. "A Board of Trade analyst remembered seeing her with Slate in Chicago before the '*Colorado* Incident'. We trailed her, and it paid off."

"Broyer looks older, but I could see them together."

Rickets clicked to the next slide. A sandstone mansion sprawled through an apple orchard atop a grassy hill overlooking the Rhône River in the south of France.

"They're not lovers," he said. "Broyer lives here with the father of her newborn, Pierre Renard. Renard used Slate to steal the *Colorado*, and now I have evidence that he's up to something with submarines again."

"What sort of evidence?"

"Nearly one billion dollars transferred from Taipei business interests to Islamabad, and then a Pakistani-built *Agosta* class submarine lands in Keelung and joins the Taiwanese order of battle."

"Sounds like an unlikely alliance," she said. "But it's circumstantial if you're fishing for Renard's involvement."

"A front-line *Agosta* is a quantum leap in Taiwanese submarine hardware. They don't have indigenous expertise, and Renard is the most qualified submarine expert on the open market with ties to both countries. He knows the players, and he knows the game."

"So he's a consultant? An instructor?"

"That's what I need you to figure out."

"Me?" Olivia asked. "Why not just bring him in?"

"We've been waiting for him to make a move, but someone just made one on him. His trail saw some orientals kidnap his son, and then Renard just went underground. We've completely lost track of him."

"What about Broyer? Can't you follow her?"

"Gone. We think she was on a helicopter that took off from the Renard estate the night of the kidnapping. He's probably got her in hiding."

Rickets clicked his remote, and the next slide showed the stucco wall of a four-story walkup apartment.

"Slate's apartment," he said.

"He's not in hiding?"

"No. The Renard child is kidnapped, with Slate risking his neck to prevent it from happening, mind you, and then Renard and Broyer disappear. But Slate goes on as if nothing happened. We trailed him to his tai kwon do studio, his gym, and his favorite bar yesterday. He doesn't look like he's going anywhere."

"You think he and Renard had a falling out because of the kidnapping?"

"Not based on the way Renard acted after it," Rickets said. "He was calm—too calm—and he was engaged in an intense conversation with Slate after the incident. It almost looked like they were planning a response to the kidnapping right after it happened. And that's what I want you to find out. I want you to use Slate to find Renard and figure out what he's up to."

Olivia swallowed.

"You didn't forget that I'm HIV positive now?"

"That's why you're perfect for this. The *Colorado*'s captain contracted HIV and knowingly gave it to Slate during an emergency blood transfusion. Revenge was a big part in the '*Colorado* Incident.'"

"How dangerous is he?"

"Third degree black-belt and strong as an ox. But he spared lives when he took the *Colorado*."

He placed his hand on her shoulder again.

"You afraid?"

"A little."

"You should be," he said. "The fear will keep you alert. You're trained for this, and you're damn good. All you did wrong last time was get unlucky."

She felt a spark within her and recognized it as purpose. It tasted better than self-doubt.

"When do I leave?" she asked.

*

Olivia pushed through a throng of HIV-positive young adults. At a sunlit buffet table, she piled wedges of sun-dried tomatoes and Camembert onto baguette slices. She scanned the small apartment for Jake Slate, but a smiling face blocked her view.

"You're new," a man said in French.

"I just began study at the University of Avignon," she said. "I found your group's flier in the lobby and wanted to meet some people."

"Then you've met the most important of the group. My name is Bertraud. I'm the group's president."

"Enchantée, my name is Olivia," she said.

Bertraud was lithe and well groomed. A gold ring and a Rolex watch glimmered as he kissed her hand.

"The pleasure is mine. You have an accent. American, I'd say, although I don't mean to be insulting."

Undercover as an expatriate, she let her Connecticut nasal twang invade her French diphthongs. Any Frenchman would recognize the violation of his native vowel sounds.

"I've been trying to get rid of it," she said.

"No, it's very slight. I only noticed because I have an ear for it. I'm earning my PhD in romance languages."

"Do they make you teach as part of your study?"

"Yes, of course," he said. "If you're studying French Renaissance literature this semester, I will be your instructor."

"I'm just taking a few art classes for fun."

He grinned and stepped closer.

"That's unfortunate," he said. "You would have been my most lovely student."

Olivia made herself blush.

"After some lunch here, will you let me give you a tour of the city?" he asked. "There is so much within these beautiful stone walls that can escape the eye without the proper guide."

She broke eye contact and scanned the room. No sign of Slate, but the energy of the conversations lifted her spirits. It reminded her that HIV wasn't a death sentence.

"I'd enjoy spending time with a man as knowledgeable as you, but perhaps you could introduce me to some of the others first," she said.

"As you wish. We are—how shall I say—a diverse group. Let me introduce you to the right people."

*

Thirty minutes of conversation with academics left Olivia drained. The group's interest in the novelty of an American had waned into the idyllic banter of savants.

Olivia spied a slender man, the apartment's tenant, opening the door. He swept a welcoming arm into the room.

Jake Slate's broad shoulders spanned the doorframe. He grinned and shook hands with the tenant and moved to the buffet table.

Olivia's heartbeat accelerated.

"Who's that, the muscular one?" she asked.

"Oh, him," Bertraud said. "He's been with us for about two years. He's never fit in."

"Looks dangerous," she said.

"Brutish."

"If it weren't for the brutes," Olivia said, "how would a lady recognize a refined man?"

"You are as charming as you are beautiful. May I give you that tour of the city I promised."

"Let me freshen up."

Olivia walked away and shifted her purse over her shoulder. In a fluid motion, she yanked out a stick of lipstick, ran it between her fingers, and dropped it. It smacked hardwood and rolled into the heel of Slate's boots.

Olivia knelt and reached.

"Excuse me," she said.

Slate turned and stooped.

"Let me get it," he said.

Olivia felt anxious as their eyes met, but his smile put her at ease. He was more handsome than his pictures and didn't seem like a criminal capable of a nuclear submarine hijack.

"Thanks," she said and smiled.

"I was hoping you were beautiful," he said in English.

"What?"

"I overheard you talking to Bertraud. He's only interested in the hotties. Now that I see you, I'm not disappointed."

Slate's directness caught Olivia off guard.

"Look, I don't mean to be rude," Jake said. "I just hardly get to speak English with anyone."

"I know what you mean," Olivia said.

They stood and Slate returned the lipstick.

"What's your name?"

"Olivia."

"I'm Jake—Jake Savin. You better get back to Bertraud. He's as jealous as he is arrogant, and we mustn't upset the son of the mayor, now should we?"

"I didn't know I was being bored to death by royalty."

"Another hour with him and you'll believe he's in line for the British throne."

Olivia noticed a slender figure approaching.

"I see that we've made the American connection," Bertraud said in English.

"Pardon your interruption," Jake said. "I was merely helping the lady pick up something she dropped."

"Perhaps you were trying to pick up the lady herself?"

"Things don't need to be dropped to be picked up," Jake said. "Nor do they need to be picked up once dropped. For example, I could drop you to the floor and leave you."

"Violence is the resort of a simple mind. I was going to give Olivia the tour of the city, but perhaps instead you should. I'm sure she'd enjoy learning which back alley walls crack the best when punched."

"Why bother, when you can reproduce Joshua's efforts at Jericho through self-indulgence? If they don't crack from acoustic energy they'll crumble from boredom."

"Olivia," Jake said, "when you need a break from Silverspoons, I'll be here tomorrow for lunch."

Slate left the buffet table.

Not sure I can wait until tomorrow, Olivia thought.

"I'm sorry, Bertraud," she said. "But I'm an American girl. I prefer the brutes."

She marched after Slate.

CHAPTER FOUR

Commander David Roth lowered his hand to the gold chain wrapped around his khaki belt, followed the chain deep into his pocket, and rubbed a gold-plated cross.

In the USS *La Jolla's* Control room, sailors in cotton jumpsuits flowed as a dark blue sea. They sat in front of monitors, streamed phone cords, and stood beside charts that reflected abstract perspectives of a seaborne battle.

"Attention in the Control room," Roth said. "The Japanese tanker convoy is nearing Taiwanese air space. One Chinese destroyer approached the convoy but turned back when challenged by the Taiwanese escort frigates. That makes me believe that the Chinese are awaiting to attack with submarines. That's where we come in."

Men turned their heads to listen better.

"Upon entering Taiwanese air space, the tankers will begin zigzag submarine evasion legs," Roth said. "The escort frigates *Kang Ding* and *Hung La* will reposition ahead of the convoy and begin active sonar searches. The *Kang Ding* and *Hung La* will stay weapons tight on all submerged contacts outside of six miles to avoid friendly fire."

Roth slipped his hands from his pockets and grasped the polished rail that encircled the *La Jolla's* elevated conning area.

"Now listen up, guys," he said. "Our rules of engagement state that we prosecute any submerged contact within fifteen miles of the convoy. We don't have to wait until a weapon is fired to attack. We fire first. I know this ship is old, but you're all capable of fighting her to her best."

"Damn right, sir!" a balding man, a senior chief petty officer said.

Sailors echoed the balding man's sentiments and a chorus of bravado and high fives broke out.

"I appreciate the confidence," Roth said. "But keep your heads in the game. Man battle stations."

*

Commander Roth watched a lanky lieutenant commander slide a sound-powered headset earpiece behind his jaw.

"The last station just reported in, sir," the executive officer said. "We're rigged for ultra-quiet."

"What's the assessment of Romeo-one?" Roth asked.

"We picked up Romeo-one's hull-popping transients," the executive officer said. "We heard his hull expand and compress as he was changing depth."

"He went to periscope depth?" Roth asked.

"Yes, sir."

"He might have just downloaded orders to attack our convoy. You got a range?"

The executive officer tapped a man in a *La Jolla* ball cap on the shoulder, whispered, and pointed at a stack of dots. The man twisted dials, and the dock stack tightened.

"Best guess is twenty miles, sir. He's got a long way to go to attack our convoy."

"Was he snorkeling?"

"Didn't hear any diesels. He might be too paranoid to risk the noise."

"Agreed," Roth said. "But if he didn't snorkel, let's assume his battery is depleted to seventy-five percent and that he wants to keep forty percent for his post-attack evasion. How fast can he go?"

The executive officer nodded at a sailor who handed him a laminated placard that correlated *Romeo* submarine battery burn rates to speeds.

"He has to cover fifteen miles," the executive officer said. "Burning thirty-five percent of his battery, he can sustain ten knots."

"Enter ten knots for Romeo-one into the fire control system. Plot a course and speed to intercept him six miles from the convoy's track, fifteen minutes ahead of him."

"What about the other *Romeos* we've been tracking?"

"We'll deal with them as opportunity permits," Roth said. "Let's stop one bad guy at a time."

*

Roth had repositioned the *La Jolla* in front of the inbound Japanese convoy.

"How's it tracking, executive officer?" he asked.

"Romeo-one's been heading for the convoy since he came down from periscope depth, sir. The solution's tracking as you assumed, only two knots slower."

"He had less juice in his battery than we estimated."

The executive officer grabbed the laminated graph.

"Probably sixty percent charge when he received orders to attack the convoy."

"That bothers me," Roth said.

"Why, sir? We've got him nailed. I recommend that we take him out with one torpedo just inside fifteen miles—"

"But if he's willing to attack the convoy with almost no juice to spare for an evasion, I question if he's alone. He didn't have to hurry. He could have waited and intercepted the convoy farther along its track."

Two sailors in blue cotton jump suits stepped aside as Roth and the executive officer stooped over a trace-paper geographic plot of the ocean. Roth pointed.

"Romeo-one is here," Roth said. "Romeo-two is here, closer to the minefield."

"You think they're waiting along the convoy's track to take turns—whittle it down ship by ship?"

"Let's look at Romeos three and four," he said.

"We haven't heard them for a while, sir. They could have received orders hours ago—long before we heard Romeo-one reach periscope depth to receive his orders."

"Give them ten hours of transit at twelve knots—one hundred twenty miles."

Roth opened a pair of dividers to one hundred twenty nautical miles and walked them over the chart.

"Romeo-four's out of range to attack the convoy, but look," he said.

"I've got you, sir. Romeo-three can reach them just before the Taiwanese anti-submarine minefield."

"So Romeo-one attacks, the convoy hits evasive maneuvers," Roth said, "and tankers fall from the convoy. What's left of the convoy keeps coming, and it happens again and again until there's little to no convoy left."

"Why not just gang up in a wolf pack?"

"You know what it's like tracking ten surface targets, each doing submarine evasion zigzag legs, don't you?"

"Pandemonium. You can't tell one target from another, and with the zig legs, a torpedo aimed at one ship often intercepts another. Plus, once the first ship is hit, the rest evade on diverging courses."

"Also," Roth said, "if shots interfere, torpedoes could be wasted on the same target, or worse, shock waves from one torpedo could destroy another."

"You think they're spread out along the convoy's track, sir? One *Romeo* inflicts its damage, surgically, and by the time the next *Romeo* attacks, the remaining convoy has regrouped into a tight circle of targets?"

"Exactly," Roth said. "And we'll have to take them out one by one, repositioning with each attack. No room for slop. No time for battle damage assessment. We shoot, cut the guidance wire, hope we aimed well, and move on."

The executive officer craned his neck and glanced at the screen that displayed torpedo settings.

"We can shoot at Romeo-one, sir," he said.

Roth reviewed the details and agreed. He stepped up to the conning platform and announced his orders.

"Firing point procedures, Romeo-one," he said. "Tube one will be the firing tube. Tube two will be the backup. I will engage with a single torpedo."

"Plot ready, solution ready, weapon ready," the executive officer said. "The ship is ready."

"Shoot on generated bearing," Roth said.

He reached for his cross.

*

Commander Hamid Hayat sipped tea as he stood. Knowing the slightest flinch would instill panic among the crew of the *Hamza*, a Pakistani *Agosta* class submarine, he tolerated no displays of fear from his men or himself.

"Torpedo alarm," he said in English with an Urdu accent.

"I've got it, sir," his executive officer, Lieutenant Commander Faisel Raja, said.

Hayat wiped his sleeve across his beard and lowered the teacup to a console.

"Read it. Silence it," he said.

"Yes, sir."

"Coming at us?" Hayat asked.

"No, sir. Signal strength is too weak. It's to our starboard and drawing right. No danger to our ship."

"Raja," Hayat said. "Torpedo seekers can adapt their signal strengths for a given sound environment, and signal strength is irrelevant. But bearings drawing to the right cannot be faked. The torpedo is no danger to our ship. The torpedo is targeting Sun's ship, not ours."

"It is drawing in Sun's general direction," Raja said.

"It's not just drawing in his direction, it's heading for him. It's an American torpedo, and it won't miss."

Raja look flustered. He tripped over a sailor's foot while returning to the torpedo alarm.

"The torpedo seeker frequency—it's American, accounting for Doppler shift," he said. "How did you know?"

"Who else would it be?"

"The convoy's frigates? An air dropped weapon?"

"No, Raja. The only way a Taiwanese platform would have heard Sun is if he had made a mistake. No submarine commander in the Chinese fleet makes mistakes. They have no imagination or intuition because they only train to do the simple things right, but they never make a mistake."

A short man in a Chinese People's Liberation Army-Navy captain's uniform exchanged whispers with a taller man in a similar uniform.

"Commander," the taller man said with a Mandarin accent, "Captain Shen states that his comrades are in danger. Why do you discuss training philosophy?"

"Because it is relevant," Hayat said. "Like all your submarine commanders, Sun was trained with discipline but with no creativity. He ascended to periscope depth at a precise time per procedure and received orders to attack the convoy. I know that he is now repositioning his ship exactly per the optimum battery burn rate and that he will die twelve miles from his ambush point."

The tall man, an interpreter, frowned and nodded.

"I will translate for Captain Shen," he said.

Hayat listened to somber words exchanged in Mandarin.

"Captain Shen appreciates your insight," the interpreter said. "He is eager to share your wisdom with the fleet, but he also urges you to take action."

"It is too late for Sun," Hayat said. "I will do what I can for the others."

More words were exchanged in Mandarin.

"Captain Shen understands," the interpreter said. "He appreciates your courage and assistance."

"Translate this for Captain Shen," he said. "You choose the words—I don't care. I'm sorry his comrades are going to die, but I don't need him questioning my every move."

The interpreter gaped. Hayat waved his fingers.

"Go on," he said. "I have work to do."

"I will do my best," the interpreter said and nodded.

Hayat sipped tea and sat.

"Raja," Hayat said. "Where is Sun's *Romeo*?"

The *Hamza's* executive officer darted to the plot.

"Twelve miles from his ambush point, sir," Raja said. "You were right."

"Of course," he said. "Now tell me the torpedo bearing rate and frequency."

"Right away, sir. May I ask what you intend to make of these numbers? We've already identified that it's an American torpedo, and we know its target."

"Frequency conversion and trigonometry will resolve the weapon's speed and course. Then I'll use Sun's position to anchor the torpedo, and I'll have its range. That will help localize the submarine that shot it."

"You mean to attack the American?" Raja asked.

"Such an attack is within our mission parameters," Hayat said. "And so I shall."

*

Hayat swirled his cup. Green leaves traced a whirlpool. He nodded at a young sailor who replaced the cup with a hot one but tripped and spilled tea.

Hayat stared at reddened skin, ignored the pain, and inhaled. His mustache tickled his nostrils.

"Get me a towel, you imbecile," he said.

The sailor ran off.

"Come here, Raja," Hayat said.

Hayat studied Raja's face. Steady dark eyes met his stare. Raja's swarthy skin appeared smooth and made him look younger than his thirty-one years.

"You appear concerned, almost hesitant," Hayat said.

"I am no coward," Raja said. "But if we attack the American submarine, we put our mission at risk."

"If I doubted your courage," Hayat said, "I would have left you ashore. Your judgment is another matter. Do you not see that the reward outweighs the risk?"

The sailor returned with a towel. Hayat wrapped it around his fingers, and its tepid moisture soothed him. He leaned over the periscope well's railing, placed a hand on the sailor's shoulder, and saw fear in the man's face.

"Mistakes are no longer tolerable," Hayat said. "We are in battle. The price for lapses in concentration is death, and we would suffer that fate together."

"Yes, sir," the man said.

"Back to your station," Hayat said.

The sailor darted away, and Hayat leaned toward Raja.

"Should we succeed, sir," Raja said, "I am concerned that the Chinese will receive credit. The Americans must know that it is the submarine *Hamza*, that defies them."

Hayat whispered.

"Keep your voice low," he said. "Allah's will unfolds according to His desires. Still, your question is insightful."

Hayat puffed his cigarette. The unfiltered tobacco taste was potent.

"The Chinese provide us weapons for our mission," he said. "Let them receive credit, or better—let the Americans wonder who kills their sons. Uncertainty creates fear, and that is our ultimate purpose."

Raja stood straight.

"Forgive me, sir," he said. "Shall I reset the torpedoes for submerged targets?"

"No, reserve them for the convoy. Backhaul tube one and load a Shkval rocket. I had that tube modified for a reason. Let us test our newest weapon against America."

*

Thunder echoed through the *La Jolla's* hull. Commander Roth accepted that he had sunk a Chinese *Romeo* submarine and killed fifty men.

"Attention in the Control room," he said. "We've just hit Romeo-one. We heard the hull shatter. We have no indication that it launched a counterfire weapon.

"We'll assume that Romeo-two heard the explosion and is alerted," Roth said. "Romeo-two is now our target of interest. I'm beginning my approach on Romeo-two.

A voice from Roth's sonar room boomed over a loudspeaker.

"High speed cavitation, bearing two-four-four. It's moving fast."

"What's the blade-rate?" Roth asked.

"No blade rate. Bad call. It's high-frequency hissing. We don't know what the hell it is!"

Roth grabbed his executive officer's arm.

"The Chinese have tested a Russian Shkval underwater rocket, right?" he asked.

"Yes, sir. But they're not operational yet."

"Not supposed to be," Roth said.

Roth placed his hands on a polished rail and yelled.

"Helm, all ahead flank, cavitate! Diving officer, take us to test depth!"

Roth's stomach leapt as the ship nosed downward. The deck plates rumbled and the digital display flipped through numbers toward the *La Jolla's* top speed.

"There's no evasion protocol for a Shkval, sir," the executive officer said. "We can't outrun a three-hundred knot rocket."

"We can make it miss," Roth said.

"Why are we going deep?" the executive officer asked. "We should be shallow in case we need to abandon ship."

"Deep backpressure stifles the shock wave."

"I hope to God you're right, sir."

"Let's get a spread of torpedoes off at Romeo-two," Roth said. "We still have a convoy to protect. After that rocket goes off, we may not be able to fight."

*

Commander Hayat studied graphical interface displays.

"The *Los Angeles* is running," he said. "We can hear it on the wide aperture sonar array that covers our hull."

"The bearing is off a bit," Raja said.

"Because they have accelerated. Look at our hole-in-ocean display. The crude, oblong shape that blocks out the background noise of marine life is their hull."

Raja bent over and bumped a young sailor who leaned aside to let him study the dual-stacked monitor.

"Transient noise from the *Los Angeles*," Raja said. "And again. They're launching a spread of torpedoes."

"A spread indicates that they're unsure of their targeting solution," Hayat said.

He puffed on his cigarette.

"Their solution is vague and they had to shoot two weapons to cover their area of uncertainty. The tactic wastes a torpedo, and neither torpedo is aimed well."

"It appears the salvo is intended for Chin's *Romeo* submarine, sir," Raja said. "Based upon Chin's patrol area, the salvo appears well enough placed."

"But by using the rocket, I forced the *Los Angeles* to shoot early. I gave Chin a chance to evade. If he recognizes the spread, bisects the incoming torpedoes, and opens range at maximum battery burn, he may survive."

Raja stared at a sonar display.

"More transients. The *Los Angeles* just shot at us."

"Yes," Hayat said. "Your assessment?"

Raja nudged another young sailor from his dual-stacked graphical interface. Multicolored lighting from the monitor's tactical scene danced through the smoke of his cigarette and reflected off his relaxed features.

"The *Los Angeles* has shot well behind us."

"Yes, Raja," Hayat said. "I steered us broadside to the American, and their weapon draws safely aft."

*

The deck plates shot into Roth's shins. His fibula burst through the skin, and he fell to the deck, breaking his sacrum and tearing the skin from his wrist.

As the explosion echoed, Roth expected the hull to crack open, but it held. The thunder subsided, darkness enshrouded him, and emergency alarms buzzed in his head.

Roth propped himself up and surveyed the control room. A man moaned, trembled, and passed out. Another lay over a control panel with his head twisted backwards. Blood oozed from a gash on the back of the executive officer's head.

He recognized the *La Jolla's* predicament: crippled by a warhead exploding several hundred yards away. But he had evaded in time to keep his ship intact.

A figure walked toward him, followed by a second carrying a flashlight. He squinted, but the face that examined him looked fuzzy.

"Easy, sir," the figure said. "You're hurt bad."

"Ship status," Roth said and winced.

"Flooding in the engine room, but they contained it. Only about thirty guys can walk. It's pretty bad."

"Engineroom … propulsion … evade."

"They're trying to get the reactor back up, sir."

"Take my keys. Override safety. Battle short the reactor," Roth said and passed out.

*

Hayat kept his gaze on tactical monitors.

"You see, Raja, it's as predicted. The *Los Angeles* class, the *La Jolla* specifically, if I believe our acoustic database, is dead in the water. We've crippled it."

A distant explosion reverberated through the hull.

"They've hit Chin's boat, sir," Raja said.

The Chinese translator moved into Hayat's view.

"The Commodore is upset that you let another Chinese submarine perish," the translator said.

Hayat drew on his cigarette.

"Express my regret for the loss, but tell him if he had engaged my services earlier, I could have trained your comrades to survive."

The translator glared at Hayat.

"Do it, man!" Hayat said.

The translator sneered and turned away.

"This leaves only us and Xiong's boat to destroy the convoy," Raja said. "I'll reload tube one."

"No, Raja. I am less concerned about the convoy than the American submarine that protects it."

Hayat pointed, and a sailor placed a new teacup in Hayat's hands. He sniffed and welcomed its bitter scent.

"You mean to finish the *La Jolla*," Raja said.

"American fear is earned by death—not by near misses. Reload tube one with another Shkval."

*

Icy pain greeted Roth as he awoke. He slipped his hand into his pocket and caressed his cross. He prayed for his wife and children, and pain yielded to numbness.

A high-pitched hiss grew louder and surrounded him. Death had come for him. His final thought was that he would be avenged by patriots who shared his ideals.

CHAPTER FIVE

Platitudes from Bertraud, desperate to keep her attention, had delayed her. As she left the HIV support group's meeting place, Olivia lifted her phone to her ear to contact the eyes and ears of the CIA that covered her.

"Where are you?" she asked.

"Outside the bookstore half a block away, playing tourist with my camera," Robert, her partner, said.

Olivia unfolded her mental map.

"You're at *La Librarie Centrale* then?" she asked.

"Yeah."

"Where'd Slate go?"

"We're following him. He's at the Wanadoo cyber café. Go check your email. You can make the meeting look accidental. It's the busiest cyber café in the city."

"What if he doesn't go for me?"

"You're hot, he's horny, and you're trained for it."

Olivia stared at the cobblestones beneath her feet.

"You okay? Say something," he said.

"Yeah, I'm fine," she said.

"You'll have three officers watching you. This'll work out fine, but not if you keep standing there."

"Okay, I'm going," she said.

"I'll stay two hundred yards behind you."

Cell phone to her ear, Olivia crossed the street. She walked for five minutes, surveying her surroundings.

"Anyone following me?" she asked. "I noticed three possible trails."

"I saw four."

"You're not counting the old British couple?"

"I did. I got a good image in my camera. The facial match came back pretty quick. He's a barrister from Devonshire. The woman—his mistress. Lucky for him we're not private investigators."

Olivia stepped around a sloppily cleaned pile of dog droppings. The pile made her aware of the faint stench of the city sewers.

"What about the other three?" she said.

"The two juveniles are local high school students. The middle-aged woman with the Gucci handbags is a tourist from Florence. They're all just randomly following your path except for one guy—the older guy in the sport coat. I'm still waiting for his data."

"That older man sticks out," she said. "Armani blazer and a nice looking tie."

"Renard dresses his men well."

"His men shouldn't be trailing me," she said.

"Not you—Slate. Renard trusts Slate, but we've seen him trail him before. And any trail on Slate would be interested in new people in his life, like you. Be watchful."

Her breaths became shallow.

"Doesn't feel right," she said.

She realized that she sounded like a coward. No combination of training or acumen beat instincts, she knew, and her instincts told her to turn back.

"I understand you're hesitant," he said. "I respect that you're back in the field after what happened on your last assignment. You'll be fine."

She slid her cell phone in her purse and hastened her pace. She wondered if the incident with Marko had made her paranoid. If so, her career was over.

Rollers squealed as a portly man with a bloodstained smock slid a metal cover over a storefront. He pointed to a glazed suckling and barked out instructions to an assistant. The assistant mounted a bicycle and brushed Olivia's shoulder as he pedaled by her.

"*Desolé, mademoiselle*," he said.

The assistant ran his eyes over Olivia's body. She frowned and pointed, and he returned his attention to the street in time to swerve around a stone post.

Men are slaves to their penises, she thought.

Her phone rang.

"Hello," she said.

"Listen up. I got a match on the Armani blazer. He's a retired French submarine chief petty officer. He's got to be working for Renard. You have a trail."

"So we call it off and try again tomorrow," she said.

"Negative. Your trail is on a cell phone, and so is Slate. Slate just left Wanadoo and is heading your way."

Olivia dropped the cell phone into her purse and felt walls closing in. The image of a slave trader holding a knife to her neck crept into her mind. She reminded herself that this was a low-risk assignment.

Behind three giggling teenage girls, Slate approached.

"Hey," he said in English. "Olivia, right?"

She tried to sound surprised and perky but heard tension in her voice.

"Oh, yeah. Hi. Jake, right? I was just on the way to Wanadoo to check email."

"I was just going to try some new games, but it's too crowded in there. So how'd you enjoy your talk with the mayor's arrogant little son?"

"It wasn't that bad," she said.

"You're too nice. I can't stand a word he says."

"I did, at least for the first two minutes or so."

"You mean the first ten thousand words," he said.

Olivia chuckled, but the tightness in her throat stifled her natural laugh. It sounded whiny, she thought, but Slate seemed unconcerned.

"Yeah, he's a talker," she said. "And there's no question who his favorite subject is."

"I wish I could have saved you," Jake said.

"You did your best, and I can take care of myself," she said.

"Yeah, I figured. I had you pegged for a tough guy."

"Tough girl."

The tension ebbed from her voice. Her phone rang and she reached into her purse.

"Who's calling you? You just moved here?" Jake asked.

"My aunt and uncle live in Aix. You better let me get this. They'll freak if they can't check on me twenty-four seven."

She placed the cell phone to her ear.

"The trail is ten seconds behind you," he said. "We tapped into his cell phone signal. We didn't get the whole conversation, but he was talking to Slate about you. You've got his attention."

"Oh, Uncle Robert," she said, "you have so little faith in me. I can take care of myself."

Olivia watched Slate. He crossed his arms and smiled.

"See, you talk like a tough guy," Jake said.

"Quiet!" she said and flicked her wrist.

"Then take care of yourself," Robert said.

"What do you want me to do?" she asked.

"Seduce the man. What else? Having an audience doesn't change anything, and we've got you covered on both ends of the street if it does."

"I appreciate your concern," Olivia said. "Give my love to Aunt Jennie."

Olivia slid the phone in her purse.

She forced a smile and tried to invite Slate's gaze, but he was looking over her shoulder. She thought she caught him winking as the trail approached behind her.

She could smell the trail man's strong cologne. The Armani blazer passed by the corner of her eye, slipped his cell phone into his breast pocket, and kept walking.

She sighed.

"A new Italian restaurant just opened. If you join me tonight, I'll treat," Jake said.

"What?" she asked.

"Italian," he said. "Let's go to dinner."

*

Three days later, Olivia dreamt.

Jolting pain filled her skull, and a knife scratched her throat. A man with a face contorted in lust and anger squinted and rammed himself into her. She felt the burning and throbbing from his hurried and careless entry.

She rose above herself and asked the naked CIA officer on the Parisian pimp's couch if the vaginal pain was a repressed memory or a nightmarish embellishment. The rape victim answered herself by pointing at her crotch and stating that the bruises proved it was real.

"The bruises are worse on your cheek because they broke your jaw," she said to her body.

"I know," her body said. *"I couldn't eat solid food for weeks."*

"Where's your pimp?" she asked her body. *"Isn't he supposed to protect you?"*

The rape victim's face scrunched in pain and disgust.

"Blown cover."

The plastic explosives in the Parisian pimp's room exploded.

Olivia awoke.

She was covered in sweat and her cell phone was ringing. She rolled to her nightstand and grabbed it.

"McDonald," she said.

"Wake up, sleepyhead," Robert said. "Mustn't blow the third date with Slate napping too long and being late."

"Yeah," she said, "I'm up."

"You, okay?" he asked. "You're panting."

"Just a bad dream."

"Recurring nightmares again?" he asked.

"Yeah," she said. "I'm fine."

"I've pulled officers out with fewer issues than you've got. After what you've been through, I'm not sure if this mission isn't asking too much."

Olivia glanced at the clock. She was running late.

"And you replaced them—the officers you pulled out?"

"Whenever possible. Sometimes you can't."

"Well, you can't," she said. "You got an HIV-positive French speaking female officer lined up?"

"You know I don't."

"Then it's me or we lose Renard."

*

Olivia walked to Jake's apartment, and the cool summer air invigorated her. She knocked on the door and he smiled and let her in. Nausea overcame her as she entered the ground floor entryway of the apartment.

"You okay?" Jake asked.

She felt weak and dizzy.

"I need to sit," she said.

He stabilized her arm, slid a wicker chair across adobe tiles, and guided her into it. Her nausea intensified as he crouched in front of her.

"You want some water?" he asked.

"Yeah," she said.

He went between a pool table and a wide screen television.

"The fridge is on the second floor," he said. "I didn't want to give you tap water from the bathroom."

"Sure. Whatever," she said.

She scanned the room for something that would make her want to vomit. The oak floor had been mopped. The stucco walls were free of water damage and mold.

The ceiling creaked as Jake fetched her water. She closed her eyes, contemplated, and realized that as her nausea passed her mind turned to thoughts of her last mission.

Jake appeared with a glass of water.

"Most women who get violently ill in my presence usually don't wait until they come into my house," he said.

She stood, grabbed his starched collar, and jabbed her nose towards his neck. Inhaling, she recognized the source of her problem and stepped back to the pool table.

"What?" he asked.

"Your cologne."

"It's Drakkar Noir. I just bought a bottle."

The guy who raped me wore that, she thought.

"What's wrong? You allergic?" he asked.

"Yeah. Maybe …"

"Okay," he said. "Sit tight. I'll shower and change. You can play pool, watch TV, or step outside for fresh air."

He darted up the stairs, and the nausea ebbed.

Her hands shaking, she arranged pool balls on maroon velvet and slammed a stick into the cue ball. She missed everything but the rail and dropped the stick on the table, then scanned the room to distract herself.

The entertainment center's black finish swallowed the overhead parlor light. A six-disk compact disk player, DVD player, and a plethora of movies and music covered the center, but too many for Olivia to draw any conclusions about Jake's tastes.

End tables at either arm of an Ikea loveseat held plants and potpourri but no pictures. A coffee table supported generic coasters from a local brewery. The room seemed sanitized of insight into Jake's history.

Sweeping balls into pockets, she drew the somber conclusion that Jake was too careful to reveal anything about Renard.

He descended the staircase.

"That was fast," she said.

"Hey, I can take n … quick showers."

He almost said 'navy showers', she thought. *He's only human. Maybe he will slip up.*

"Tommy Hilfiger okay?" he asked.

She grabbed his shirt and nudged her face in it. The scent was invigorating with a jolt of citrus. She smiled and drew him into a kiss. It was their first deep kiss, and taking command of it rekindled her confidence.

He seemed uncertain—even nervous, but he didn't pull back until she broke contact. She had owned the kiss from start to finish and felt ready to take ownership of him.

"Do I get a kiss after every shower?" he asked.

"You'll get one every time I think you've earned one."

"How do I earn one?" he asked.

"That's for me to know and for you to find out."

CHAPTER SIX

His thighs burned, but with each step, he gained energy. Despite being HIV positive, Jake felt invincible. He wondered if he were in love with Olivia.

The twisting dirt path took him by an elderly couple resting against a rock outcropping.

"*Bonjour,*" he said.

"Good morning, young man. It's a wonderful morning for a climb," the old man said in the sunny French of the country's southern provincial region.

"You must have started at dawn," Jake said.

"We've done this every Sunday at daybreak for forty years, weather permitting. From up here I can see all my land and my sheep. Doing this keeps us young."

"I think it's worked," Jake said.

He bid the couple farewell and kept climbing toward the summit of Mount Saint Victoire, the peak glorified by Cézanne.

At a turn, a chapel came into view. Jake crossed the doorstep and smelled the damp oak. Except for a statue of Christ and a few rows of pews, the chapel was bare.

In the grassy yard outside the chapel, a well attracted his attention. He moved to it and peered between the bricks. Dirt covered the dried up hole.

He glanced at a natural rock wall and moved to a gap that yielded a view of distant valleys. Although he knew a sheer cliff awaited, he could not resist dangling his toes over the edge and looking down. Danger enticed him.

An updraft from the valley blew the scent of lilac across his face. He inhaled and turned back to the yard. The older man who had trailed Olivia trough the streets of Avignon had exchanged his Armani blazer for hiking boots, jeans, and a flannel Abercrombie and Fitch shirt.

"Good to see you, Henri," Jake said in French.

Henri ran a wand over Jake's clothes.

"Checking for bugs," Henri said. "Pierre's orders. He's inside with the others."

"Others? How many?"

"See for yourself. Come on in."

Jake entered the room that would have passed for a misplaced barn had the wooden tables and chairs been bails of hay. Six men sat at a table eating croissants with Brie and Camembert while sipping coffee from tin cups.

Upon Jake's entry, the conversation died. Six faces looked at Jake, and he recognized all but two.

"What the hell's going on?" he asked. "A submarine sailor reunion?"

"And now all of our guests have arrived," Renard said.

Wearing garb similar to that of Henri, Renard stood.

"Shit, Pierre," Jake said, "you and Henri could pass as twins."

"My dear man," Renard said. "Henri's ego is big enough. Don't suggest that he's more handsome than he already thinks he is."

Jake and Renard exchanged kisses at each other's cheeks.

"What's going on?" Jake asked. "Why the party?"

"I'll explain after breakfast," Renard said.

A stranger's hand emptied a thermos into a cup. Jake thanked the man and sipped back coffee.

"Jake, that is Claude LaFontaine," Renard said. "He was the Engineer Officer when I was the Executive Officer on the *Rubis*. He's just retired."

Jake shook LaFontaine's hand.

"And this is Antoine Remy," Renard said. "He was my best sonar operator when I commanded the *Améthyste*. I believe you know the rest."

Jake greeted the sonar operator and sat. The conversations remained lighthearted and centered around memories of the French submarine force. When the plates were empty, Renard stood.

"Gentlemen, please," he said.

As if rehearsed, the men left Renard alone with Jake.

"This is our place to discuss things in private," Jake said. "I thought you had called me up here so I could transfer Marie and little Jacques from their Taiwanese captors to our hideaway while you were shaking down your *Agosta*. I didn't expect your mercenary crew."

"Marie and Jacques will stay where they are," Renard said. "Their best protection is to follow Li's agenda."

"Then why'd you summon me here?" Jake asked.

"I need you for my mission," Renard said

"No way. I'm not setting foot on another submarine."

"My debt to Taiwan is also yours."

Jake jammed his finger into Renard's sternum. The Frenchman coughed.

"You came to me," Jake said. "You brought the whole *Colorado* thing together."

"You would prefer that I rewind time and leave you with your career as an American naval officer in shambles and your navy's betrayal gnawing at your soul? I rescued you in exchange for helping me sell warheads to Taiwan. We failed, and you share the burden of that failure."

"Things change," Jake said. "I've got a life now."

"I'm starting to sense that," Renard said.

"Is that why you had Henri following me?"

Renard lit a Marlboro.

"I was candid that I had men following you during the first months after the *Colorado*. This is nothing new."

"I thought you had stopped," Jake said.

"I did, for a time, but I started again. I never should have stopped, actually. The more people you meet, the greater the danger. You may have a surgically altered nose, but someone from your past could recognize you. Too many Americans are starting to tour the south of France."

"I don't like being followed without knowing it."

"Now you know," Renard said. "I'll have someone watching you as often as I can spare."

"Why not always? Henri could help wipe my ass."

"I only use those who know of our past to watch over you, and most of them are graduates of the French submarine fleet. They are not surveillance experts. You need to protect yourself, and I fear you've forgotten to be wary of new people."

"So I can't get close to anyone?"

"No, indeed you may not. Not in our present situation. You would risk ruining us all. You can trust no newcomers with our secrets."

The elderly couple that Jake had passed during his ascent strolled into the room. Jake smiled and waved.

"Switch to English," Renard said. "Keep your voice low in case they understand. I'm concerned about people you meet, such as the young American lady."

"Olivia," Jake said. "We've been on a few dates."

"Who is she?" Renard asked.

Jake wanted to tell him it was none of his business but knew he couldn't. Renard was making it clear that everything was his business.

"Just an unemployed psychology PhD. She's taking courses at the university to learn how to draw, and she parked in Avignon to make some sketches of gothic architecture. Cool way to pass the time if you ask me."

"A perfect life, indeed," Renard said. "Too perfect."

"She's had some hard times."

"I sacrificed many of my intelligence channels when we stole the *Colorado*, but I still have a few. None of them, however, could produce a shred of data about her after she earned her PhD from Yale University three years ago."

"I don't like you looking over my shoulder."

"It is for your protection."

"You sure you've got the right Olivia McDonald?"

"Certain. Henri may be a hopeless romantic who telephones you to help you meet a new lady he's supposed to be surveying, but he's competent enough to capture a digital image of her face."

"You can't find anything on her after 2005?"

"Nothing," Renard said.

"So what does that mean?" Jake asked.

"It could mean nothing," Renard said. "The entire world is no longer at my fingertips, but I am concerned."

"I'm not blowing her off because you're concerned."

Renard stamped out his cigarette and withdrew a gold plated Zippo lighter. His thumb whipped across a gear. A spark jumped and flame danced across the tip of a Marlboro.

"How well does she know you?" Renard asked.

"She believes my cover," Jake said. "Everyone believes my cover. Shit, Pierre, it's not that hard to swallow. I tell everyone my rich father died and left me millions and that I got HIV from a cheating girlfriend."

"The cover is workable, but my concern is the better people know you, the harder it is for you to separate your real history from the lies."

"I'm not going to hide in an ivory tower."

"Nor should you," Renard said. "But have you considered hiding in a Taiwanese *Agosta* class submarine?"

"I'm not going with you."

"Then this is it," Renard said. "After today, I return to hiding, and I'm not sure when I will see you again."

Henri's head popped through the doorframe again.

"Come in," Renard said. "Bring the others."

"I'm serious," Jake said. "You're on your own."

The five French submarine fleet veterans entered the room. The elderly couple waved and departed.

"At least stay and help us plan, Jake. When you hear what I'm up to, you'll know why I need your input, and you may change your mind about joining us."

"Sure," Jake said and sat. "I'm not going to join you, but I'm sure you dumb asses need an American's input on your anti-China submarine tactics so you don't get yourselves killed."

CHAPTER SEVEN

Olivia studied her translucent image in a glass storefront. The French summer sun had started to tan her skin—a difficultly for a redhead from Connecticut.

She focused beyond her image into the store. Beside a carousel of men's slacks, a shapely blonde woman stared back at her. The blonde removed an emerald ring from her right finger, slipped it over her left, and turned.

CIA Officer Rebecca Daman, I presume, Olivia thought as she stepped back from the window.

"I'm buying you a tie," she said.

"I have enough ties," Jake said.

"You've spent a lot of money on me, but you haven't let me buy you anything."

"Then buy me some chocolate. I'm hungry."

Rebecca Daman appeared at the store entrance.

"Hello," she said in French. "Do you desire anything?"

Olivia noticed a hint of a Long Island accent in her French but trusted Jake did not have the ear for it.

"No, thank you," Jake said.

"Yes," Olivia said. "Don't you think he'd look fantastic in a blue Italian tie?"

"I think he looks fantastic already, but if you put him in a Villa Bolgheri, you'd have to fight off every woman in *Provence*."

Rebecca smiled, tilted her head, and swept back her blonde hair. Jake started toward the store.

"I don't suppose I'm getting out of this?" he asked.

"Not a chance," Olivia said.

*

Jake flipped a navy blue tie over the collar of his starched white shirt. Olivia knew that Rebecca had chosen the tie because it was too dark. While Jake assessed his image in a mirror, Olivia slid out of his view.

"Third tie, right?" she asked.

"Yes," Rebecca said, "Ready for the control unit?"

"Do it."

Olivia opened her purse and presented it. She frowned as she felt Rebecca insert and withdraw her hand. Although it was Rebecca's first assignment, the motion should have been indiscernible.

Followed by Rebecca, Olivia walked behind Jake.

"Hey handsome," she said, "that doesn't look right."

"No, it's too dark," Rebecca said. "Try this one."

Jake exchanged the dark tie for one of pale blue.

"I don't like this one either," Olivia said.

"Too pale," Rebecca said. "Perhaps this one."

Jake tried the third tie.

"Perfect," Olivia said.

"The blue matches his eyes," Rebecca said.

"I'll take it," Olivia said.

"Don't I get a say in this?" Jake asked.

Olivia wrapped her arms around him and kissed his cheek.

"Nope. You're wearing this to dinner."

"That reminds me," he said. "We need to hurry. It's going to take us a few hours to get there."

"Yeah, and I want to see Nice. Let's buy this thing and get going."

"Your pretty pushy for a new ..."

She stepped in front of him.

"A new what?"

"Friend."

"Okay, good," she said. "I was afraid you were going to admit that you liked me."

*

After a limousine ride to France's southeast corner, Jake strolled through the streets of Nice. European wealth made him feel like he could spend his money liberally, and Nice's gaudiness provided him a place to meet Renard without drawing attention.

His new tie around his collar, he grabbed Olivia's hand. A lady wearing an apron and jeans stepped out of a candy store's front and reached upward.

"Hurry," he said. "The store's closing."

His grip slipping, he realized that the subject of his new infatuation didn't share his zeal for chocolate.

"Go on," Olivia said.

"Wait!" Jake said.

"Okay, take your time," the lady in the apron said.

"Thanks," Jake said. "I'm dying for a chocolate animal. What do you have?"

The lady stepped behind a glass display and pointed at pairs of chocolate-sculpted pigs and frogs nestled between éclairs and napoleons.

"The frogs, please," Jake said.

He dropped euro into the lady's hand, transformed his hand into a lily pad for his chocolate treats, and sauntered towards Olivia.

"Couldn't you at least get them wrapped?" she asked.

"They're not going to last long enough," he said.

"Dinner's in two hours."

"Dear God, woman. Haven't you seen me eat? You're lucky I'm even thinking about giving you one."

He rammed a frog head first into his mouth. Even after two years in France, he always enjoyed the sweet explosion of chocolate from French pastries.

"That frog died for a good cause," he said.

"Close your mouth. You're being American."

"You want the other one?"

Olivia shook her head.

"You sure?"

He jammed the second head in his mouth.

"Well, maybe half."

He shrugged his shoulders, grabbed hers, and pulled her to his mouth.

"Jake, this is gross."

He nudged the frog's butt into her nose. She blushed but bit into the frog. He inhaled his half of the chocolate amphibian and pressed his lips against hers.

She pulled back, covered her mouth, and chewed.

"It's sad," she said. "But I think that's the most romantic kiss you've given me."

He handed her a napkin. She cleaned her face and swallowed. He wrapped his arm around her waist, drew her in, and kissed her again.

She grabbed his ribs and embraced him, and he let himself become lost in her. She was the most amazing woman he had met in his life, and he didn't want to let go.

✱

As Pierre Renard came into view, the butterflies in Olivia's stomach went hysterical.

She stood, exchanged a southern French cheek-to-cheek greeting kiss with Marie and Pierre, and sat back down. A waiter poured the house's red wine into four glasses. Olivia tasted it and found it bitter.

"Ah," Renard said in English. "Dry. Crisp. The vineyard that supplies this restaurant has been in the same family for eight generations."

"I think it's a bit too strong," Marie said.

"Me, too," Olivia said. "A bit bitter for me."

"More for us," Jake said.

Olivia rubbed Jake's knee. He was wearing a two-tone gray and black dinner jacket over his white dress shirt. He had worn her blue tie, and that's all she cared about.

"So," Renard said, "English or French tonight?"

"I could still use the French practice," Jake said.

"I was asking the lady," Renard said. "Some day, I will turn you into a gentleman."

"French is fine," Olivia said.

"Where to begin?" Marie asked. "We've been dying to meet the new love of Jake's life."

"Love of his life?" Olivia asked.

"Of course," Marie said. "We've known that boy long enough to know when he's head over heels."

Jake blushed, groaned, and put his head in his hand.

"You're embarrassing the poor boy," Renard said.

Olivia ran her hand across Jake's back.

"It's okay," she said. "It's fun to watch him squirm."

"Maybe we should rescue him," Renard said. "Tell me, then, what brings you to Avignon?"

Olivia recited the combination of truths and lies that she had internalized as her cover.

"The architecture. I'm supporting my new hobby with a few drawing courses, but it's really just an excuse to keep traveling. I'm sure Jake told you that my father was a cop in Hartford and died in the line of duty. Between his insurance and pension, I've had some financial freedom."

"That must have been devastating," Renard said. "I lost family when I was young."

"So you understand," Olivia said. "It turned my whole life around. I had just earned my PhD in psychology and was going to be a criminal psychologist for the Hartford Police Department. When my father died, I needed time off to rethink things. I guess I'm still just rethinking."

"And why not?" Marie asked. "Life is too short to do what one dislikes."

The wireless phone in Renard's breast pocket rang. He excused himself and walked under the incandescent lights of the cobblestone street. Olivia sensed an opportunity.

"What does he do?" she asked.

"He's a broker," Marie said. "Always arranging for someone to sell something to someone else, and the goods hardly seem to matter. I keep begging him to retire, but he seems addicted to his network of business associates."

I'm not alone in telling rehearsed lies, Olivia thought.

"Sounds exciting," she said.

Renard reappeared at the restaurant's entryway and pointed at Jake, who excused himself.

Olivia reached into her purse and withdrew the compact mirror that the undercover sales associate had slipped her. She flipped it open, saw her reflection, and watched a tiny digital display inform her that the transceiver in her compact was linking to the microphone and transmitter woven into the silk threads of Jake's tie.

The short-range, high frequency signal from the compact engaged the antenna in Jake's tie and commanded a transmitter to life.

She worked lipstick across her mouth as she studied the compact's digital display. It stated that the compact had linked to the bug in Jake's tie and was recording data.

Confident she was capturing the conversation between Jake and Renard, she slid the compact into her purse.

"With the only people dining at this table who possess doctorate degrees being ladies," Marie said, "you'd think that they'd ask our opinion instead of storming off alone."

"It has to do with testosterone," Olivia said.

"I love them both dearly, but they are restless. I fear that Jake is like Pierre. The moment you think you've earned his undivided attention is precisely when he'll decide that business is more important."

Olivia sat in silence until Marie breached the subject of European politics. The latest scandal was suspected kickbacks from France Telecom to an officer of the European Union, and as an educated woman, Marie had plenty to say about it.

Jake and Renard returned and made no mention of their conversation other than that it had been business. Olivia passed the evening discussing world events but nothing more about Renard's affairs. She trusted that her compact held insight into the secrets of his life.

*

After the return trip to Avignon, Olivia kissed Jake goodnight at her door and trotted to her laptop. She placed the compact next to it and waited for the wireless connection between the machines.

As the laptop wrote an encrypted file to its hard drive, she slipped on a headset.

Her cell phone rang. She stopped the file and pushed the headset behind her ear with the cell phone.

"McDonald," she said.

"What did you get?"

She recognized the voice as Tommy, her midnight support. 'Cousin Tommy' if questioned.

"If you'd leave me alone," she said, "I'd tell you."

"You're supposed to transmit before listening."

"I know," she said. "I'm just tired."

"Don't go to sleep until we've both listened. If this is as big as we hope, I'll have to wake Robert up."

"I've been dying to listen to this for hours."

"Transmit. Then listen."

"Fine.

She hung up, transmitted, and put her headset on.

*

She heard the bustle of tourists trekking through the streets of Nice, but the recording produced a crystal-clear rendition of Jake and Renard's hours-old conversation.

"What's Marie doing here?" Jake asked.

"I convinced her to leave Jacques for a few days," Renard said. "Minister Li is treating my family well enough, and as long as one of them stay with him, he will be satisfied of my commitment. Marie is free to come and go as she pleases, and I wanted her to help us assess your new love."

"What do you think of her?" Jake asked.

"Stunning, indeed," Renard said. "A pleasure to meet her in person, finally."

"But you still don't trust her."

"I have nothing but her word that she's been wandering across the globe for three years."

"You verified her father's death and her PhD?"

"Yes, they checked out," Renard said.

"And her stories of world travel are pretty impressive. I'll ask her to tell one tonight."

"Those could be memorized. Perhaps we should—"

"Perhaps you should just back off," Jake said. "I hope you didn't call me over here just to talk about her."

Olivia heard Renard flip the gears of his lighter.

"Of course not. I just received word from Admiral Khan that a Pakistani *Agosta* class submarine is missing."

Olivia's pulse accelerated. From her research she recognized Khan as the Pakistani Navy's Chief of Staff.

"Lost at sea?" Jake asked.

"No, the *Hamza*, the third Pakistani *Agosta* 90B hull, is four weeks late returning to Karachi. Khan has admitted that the submarine is outside of Pakistani control and has been so for at least a month."

"That's nuts," Jake said. "What's it doing?"

"If the *Hamza* has indeed gone rogue," Renard said, "it has an unknown agenda."

"If I were a renegade Pakistani submarine commander," Jake said, "I'd launch a sneak attack against the Indian Navy. You could take control of the food sources and trade routes. It would cripple the Indian economy."

And kill thousands, Olivia thought.

"Perhaps," Renard said. "But you assume a commander of sound mind. Such a man does not take his submarine rogue."

"I did," Jake said.

"Proving my point."

"You're hilarious. Who's the skipper?" Jake asked.

"Commander Hamid Hayat. He's a brilliant man, the Admiral tells me. He earned a masters degree from Harvard and learned western submarine techniques at the U.S. Naval Submarine School before exchange programs were restricted. Khan is scared and wants the *Hamza* stopped."

"Stopped?" Jake asked. "You mean sunk."

"Khan has sent assets to patrol the Arabian Sea and the Bay of Bengal in case the *Hamza* attacks Indian ports."

"Why'd Khan tell you?" Jake asked.

"Because when I take command of the *Hai Lang*, I will be on an exact replica of the *Hamza*. It is vital that I know that at least one nation is hunting my twin and that my twin is hostile with an unknown agenda."

Take command of the Hai Lang, Olivia thought, *the official name of the Taiwanese Agosta. Renard's no sideline consultant. He's right in it!*

"So what are you going to do?" Jake asked.

"Nothing different for now. My debt and risk is to Taiwan. Beyond that is mere conjecture. I will make haste, however. I'm taking my crew to Taipei tomorrow. We'll meet the *Hai Lang* at Keelung, familiarize ourselves with the vessel, and begin hunting Chinese submarines."

"And this is where you ask me to go with you."

"You must join me. You will before this is over. Damn it, man, I swear you will."

Olivia noted that Renard sounded less afraid of Slate than afraid of being without him.

"You threatening me, Pierre?"

"I never would. You just leave me with no choice but to trust that you will realize where your loyalties lie."

The rest of the tape held no intelligence. Olivia dropped her headphones and picked up her cell phone.

"I heard it. I already woke Robert," Tommy said. "You just blew this wide open. There'll be some action in Islamabad and Taipei tomorrow. This is huge."

"There's going to be plenty of action right here," Olivia said. "Renard's still trying to recruit Slate."

"Renard owns him," he said. "Slate will join him."

Her confidence spiked.

"Except that Slate's falling in love with me, and I've got him off balance," she said. "We can play this out for some prime intel. The fun's just getting started."

CHAPTER EIGHT

HAYAT PLACED HIS TEACUP ON a podium and aimed a laser pointer at a wall-sized monitor. Square symbols represented surface ships of the Japanese convoy and its Taiwanese escort frigates. Inverted triangles represented submarines. Color differentiated friend from foe.

"The *Hamza* was on its third day of a seven-day patrol with your commodore onboard for observation," he said. "Intelligence suggested that a large convoy of Japanese tankers was loaded with fuel and possible weaponry with the ultimate destination of Keelung, Taiwan."

Beside him, the same interpreter who had accompanied him on patrol translated his debrief into Mandarin.

"The Taiwanese frigates '*Kang Ding*' and '*Hung La*' left port two days prior to the event," Hayat said. "Chinese maritime reconnaissance aircraft spotted the Japanese convoy a day prior to its rendezvous with the frigates."

Hayat surveyed his audience while the interpreter translated. The captains and executive officers of China's East Sea Fleet submarines were jammed into the small auditorium. The most capable officers—the half of the dozen who commanded China's state of the art Russian-built *Kilo* class submarines—sat in the front row with the Commodore. The other half dozen were at sea enforcing the blockade.

Interspersed with the *Kilo* commanders sat half of the ten captains of indigenously-built *Songs*, respectable submarines less capable than the *Kilos*, and one commander each of the pre-commissioning crews of the anticipated stealthy and capable *Yuan* diesel and of the next-generation nuclear attack submarine, *Shang*.

A few captains of the older *Ming* and *Romeo* submarines, younger and of lower rank than the leaders of the more capable vessels, sat behind the rest. Hayat realized that the young captains, who appeared eager and sharp, had been recalled to port for his training session.

Very wise, he thought. *With my enlightenment, these capable men may soon join the world's elite.*

"The maritime aircraft estimated the convoy's course, and the *Hamza* was summoned to the surface so that the Commodore could broadcast the strike plan."

The interpreter's translations became a drone as Hayat relived and taught his tactics to attentive listeners.

"Five submarines were within range to intercept the convoy—the *Hamza* and four *Romeo* submarines, commanded by Commanders Sun, Chin, Xiong, and Hou. But Hou needed to snorkel, and he could not take part in the attack."

As Hayat mentioned the names, he swept a laser dot over each submarine on the monitor.

"Sun took position to the north, followed along the convoy's track by Chin, me, and Xiong at eight-nautical mile intervals. We knew American submarines had been reconnoitering the area and that interference was possible. Knowing this, I was able to respond when the *La Jolla* revealed itself by launching a weapon at Sun's boat."

The crowd stirred, and he realized those present were reacting to the two lost Chinese submarine crews. Hayat continued.

"I used the knowledge of Sun's position, Doppler effect, and knowledge of American torpedo speeds to solve the *La Jolla's* position. I verified the position with hole-in-ocean display in the lower broadband frequencies. Targeting was adequate to engage with a torpedo, but I opted to employ a Shkval rocket to reduce time-to-target with hopes of pre-empting the attack against Chin.

"My weapon arrived too late for Sun, but it flustered the *La Jolla* as it targeted Chin. Stop play here."

The symbols on the monitor froze.

"Evidence suggests that Chin performed a textbook evasive maneuver for the first torpedo. Unfortunately, the first torpedo was the leading weapon of two. As Chin turned one-hundred and forty degrees, he successfully opened range from the lead torpedo. But this placed him on a collision course with the second, lagging, torpedo.

"In multiple-vessel engagements, submerged adversaries may not have time to resolve tight solutions and may compensate with a lead-lag two-weapon salvo. Chin could have optimized his evasion by turning one hundred degrees and seeking the edge of each weapon's seeker's acoustic acquisition zone."

Members of Hayat's audience nodded, pointed, and whispered. Some scribbled notes.

"Your *Kilo* submarines and probably your *Songs* can defeat a capable submarine as I did with the *Hamza*, except for launching the rocket which is too large for conventional tubes. Given the results of the Shkval, I recommend that you modify one tube per ship to support using the rocket, as your shipyard did for the *Hamza*. Continue play."

The symbols moved again.

"After crippling the *La Jolla*, I finished it with a second Shkval. Then I was able to re-engage the convoy."

A wireless phone vibrated in his pocket.

"I need to answer this," Hayat said.

The interpreter nodded as Hayat lifted the phone to his ear.

"Modifications are complete, sir" Raja said.

"The second sixty-five centimeter tube?"

"Welding and hydrostatic testing are complete."

"The Shkvals?"

"There are four onboard. One in a tube, three on the racks."

"And the special heavyweight torpedoes?"

"Four weapons, sir, as the Commodore arranged. One each loaded in tubes one and two, both tubes flooded. We have continuity between the weapons and the fire control system. I am ready to carry out your order."

"Well done, Raja," Hayat said. "If you do not hear from me in an hour, you know what to do."

Hayat slid the phone into his pocket and noticed that the scene on the monitor had run to its end. The Commodore had climbed onstage and stood beside him, speaking. The interpreter translated.

"Thank you for the debriefing. We would like to focus the question and answer session on anti-submarine warfare. The opportunities of the next patrol—"

"There will be no more patrols for the *Hamza* in support of Chinese efforts," Hayat said.

The interpreter remained silent.

"Tell him," Hayat said, "that I've fulfilled my obligation by establishing Chinese subsurface dominance in the waters surrounding Taiwan."

The interpreter exchanged words and spoke for Captain Shen, the Commodore.

"There will be more convoys, and there is no guarantee that the Americans will not return. You must stay."

"You are skilled at anti-surface combat and don't need my help. And by sinking the *La Jolla*, I have forced the Americans to shy away from the region."

"If they don't?" the Commodore asked through the interpreter. "Then what? You are obliged to patrol our waters until Taiwan falls."

"I drove back your greatest adversary, and if America comes again, I've taught you how to fight them."

Hayat started off the stage.

"You are forbidden to leave."

"Forbidden?" he asked.

"We have invested many resources into your submarine at great diplomatic risk. If you will not honor your obligation, we will detain your crew, take back our nuclear torpedoes, and confiscate your submarine."

Hayat looked at his watch.

"I have honored my obligation," he said. "But if you insist on disagreeing and restrict me, my executive officer will destroy the *Hamza* in fifty-five minutes."

"You would destroy your own ship?"

"No," Hayat said. "I will detonate two of the heavyweight nuclear torpedoes you just loaded. I will destroy not just my ship, but your base, your East Sea Fleet Command, and many of the inhabitants of the city of Ningbo. The fallout will carry as far as Shanghai."

The interpreter glared at Hayat.

"I won't embarrass you by translating that. It's a bluff. The physical safeguards are—"

"Irrelevant," Hayat said. "I can create conditions to simulate a true nuclear-tipped torpedo attack."

The interpreter smirked.

"Impossible. The *Hamza* is in drydock."

"My tubes are flooded from my interior tanks, and the weapons' water sensors believe they are immersed. Raja will launch the weapons into your drydock, and the impulse of the launch will suffice for the accelerometer interlock. Before the weapons land in the concrete basin, Raja will command-detonate them through the guidance wires."

The interpretor's face betrayed his concern.

"You wouldn't," he said.

"Safeguards are designed to prevent unintentional launch," Hayat said. "With tactical weapons, even nuclear-tipped ones, it's quite simple to purposely set them off. Do not doubt my resolve."

"I will inform Karachi of your whereabouts," the interpreter said. "That would hinder your plans."

"If any Pakistani asset approaches me, I will know it was your doing and will return to make Ningbo the victim of my attack. Begin flooding your drydock immediately and have tugs standing by to enable the *Hamza's* egress to open ocean by nightfall."

"Why?" the interpreter asked. "Why such an extreme act? What is your urgency?"

The question made Hayat aware of the constant pain he normally ignored. Cancer cells metastasizing from his pancreas to his stomach, liver, and vertebrae compressed the bundle of nerves at the base of his spinal cord. Codeine kept the pain tolerable, but Hayat felt his biological clock clicking away.

"I have a destiny to fulfill," he said, "and Allah demands that I hurry."

CHAPTER NINE

Olivia swiveled the camera atop her laptop screen.

"That's better," Director Rickets said. "I can see you now. Are we secure yet?"

"Yeah," she said. "Go ahead."

"That was great work, Olivia. Fantastic."

"Thanks," she said. "Does it match up with anything else we've got?"

His smile spanned her laptop monitor.

"Sure does," he said. "Check this out. We weren't sure which hull this was until we had Renard's insight."

The image of a submarine's bow jutted from the shade of a drydock canopy. Olivia recognized it as a satellite photograph from a steep slant angle.

"Where is this?" she asked.

"China East Fleet shipyard near Ningbo," he said.

"And that's the *Hamza*?"

"We thought it might have been a *Song* class guided missile shooter undergoing a mod, but the hull we suspected turned up in port after a five-week patrol. We were stumped until you got your intel from Renard."

"So what's the *Hamza* doing there?" she asked.

Rickets' face displaced the satellite photograph.

"We know the Russians have sold many special weapons to the Chinese," he said. "And that includes nuclear weapons. It's unconfirmed, but the *Hamza* likely picked up at least one ET-80 Russian nuclear-capable torpedo."

"Shit," she said.

"'Shit' is right," he said. "But at least we know. We couldn't have pieced this together without you."

Olivia wiggled in her chair. For reasons she didn't understand, she feared where Rickets was going.

"You're not shutting this down, are you?" she asked.

"You uncovered everything Renard was up to and then some. You hit pay dirt."

"Follow-on mission," she said. "Figure out why a front-line Pakistani submarine is outside of the Pakistani Navy's control and refitting in a Chinese drydock."

"The longer we wait," he said, "the greater the risk that Renard gets away. Don't forget that we have to bring him to justice when this is all said and done."

Olivia tapped the nose of a small red teddy bear that Jake had given her. She knew better than to let her emotions dictate her actions, but she was concerned.

"What about Slate?" she asked.

"You know what's going to happen to him. The Navy will take him to Court Martial, and he'll probably spend that rest of his life in jail. That's if he's lucky."

She accepted Slate's fate but didn't like it.

"You're not emotional, are you?" Rickets asked.

"No, I'm fine," she said. "He'll get what he deserves. I'm just wondering if we'll be leaving information on the table if we call it off now."

"What are you getting at?"

"Renard still has connections with Admiral Khan, and I think he's going to know a lot more about the *Hamza*, like what mods it received and what its intentions are. Some of it will trickle to Jake, and I can intercept it."

"You mean 'Slate.'"

"What did I say?"

"You called him 'Jake,'" he said.

"Didn't mean to."

"He's a traitor and a murderer. Don't forget that. But you have a good point. We know where Renard's going to be, and we can always pressure Taipei to hand him over. I'll give you another week to work on Slate for more data."

"Thanks, Jerry. I won't let you down."

"You never have. But if you don't find anything after a week, we move on Slate and Renard, wherever they are. Get moving. The clock's ticking."

*

The next day, Olivia scanned her apartment.

Window shades blocked setting sun's rays. Backlit by a corner lamp, the tiny den darkened as Jake's silhouette swallowed the light. Even if her support team could see into the room, they'd see nothing but shadows.

Two eavesdropping bugs—one embedded into stucco and painted over, the other sewn into cloth of the couch upon which she lay—offered her comfort that she had support, but she felt alone. Nothing stood between Jake and herself, and she knew his intent was sex.

"You ready?" he said.

"What do you have in mind?" she said.

"You'll see."

She felt the couch sink as he curled up beside her. She felt his strength as he pulled her to his chest. "Hey, where's the remote?" he said. "I left it right there. You're sitting on it."

"No, I'm not."

He wiggled and slipped his hand under her leg. He pinched her.

"Hey! Ouch!" she said.

"And voila," he said and yanked the remote from under her. He pointed it at the television. Images rolled by.

"I always skip the previews," he said.

"I can hardly wait to see what you got."

"And here it is."

Olivia read the credits and watched the opening scene.

"Vin Diesel?" she asked. "Is this your idea of romance?"

"I only promised you a romantic dinner. I mentioned nothing about the movie."

"Fair enough. It was a nice dinner. I didn't know you could cook, and not a bad job for using my kitchen."

"Wasn't that hard."

"Lasagna with Caesar salad, pine nuts, and dried tomatoes? I was impressed. I expected runny spaghetti."

"Hey, I go all out for the women I care for," he said. "I got Vin Diesel because I thought you might be homesick for some mindless American sex and violence."

"You are a sweetie," she said and drew him close.

*

The movie ended. Olivia swallowed a strawberry and flipped a fondue stick into a bowl of chocolate Jake had melted during the movie. She waited until he went to the restroom and darted into her bedroom. After closing the door she reached for the telephone beside her bed.

"You're doing fine. Everything's fine," Robert said.

"He's expecting sex," she said. "I've given him all the signals."

"You don't have to. He's already eating out of your hand."

"But I've got to play this like it's real."

"And if it were real? Would you sleep with him?"
"This is real."
"You know what I mean."
"How the hell should I know? I don't know what my real love life is anymore. I don't have one."

She realized she was being unprofessional, but Robert would understand. Director Rickets had chosen Robert, a veteran team leader, because he had seen it all. He had counseled many CIA officers through harm's way.

"It's tough coming back after what you went through. It's your call, but there's no right answer. Follow your instincts. I'll support whatever you want."

"Thanks," she said.

"I got two bugs in your bedroom and we're watching you through the television control console. You so much as knock the phone off the hook, I'll have Tommy and Rick in there in fifteen seconds. No one gets hurt on my watch."

"I'm going to play this to its end," she said. "I'm sleeping with him. It'll sell my cover better if we do this, and ..."

Olivia lay back on the bed, placed her palm against her forehead, and sighed.

"And?"

"And if I can't do an operation like this, my career is over. I need to get this behind me."

*

Olivia checked her hands. They had become steady. She unbuttoned the top button of her blouse and opened the bedroom door. Jake looked up and leered. She leaned against the doorway and flicked her hair behind her ear.

"You ready for your fifth course?"

He appeared before her. His strength drew her in. She tasted the warmth of his mouth.

Within minutes, she was naked with a man for the first time since her incident. Emotions overcame her—too many to grasp—but she held the ones that reminded her who she was. She focused on her pride, sense of duty, and ambition to succeed as a CIA officer.

*

Two hours later, Jake lay behind her. The arm draped over her ribs felt like boa constricting her.

"Can you move your arm, Jake?"

"Sure," he said.

He rolled out of bed. His belt buckle clinked while he slipped into his jeans.

"I didn't mean you had to leave," she said.

"You want me to stay?"

"I don't know. Maybe it's too soon. Staying the night would be a big step," she said.

"We just took a big step."

You have no idea, she thought.

Banal animalistic drive had affected his technique as a lover, but she judged him as being otherwise giving and skillful. Her orgasms might have been real had she been ready to enjoy sex again.

"I'm not going to get sappy and ask you to spend the night," she said. "We'll know when it's time, I guess."

"Yeah, okay. Let's sleep on it."

*

At her apartment door, they kissed. The fingers on the small of her back drew her in but did not crush her. She felt desired but free. She stepped back, and his hands dropped to her waist.

"When will I see you again?" he asked.

"Call me."

She closed the door. She picked up a phone from its cradle, placed it to her ear, and flopped onto the couch.

"Just checking in," she said.

"I had your back the whole time," Robert said.

"I know. That feels kind of weird," she said.

"It's all background noise to me. How you doing?"

"Tired but okay. My head's kind of a beehive."

"You took a bold step tonight. I'm sure it'll pay off."

CHAPTER TEN

Pierre Renard sat in a Lincoln Town Car beside a smallish dark-skinned man in a white uniform. Renard had met Pakistani Admiral Sardar Khan a decade earlier when he managed the transfer of the *Agosta* 90B class submarines for France's national shipbuilding company, *Direction des Constructions Navales*.

"It's good to see you again," Renard said.

"And you, old friend," Admiral Khan said.

"I appreciate the jet fuel."

"Anything to help you reach Keelung."

The car stopped, and a uniformed guard peered inside.

"The next three cars are with me," Khan said.

The guard waved the car through, and a chain link fence slid open. As the Lincoln descended to the lower base, moonlight illuminated a three-story boxy building Renard remembered as squadron command. The waterfront came into view, and the moon shimmered on the Arabian Sea beyond the conning tower sail of an *Agosta* class submarine.

"Seeing an *Agosta* brings back memories," Renard said.

"That's the *Hurmat*. I believe you know it well."

"Indeed! Known in the French Navy as the *Adventurous* nearly twenty years ago when I was its executive officer."

"Beside it is an aging *Daphne*," Khan said. "I fear I may need to squeeze a few more years of life out of it."

"It's a shame the rest of your units are indisposed." Renard said. "Searching for the *Hamza*, I believe."

"I make do with my limited resources."

The car pulled up to an officer barracks and Khan stepped out. Renard shut the door behind him.

"Yet your president won't ask other nations for help."

"It is still too delicate a matter to share," Khan said. "I'm protecting him from the details."

"That's bold of you," Renard said.

"The true test of my courage will come when I tell him that the *Hamza* is unaccounted for and I've deployed half the fleet to find it."

"I thought you were going to protect him?"

"I will tell him the *Hamza* is missing, and when the president presses for information, I will be truthful and tell him I know nothing. If Commander Hayat has malevolent intent with the *Hamza*, the first true indication will likely be attacks against Indian warships."

"I sense that you wouldn't mind if that happened."

"My father was an officer on the destroyer *Khyber* in the 1971 War. He was killed when the Indians sank it during their patrol boat raid on Karachi."

"Few of your adversaries on the subcontinent were even born then. I myself was only a child."

"I would make a poor leader if I acted upon emotion, and I've done my duty in dedicating my assets to prevent the *Hamza* from launching an unprovoked attack."

Renard pulled his Armani jacket tight over his shoulder, reached into the Town Car's trunk, and hoisted a canvas bag over his shoulder.

"I can find you a porter," Khan said.

"No," Renard said. "I am a sailor headed to sea. I will carry my own sea bag."

Renard's entourage of French submarine veterans were lifting bags from their cars. Henri nodded.

"Get them checked in, Henri," Renard said. "Then get straight to sleep. We leave for Taiwan at dawn."

Renard followed Khan into a barracks that resembled a clean but modest hotel. Lamps extending from cherry wood walls provided soft lighting, and the turquoise carpet with salt air stamped into it seemed like a replica of a calm sea. Khan turned a corner into a passageway.

"This building should bring back memories," Khan said.

"Nightmarish long nights," Renard said. "I remember hardly sleeping for months."

"And we had thought we were already old," Khan said.

"If you have nothing of the *Hamza's* intention to share with the president, what do you intend to share with me?"

"The president discourages guessing. He wants facts, and that is what I will give him," Khan said. "However, Agent Zafar Malik of the Directorate for Inter-Services Intelligence has an interesting theory that I will share with you."

"Why should we trust the ISI?" Renard asked.

"Most ISI officers with ties to fundamentalist organizations have been purged," Khan said. "Malik is aligned with the President."

Renard followed Khan into a conference room. A tall man in a conservative suit stood by a pile of folders. He extended a hand but seemed incapable of smiling.

"Agent Zafar Malik," he said.

"Pierre Renard."

The trio sat around a polished table. More lamps provided soft lighting, and a wall clock embedded into a carved wooden anchor indicated that midnight approached. Khan poured tea into pewter cups on a silverware tray.

"Mister Renard," Malik said, "I understand that you will be an advisor on the *Agosta* that we recently sold to Taiwan, now commissioned as the *Hai Lang*."

"Officially an advisor," Renard said, "but I will be in command. One submarine against many, but I believe I can make my presence well enough known to crack the undersea threat from China, at least long enough to allow significant replenishment by sea to the island."

"How fast can you achieve this?"

"There is no deadline," Renard said. "I have as long as Taiwan can withstand the blockade. Months if needed. Weeks or quicker if I can defeat a *Kilo* class submarine or two early enough to scare the bulk of their submarine fleet back into port while they assess their losses."

Malik leaned forward, and his face hardened.

"You may wish to impose a deadline. As soon as possible, we desire your assistance with the *Hamza*."

Through the fatigue of a transcontinental flight, Renard felt a spike of adrenaline followed by hesitation.

"Ten years ago, I would have jumped at this," he said. "But today, the work with Taiwan is my final act."

Malik slid folders and compact disks across the table.

"These are copies of Commander Hamid Hayat's dossier," Malik said. "Perhaps they will change your mind when you have a chance to read them. Guard them well."

"I'll be busy learning the workings of the *Hai Lang*," Renard said. "Could you give me the summary?"

"It wasn't evident until Admiral Khan informed me of the *Hamza's* disappearance, but we fear that he's been recruited by a fundamentalist extremist group that supports terrorists and undermines the President's rule."

"You suspect him to have adopted the agenda of a terrorist organization?" Renard asked.

"I noticed a pattern of dangerous behavior in recent months—increases in the personal finances of his family, travel to locations frequented by fundamentalist leaders, and telephone calls. I will keep questioning those who know him and pressing informants. The answer will come."

"This is why you assume the *Hamza* is rogue instead of in distress?" Renard asked.

"The *Hamza* could be at the bottom of the sea serving as a tomb for thirty six of my finest sailors," Khan said. "I dedicated three ships to search its patrol area but found nothing. There is no evidence of the *Hamza*'s fate, but given Malik's discoveries, I assume it to be rogue."

"It is sad irony that a submarine's submerged stealth advantage can preclude its distress calls," Renard said.

Renard reexamined the folders. The pile was thick.

"May I smoke?" Renard asked.

Khan nodded. Renard withdrew his Zippo and massaged the end of a Marlboro with its flame.

"Let's assume the *Hamza* has gone rogue," Renard said, "and the primary target is the Indian fleet. Why now?"

Malik emptied his teacup and set it on the tray.

"China," he said. "Our allies of necessity have turned their attention toward Taiwan, opening the opportunity for the Indians to redeploy forces from the Chinese border."

"China is far from mobilizing troops for a possible assault on Taiwan," Renard said. "The blockade scenario must fail, followed by missile strikes, before they would attempt the amphibious assault. Even then, China still would have enough manpower to threaten the Indian border."

"It is less a matter of resources than a matter of diplomacy," Malik said. "Aggression against Taiwan can be explained as a civil affair, but a simultaneous assault on Indian territory is outright imperialism. India is now free to turn their attentions towards us."

"I see," Renard said. "Then if India chooses this opportunity to claim land to which they believe they have rights, Kashmir for example, you face a discouraging land campaign with no hope of Chinese support."

Khan stood and walked to antique desk upon which rested a model of the thirty-year old Pakistani frigate, *Shahjahan*, a second-hand British unit serving as Pakistan's frontline major surface combatant. Khan ran his finger across the model's rakish lines.

"If unrestricted in my actions," Khan said, "I would consider crippling the Indian fleet—blockade their ports, deny their fishing havens, halt their trade.

Their army would starve and their economy would crumble. This would prevent a land campaign that could only end in terrible bloodshed and embarrassment."

"Embarrassment?" Renard asked. "History has proven your army competent at taking ground."

"Against the numbers we face, the outlook is grim."

"Not to mention," Renard said, "international sympathies would favor your adversary."

"My nation is held responsible for terrorism," Khan said, "and until the extremists who protect and support them can be contained, it is a stigma Pakistan will bear. India is free to move against us, and the only hope to stave off their aggression is to weaken them from the sea."

"Yet why do you see yourself as being restricted?" Renard asked. "Why not act?"

"I serve the president," Khan said. "And he has chosen diplomacy and restraint. Commander Hayat, however, appears to have chosen the unrestricted route."

"And you would have him destroyed before carrying out that which you might otherwise see done?" Renard asked.

"It is my duty as much as it is his folly. One submarine's conventional attack against a fleet is a tactical victory but a strategic failure. If he attacks—alone and without a crippling coordinated effect—he will incite the world's seventh largest fleet against us and erase any shred of international sympathy we may have."

"But it would destroy the President's rule and open the door for the fundamentalist regime," Malik said. "And that is likely Commander Hayat's intent."

"Then you're doing all you can by searching for him on the approaches to the Indian coast," Renard said. "Why would you need my help?"

"Intelligence is a tedious business," Malik said. "As tedious as it is ambiguous. We have evidence that Commander Hayat has ill intent, and we can conclude with confidence that he targets India. But we may be wrong."

Renard blew smoke.

"This sounds like where I come in," he said.

"If we are wrong and you find the *Hamza* outside the Indian Ocean," Malik said, "we will pay you twenty-five million euro to destroy it."

"You are approaching my price range," Renard said, "but I fear you've spotted me a submarine I do not have."

"We are arranging to lease the *Hai Lang* after you enable Taiwan to break the blockade. They paid enough for the vessel so that we have a surplus for such an arrangement."

"What business would the *Hamza* have outside the Indian Ocean?"

Khan turned his back to the model frigate.

"Japan, Singapore, Australia, maybe even America … use your imagination, Renard," he said. "Because if Hayat has intent beyond the subcontinent, we have nothing else to go on."

*

Renard awoke the next day as his Gulfstream jet touched down on a runway at Keelung naval base. He felt numb after taking off in Pakistan and landing in Taiwan with only a vague sense that it was before noon.

Henri bumped him while reaching for his sea bag.

"Time to earn your pay, Henri," Renard said.

"For adventure on a solid submarine, I would have done this for free."

"You jest."

"Yes, old friend. I do."

Renard hoisted his sea bag over his shoulder and descended into sunlight. Heat from the tarmac lifted moisture and the scent of salt air to his face. He lit a fresh Marlboro and squinted.

White naval vehicles pulled beside the aircraft. A black limousine darted between them, and a thin man in a three-piece suit stepped out.

Renard recognized Young Li, the Deputy Defense Minister for Operations who held his infant son captive. A second man appeared beside him in a Taiwanese naval officer's uniform.

Li extended a hand. Renard thought for a moment and then accepted it.

"Welcome to Keelung, Mister Renard," Li said.

"Anything to get my son back," Renard said.

"This is Commander Danzhao Ye, commanding officer of the submarine, *Hai Lang*."

Ye stepped forward and extended a hand. He wore thick glasses, and Renard thought his head was shaped like an onion. He smiled and exposed crooked teeth.

Renard shook Ye's hand.

"It is an honor to meet you," Ye said.

"I thought I was the commanding officer," Renard said.

"You are in command once the vessel is in international waters," Li said. "For appearance and matters of diplomacy, however, Ye is in command."

"Logical," Renard said.

"Did you bring an executive officer?" Ye asked.

Renard lamented that Jake had held firm in his decision to stay in France.

"No, Commander Ye, I did not. At least not yet. I suppose you're the top candidate."

"My anti-submarine warfare capabilities are limited," Ye said. "But I am capable in anti-surface warfare and basic seamanship. Any my English is strong. Masters in Physics from University of Washington."

"You're hired," Renard said.

"Commander Ye is being modest," Li said. "He circumnavigated the route from Karachi to Keelung spending eighty percent of the time submerged."

Renard exhaled smoke.

"Impressive," he said. "You personally saw to the sea trials?"

"Yes, quite rigorous," Ye said. "I've run the ship through its testing."

"And the crew?" Renard asked.

"The best from the *Sea Dragon* and *Sea Tiger*," Ye said. "We could only spare eighteen men, though—half the standard crew. I was hoping your men could help."

"Oh, they will," Renard said. "Henri will see to it. Your men, Commander Ye, are they prepared to take orders from mine? It is a delicate formality we must overcome."

"Yes," Ye said. "They are looking at you and your crew as veterans and instructors."

"You mean we all look very old," Renard said.

"I only ask that your men also trust mine. They will voice opinions in their areas of expertise."

"Agreed," Renard said. "May I see my ship?"

"Not yet," Li said. "But send your crew. I need you and Ye to come with me. The briefing for your first mission has been delayed pending your arrival."

Li snapped words in Mandarin. Commander Ye nodded, bid farewell, and stepped into a white van.

"Please, Mister Renard," Li said. "Ride with me."

Renard ducked into the limousine and sat facing Li.

"What's the first mission?" he asked.

"The last Japanese convoy lost three of eight ships with a fourth crippled," Li said. "Our generous Japanese neighbors will no longer risk their own vessels, even when assured by Taipei companies. We must now escort our own tankers out of the blockade and back home again."

"This blockade must be costing you a fortune."

"This war," Li said, "is straining our economy, our reserves, and the resolve of our people."

"I'll do what I can to help," Renard said.

The limousine turned toward the Keelung command center. Renard steadied himself against the door.

"I know how you tried to help us the last time," Li said. "With the loss of the lead ship of our stealth patrol class and the forfeiture of one hundred and twenty million dollars for nothing, enough ranking people discovered the truth of your failure."

"Pity it cost your boss his job," Renard said. "Before you cast stones, why don't you tell me who is first in line to replace him? You are the acting Defense Minister in the position's vacancy, are you not?"

"The young must replace the old, Renard," Li said, "especially in time of war. I have made the Prime Minister aware that I am ready to assume the Defense Minister role permanently."

Darkness enshrouded the limousine as it entered an underground parking lot.

"If you are so dismayed by the so-called failure that ruined your old boss, why do you trust me now?"

"You are still among the world's best in military planning and submarine operations."

"Among the best? I am aware of none better."

"There are other qualified candidates," Li said, "but none of them are in my nation's debt. You are the obvious choice, but remember that I can replace you, and remember that I am your son's caretaker."

CHAPTER ELEVEN

Drugs helped her sleep through the night, and Olivia awoke early. She had maintained her composure during intercourse with Jake, but beneath her acting, her lovemaking had been rote. She had denied herself feeling love or desire. She tried to ascertain if professionalism or the inability to feel had made her numb.

Having showered, she sensed life infusing itself into her again. Her first sip of coffee brought color to her face.

A knock at her door startled her. She scooped her cell phone and thought about asking her lookout to identify her visitor, but she opted to just open the door.

"Jake?" she asked.

"Hey, look, Olivia, I uh …"

"You look like the X-games poster boy."

A black leather jacket and riding pants covered him from shins to neck. His accessories were also black—the gloves, the leather boots, and the helmet with a microphone under the shaded visor he held under his arm. Over his shoulder she saw the morning sun beaming off a black Kawasaki Ninja squeezed between two Citroëns.

"You remember that I told you my dad left me a lot of money?" he said.

"Yeah."

"I don't like to throw it around, but I'm getting ready to blow some."

"So you're sponsoring yourself in Grand Prix racing? I hope you're not looking for me to join your pit crew."

Jake chuckled.

"Nothing like that."

"So, what are you up to?"

"I'm taking a bike trip. I'm staying in the best hotels, eating the best food, and drinking the best beer and wine I can get my hands on."

"You're kidding. Just like that?"
"Yeah."
"Any idea where you're going?"
"Don't care. Probably head into the Alps."
"That's awesome. Just don't get yourself killed. I'll miss you, though. How long are you going to be gone?"
"A few days. Maybe a couple weeks."
"So you came by to say goodbye?"
"Well, I was hoping you'd come with me."
His face reminded her of a puppy dog's.
"You serious?"
"Yeah," he said.
"I have school."
Her protest sounded lame the moment she said it.
"You've got a PhD in psychology. I'm not taking art classes as an excuse."
"Jake, this is so sweet. I just don't know if I'm ready. I'm not much for riding on the back of a two-wheel pocket rocket."
"You don't have to. I rented you your own bike. You can follow me—if you can keep up."
"You want to race me through the Alps?"
"You said you had your dad's bike up to over a hundred miles an hour. I'm going to hold you to that."

The concept of running off with him scared her. She'd have less surveillance coverage, and she hadn't pushed a cycle to its limits in years. But she sensed that the reward would be Slate's deeper confidence. She could feel the relationship blooming. Even though the professional voice in her head told her not to, she began to trust him.

"What brought this all on?" she said.
"I just want to get away," he said.
"A life of financial independence in a sunny French city full of art and culture is too much to bear?"
"No, I'm actually pissed off at Pierre, if you must know. We're having a pretty big argument. I need to clear my head."
Bingo, she thought.
"I sensed a little tension during dinner."
"You did?" he asked.
"Remember, I am a psychologist."
"I don't really want to talk about it."
She caressed his shoulder.
"It's okay. You don't have to."

"I'm feeling the itch of the road. You coming?"

Olivia raised her hand over her mouth to hide a giggle. She blushed, and her giddiness was half real.

"Okay."

He sighed through a smile.

"Serious?"

"Yeah."

She reached out, hugged him, and kissed his neck. He wrapped his arms around her. She strained to breathe but didn't care. She pushed back and he released her.

"I need to pack some things," she said.

"Okay, but not too much. We can buy or rent anything we need, and I want to travel light."

"You mean fast," she said.

"Whatever."

"What do I wear? I mean for riding?"

"Got it taken care of," he said.

"Oh, yeah?"

"If you'll permit me the luxury—I used the help of a female salesperson at the apparel shop to reserve you an ensemble like mine. Except I decked you out in bright blue. It goes with your red hair."

"That's gaudy!"

"No, you're going to look hot!"

His grin became impish. She rolled her eyes.

"Yeah, I'll look pretty cute. Did you also rent me a bright blue bike?"

"Of course. Just got to catch a cab to go pick it up. I'll be back."

He sauntered away with a spring in his step. He had to be falling in love with her, and, for a moment, Olivia forgot she wasn't supposed to be doing the same.

*

She rummaged through underwear and toiletries and pinched a phone receiver between her shoulder and ear.

"How much of that did you hear?" she asked.

"Enough," Robert said. "I don't like it."

"What can he do to me on the road that he can't do here?"

"Who knows? It won't take much if you're doing high-speed turns in tight mountain roads. This is dangerous."

"This mission's dangerous. Life's dangerous. Just cover me the best you can."

"You think I'm going to keep up with you in a Renault Scénic hatchback?"

She grunted as the cap popped off her toothpaste and smeared a pair of panties.

"You okay?" he asked.

"I'm making a mess. He'll be back with my bike soon."

"I don't like my options for keeping an eye on you while you're tearing through mountain roads on one of the fastest stock motorcycles in the world."

"We'll take breaks. Your shoulders get tired riding hard. If he doesn't stop enough, I'll ask him to."

She intuited that Robert was thinking through scenarios. She knew he was a genius at visualizing future risks that CIA officers in the field could face.

"I'll contact the field office in Geneva," he said. "We can get some help. We have high enough priority. We need a helicopter, too. The local authorities should cough one up if I can get the right people talking."

"Okay."

"And when's the last time you rode?" he asked.

"About four years ago."

"Here's the plan," he said. "You buy a day to practice riding that rocket he's renting you. I need the time to arrange your backup, and you need the practice."

"Fine," she said. "That's probably a good idea."

"It's the least you can do after agreeing to this."

With the extra day to prepare, she gave up on the toothpaste and released the tube.

"I know you don't see it, but this is the right thing. It just feels right."

"Your feelings are what bother me. He's not your lover. He's your pawn. Don't forget that."

She raised her voice.

"I know what I'm doing!"

She hung up, dropped the phone to her mattress, and cupped her head in her hands.

"No I don't," she said.

CHAPTER TWELVE

HAYAT SWALLOWED BITTER PILLS WITH a mouthful of water. A middle-aged man, Hayat's handpicked corpsman, took his empty plastic cup and gazed with concern.

"Captain," the corpsman said, "I see the pain in your face increasing daily. We must increase your dosage."

I brought this pain upon myself by turning my back on Allah, Hayat thought.

"What are the risks?" Hayat said.

"Codeine poses an addiction risk, but we need only fear the acute lethal dose. You are far from it."

"I do not want my thoughts clouded," Hayat said.

"Let me maintain the dosage at sixty milligrams but double the frequency. This will minimize the effect of a high dose but will keep the concentration in your blood high. I can have pills dissolved in your tea to keep it discrete."

Nausea swelled throughout Hayat's chest. He cringed and waited for the sensation to pass.

"Very well," Hayat said.

"I also want you to drink the bismuth fluid."

"And how would you hide that from the crew?"

"Private doses when in your stateroom. While you are elsewhere, perhaps I can hide it in your food or drink."

"You will think of something," Hayat said. "You are a resourceful man."

Hayat sent the corpsman from his stateroom. A bell jingled on the wall, and he picked up a phone receiver.

"Captain," he said.

"Sir," Raja said, "I request permission to take the ship to periscope depth and attempt a message download."

Hayat glanced at the wall clock and realized that all but a handful of his crew were sleeping.

"Very well," he said. "Ascend to periscope depth."

He left his stateroom and followed the tight passageway forward. With Raja taking the ship shallow, Hayat stabilized himself against the tilting deck. Stopping short of the watertight door, he sat before electronic modules and reached for a keyboard.

He called up a screen that controlled the interface between radio mast downloads and the operations room then typed a message header that indicated urgent traffic from squadron command destined for his eyes only.

Sliding a compact disk into the radio console, he launched an encryption scheme. He formatted the message like a formal naval template but typed gibberish into the body and scrambled it.

He pushed the message to the front of the queue and smirked as he noticed a real message being downloaded. He released his fabricated message to the operations room but froze the real message from Karachi at his console.

The unencrypted message from Karachi demanded that he contact squadron command and return to port immediately. He deleted the message, returned to his stateroom, and waited.

His phone jingled.

"Captain," he said.

"Sir," Raja said, "urgent message from squadron command. For your eyes only—the body is encrypted."

He walked forward again, opened a watertight door, and set foot in the *Hamza's* operations room.

Automation permitted Hayat a small crew of thirty-six men, and he noted this manning advantage in the ship's nerve center. The French-designed Subtics—submarine tactical integrated combat system—simplified the housekeeping and the tactical dissection of data to track, analyze, and attack adversaries. It permitted few men to achieve with efficiency what used to require dozens.

With the Subtics automation, Hayat's minimal midnight watch crew consisted of five men. Raja stood behind the periscope, a chief petty officer sat beside a sailor at the ship's control panel, and two sailors sat side by side on a long row of seats spanning the six Subtics displays along the hull.

"Welcome, captain," Raja said.

"Lieutenant Commander Raja," Hayat said and nodded.

A sailor stood and walked to a compact disk burner. He withdrew the disk, encased it, and extended it to Hayat.

"Your message, sir," he said.

The sailor's body language and vocal pitch carried confidence. Hayat sensed that his crew believed in their ship, their abilities to fight, and—most importantly—their captain. He banked that they'd follow him anywhere.

"Another urgent message from Karachi?" Hayat asked.

"Yes, sir," the sailor said. "We're seeing a lot of them lately. There must be some action headed our way."

"Let me decode it on my stateroom laptop," Hayat said, "and perhaps I will have news to share."

Hayat returned to his stateroom, placed the disk on his desk, and drank from a bottle of bismuth fluid. He flipped open a leather-bound copy of the Qu' ran and read a chapter.

He closed the book and returned to the operations room. Expecting news, each man on watch turned to him except for Raja who kept his eye on the periscope optics.

"Lieutenant Commander Raja," he said. "I relieve you of the deck."

Raja released the periscope.

"I stand relieved, sir."

Hayat handed Raja the compact disk.

"The orders require your concurrence," Hayat said. "I decoded my half of the message, but you need to decrypt your portion with your personal codes."

As Raja stepped away, Hayat placed his eye against the periscope optics. The Western Pacific Ocean's placid waves shimmered in the moonlight.

"Shifting periscope to automated mode," Hayat said.

He steadied the elevation angle and pressed a button on the periscope control console. Electronic relays snapped shut, valves porting hydraulic fluid clicked, and the periscope twirled a full revolution.

A printer produced a panoramic image of the world above the *Hamza*, and Hayat lowered the periscope. As he studied the image of the ocean's surface and convinced himself the *Hamza* was alone, the chief petty officer spoke.

"Sir," the chief said, "do you wish to stay at periscope depth? Since the MESMA propulsion unit is secured, perhaps we should snorkel."

"We have enough battery charge to last the night," Hayat said. "Let the resting men remain asleep."

The chief pointed at a meter and instructed the sailor seated beside him to pump water overboard from the ship's centerline tank. He returned his attention to Hayat.

"Do you need to broadcast a response to your message, sir?" he asked. "I'm holding depth easily."

"No," Hayat said. "We are out of range for a secure transmission, and our mission parameters include remaining undetected. Lower the radio mast and make your depth fifty meters."

Hayat grabbed a polished rail for balance as the *Hamza* dipped forward. Raja passed through the watertight door.

"These orders are indeed urgent, sir," he said.

"We'll announce them to the crew in the morning. If we tell them now, none would be able to fall back to sleep, and I want a rested crew to carry out these orders."

★

Bothered by body aches, Hayat slept fitfully and awoke tired. Having showered, he was zipping his jumpsuit when a knock on the door startled him.

"Come," he said.

Raja entered.

"I am concerned, sir," he said. "Overcoming an enemy in battle is one thing, but convincing a crew to follow a lie is something for which I have little talent."

"You knew this time would come," Hayat said.

"I will follow your lead, sir," Raja said. "You have never let me down. I'm just not sure what to do."

"Follow my cues. We will convince them."

Hayat led Raja out of his stateroom and into the operations room. A lieutenant stood upon his arrival.

"Good morning, captain," he said.

"Good morning, Lieutenant Walid," Hayat said and reached into the overhead for a handset to speak to his crew.

"Attention, crew of the *Hamza*, this is the captain. We've etched our place in history through our gallantry and success in combat, but there is much more for us to achieve. We may soon be called to combat again, but this time in direct defense of our home.

"The torpedoes we loaded in Ningbo are nuclear-tipped, earned in exchange for supporting our Chinese allies. I do not have launch authority, but the threat of an Indian offensive has heightened tensions. It is expected that the Indian aircraft carrier, *Viraat* will deploy to launch a pre-emptive air assault on Karachi.

"The Indians, however, know that our brethren in the submarine fleet will seek their carrier. Our countrymen would send them to the bottom before it could approach Karachi. With that risk, the Indians have asked the Americans to assist with air support against Karachi.

"If events unfold as feared, squadron command will task us with conducting an approach on the American aircraft carrier, *Stennis*. We will stand ready to prevent the *Stennis* from interfering with the defense of our port.

"I predict that Karachi will order us to launch a conventional attack against the carrier and reserve the nuclear weapons for a demonstration firing as a warning. However, we will be ready to use nuclear weapons in combat.

"The American carrier is performing a workup in the Eastern Pacific Ocean and is expected to make a port call in Pearl Harbor in the next few weeks. If hostilities increase, the *Stennis* will steam for our home waters. Our immediate order is to return to Pearl Harbor, shadow the carrier, and stand ready to attack it."

Hayat passed the handset to Raja.

"This is the executive officer, Lieutenant Commander Raja. I have read our latest orders from Karachi and concur with Commander Hayat."

Hayat took back the handset.

"I am proud of the valor you showed in battle, and I will be honored to lead you into battle again."

CHAPTER THIRTEEN

Renard followed Li up an escalator and through two security checkpoints. At a third checkpoint outside the entrance to the command center, Commander Ye awaited.

"It is here that I will leave you with Commander Ye," Li said. "Enough men inside that room remember you and are expecting you. Introductions are unnecessary."

"I had expected you to join me," Renard said. "Minister Zhao often accompanied me in the command center."

"I am not Zhao."

"Nor do you enjoy the same respect he earned with his operational commanders."

"They are now my operational commanders," Li said, "and I will leave you to them. I will watch from the overheard observatory. I would only get in your way."

The acting Minister of Defense stormed away. Renard patted Commander Ye between the shoulder blades.

"Have no fear, man," he said. "Somewhere within this mess lies a path to victory, and we shall find it."

*

Renard entered the command center and felt two dozen eyes shift from an electronic navigation chart to him. The highest-ranking man, the Chief of Staff that Renard remembered from years ago, announced his arrival.

"If my eyes are not too old," Admiral Kuotong Yang said in English, "two heroes have just entered the room."

Renard had expected center stage.

"Two heroes?" he asked.

Ye whispered.

"When I commanded the *Sea Tiger*, I sank a *Romeo* class submarine five miles off the coast of the Kaohsiung's Tsoying naval base. It was trying to lay mines, but I stopped it. It was a noteworthy mission."

"Noteworthy?" Renard asked. "Dear God, man. You and I may indeed have a bright future together."

The Admiral opened his arms.

"Come down here and join us," he said. "Commander Ye needs no introduction, but Mister Renard may be unfamiliar to a few of us. I will explain your deeds in planning the destruction of the Chinese destroyer, *Hefei*, to those who do not remember."

The admiral switched to Mandarin. Eyebrows raised on the faces of the who had been ignorant of Renard's plan two years earlier that had sunk a Chinese destroyer with the risk of only two divers and a patrol craft.

Ye craned his neck as he led Renard down stairs into the sunken command center.

"I was not aware you had plotted the operation against the *Hefei*," he said. "No Taiwanese lives lost—a capital ship taken completely by surprise—your work is legend."

"Let's pray that my work today proves equally sound."

Renard glanced over the shoulder of a sailor seated at one of the monitors encircling the center. He recognized three pairs of blue triangles overlaying a map of Taiwan's northern half and its surrounding waters as F-16 combat air patrols. The Chinese coast set the western end of the map, and a pair of red triangles paralleled one of the blue over the Straits of Taiwan.

The sailor pressed a button, and the triangles disappeared. Squares appeared, dotting the water, and Renard assumed they represented surface combatants. Blue friendly forces were concentrated within twelve miles of the Taiwanese coastline. The red squares—Chinese vessels—lined the shipping lanes to the harbor.

Before Renard could inquire, Ye clarified a question growing in his mind.

"The two friendly surface combatants you see beyond the international boundary are patrol vessels of the *Tai Chiang* class," Ye said. "Their speed and stealth let them escape detection and prosecution by submarines. We have only five of its class and cannot build them fast enough."

"I'm not surprised," Renard said. "I know the *Tai Chiang* class quite well."

Inverted triangles caught Renard's eye. He pointed at a red one that represented a Chinese submarine.

"If you know where it is, why not prosecute it?" he asked. "Your rules of engagement support such action."

Ye exchanged words with the seated sailor. The sailor tapped a keyboard and the triangle faded away.

"The *Tai Kuang* detected the submarine with its blue-green undersea laser, but its torpedo missed. The submarine escaped, and the targeting data is now stale."

"And what of the blue inverted triangles?" Renard asked. "There are three of them deployed, but that cannot be correct. You don't have enough submarines for that."

"Those are unmanned undersea vehicles," Ye said.

"Unarmed, I hope," Renard said. "Perhaps I am old-fashioned, but I don't trust robots in combat."

"They carry no weapons. They broadcast active sonar pulses and have proven effective at detecting submarines. After we detected one submarine, the Chinese have not sent submarines near our harbor."

"I thought your anti-submarine minefield would have taken care of that itself."

"The unmanned vessels patrol beyond the minefield. It is necessary to push them as far as we can."

A voice rang out over the murmur behind Renard.

"Mister Renard," Yang said, "we are ready for you."

Flag and near-flag ranking officers created an opening for Renard and Ye to view the central horizontal monitor. A map showed an egress route from Keelung to distant international water. Triangles and squares represented tankers, surface combatants, helicopters, and a submarine.

Renard recognized Mandarin characters beside the *Hai Lang* and disliked its placement at the head of the convoy.

"The Chinese have been engaging shipping fifteen nautical miles from the coast," Yang said. "Once twelve miles out, the tankers will accelerate to seventeen knots and begin forty-five degree zigzag submarine evasion legs, slowing convoy speed of advance to twelve knots.

"The frigate *Kang Ding* will protect the port side of the convoy while the patrol craft *Tai Ping* will protect the starboard. The helicopter from the *Kang Ding* will patrol the port side, as it is the expected threat vector for submarines. Four F-16 aircraft armed with anti-shipping missiles will take primary responsibility to suppress surface combatant intervention."

"Preemptive or reactionary suppression?" Renard asked.

"Reactionary," Yang said. "Better to minimize attention to the convoy. The Chinese cannot enforce the blockade to all shipping. If tomorrow is our day, we may be fortunate enough to pass unnoticed."

"You risk that a surface combatant's first sign that it is engaging us is the launch of its anti-ship missiles."

"The frigate and patrol craft would then engage their incoming missiles," Yang said.

"A difficult task for crews searching for submarines and possibly shooting retaliatory anti-ship missiles."

"These are our best crews, Mister Renard. Three months ago, the *Tai Ping* sank a *Romeo* as it was preparing to fire on an inbound tanker, and the *Kang Ding* recently was able to harass a *Romeo* enough to keep it from completely destroying an inbound Japanese convoy."

"And the *Hai Lang*?" Renard asked.

"It will sweep for submarines ahead of the convoy."

Renard furrowed his brow and contemplated.

"Your opinion, Mister Renard?" Yang asked.

"This is all wrong."

The officers broke into side conversations. Admiral Yang shouted in Mandarin, and the table fell silent.

"You've thrown the *Hai Lang* into this operation as an afterthought," Renard said.

"Mister Renard," Yang said. "The men around this table have planned many successful blockade runs."

"I see this as an optimal egress escort scenario for a navy that can spare only a stealth patrol craft, a frigate, and helicopters," Renard said. "I commend you and your staff for outlining a plan that I believe has more than a fifty percent chance of success."

"Do not mince words," Yang said. "We do not have the luxury of subtlety. What's wrong with the scenario?"

"First, I would triple the helicopter coverage. You would stress the *Kang Ding's* flight support crew, but if you station helicopters ahead of the convoy, you can average two and half helicopters on station while the third is in transit, refueling, or reloading sonobuoys."

"That would conflict with the *Hai Lang's* search," Yang said. "We would need to set exclusion zones to prevent the *Hai Lang* from becoming a target of our own helicopters, and that is a complex matter."

"But helicopters can use active sonar where my submarine would have to search passively for fear of counter detection," Renard said. "Active sonar from helicopters can detect submarines of all classes and negate the quieting advantage of a *Song* or *Kilo*, should one threaten the convoy."

"They rarely risk their best submarines against convoys for that very reason."

"Indeed," Renard said, "The helicopters' main purpose, achieved by repositioning frequently, is to force any submarine lying in wait to turn from the convoy's track. If you're a submarine commander, a helicopter can be pinging loudly in front of you one minute, and minutes later it can be behind you. A submarine commander is safe only by disengaging."

"Then what of the *Hai Lang*?" Yang asked.

Renard lifted the Zippo lighter and lit a Marlboro.

"The *Hai Lang* should not participate," Renard said. "At least not directly as you have it here."

"And why not?" Yang asked.

"I did not come here to be passive and wait," Renard said. "I came here to hunt submarines for you. I feel confident in your ability to detect and engage Chinese *Romeo*, *Ming*, and *Han* submarines with your surface and air fleet. You've had success with them, have you not?"

"Yes," Yang said. "We've detected twelve with possible hostile intent, sunk five, and forced two to surface."

"That is commendable," Renard said, "but I must ask if any of your quarry have been a quiet *Kilo* class submarine?"

Yang lowered his head.

"No," he said and lifted his gaze. "We have yet to detect a *Kilo* on patrol. We had questionable contact on a *Song*, but classification was unconfirmed."

"My services were engaged to alleviate this submarine threat that is the backbone of the blockade. I believe I can achieve this most effectively by taking the *Hai Lang* against a *Kilo*, and nothing less," Renard said.

"Then you wish a separate operation?" Yang asked.

"Yes, sir," Renard said. "Separate but related. If you will lend me the use of the patrol craft, the frigate, and the helicopters, I will reduce the Chinese submarine order of battle by at least one *Kilo* class submarine. As a byproduct of that effort, I shall present you a corridor through which you can send the convoy."

The admiral's face hardened.

"I remember your successes in our past," he said, "but this is bold. Show us your plan."

Yang rolled a shiny stainless steel pen onto the table and Renard picked it up.

"It's magnetic," Yang said. "Just touch and drag."

Renard pressed the pen against the triangle that represented the *Hai Lang* and dragged it. The triangle followed.

"Two operations, each complementing the other," Renard said. "The first is to hunt Chinese submarines. Once that's done, the convoy begins its egress under the protection of the same friendly assets as used in the hunt. Any adversary that survives the first operation will be disoriented, poorly positioned, and in need of snorkeling."

Renard pushed the tankers back into port and shuffled the surface combatants and helicopters to his liking.

When he was done, heads began to nod in approval.

"This is impressive," Yang said, "but it relies heavily upon the success of the *Hai Lang*. It is still unproven in combat."

"But its leaders are proven," Renard said. "And you have no choice but to trust that we will succeed. If you do not take the offensive, the Chinese will whittle your convoys away until your island starves."

"I must review this new plan," Yang said.

"Yes," Renard said. "Of course."

"With my staff," Yang said. "Alone."

CHAPTER FOURTEEN

COMMANDER DIEGO RODRIGUEZ STARED AT the man beside him. Although the ensign had picked a movie for the off-watch officers, he spent more time glaring at the electrical system diagram he had opened on the table. Rodriguez pushed the diagram into the ensign's lap.

"There'll be plenty of time for training later," Rodriguez said. "Relax and watch the movie."

The faces lit by the television monitors tried to smile at Rodriguez' attempt at levity, but each officer was too stressed to do more than smirk.

The USS *Hawaii*, the third hull of the *Virginia* class attack submarine, was on station in waters claimed by China as an economic exclusion zone. Tasked with monitoring Chinese submarine activity, Rodriguez had the crew on a port and starboard two-section watch. Rodriguez considered the *Hawaii* the most advanced and automated submarine but could see that his crew grew fatigued.

Four more weeks, he thought, *and we'll be relieved. I'll be able to give them a port call. They've earned it.*

The *Hawaii* had tracked five distinct *Romeo* class submarines and one *Ming*, and Rodriguez believed that he knew their patrol areas as well as the Chinese. His crew had collected useful data, and they had operated their magnificent war machine well, he decided.

At the expense of speed and depth, the *Virginia* class had been built with every other advantage. Sonar configuration and sound quieting optimized it to defeat diesel submarines in short-range or coastal combat. Rodriguez' submarine could defeat anything in the Chinese fleet.

Although he had yet to discover a coveted *Kilo*, Rodriguez wanted to test his ship and crew against the best his adversary could offer. But his rules of engagement precluded him from attacking unless in self-defense. After the loss of the *La Jolla*, presumably at the hands of a Chinese *Kilo*, American submerged combat protocol had become conservative.

Light from the passageway shined into the wardroom as a sailor popped his head through a door.

"Captain," the zit-faced sailor said. "The executive officer wants you on the conn."

Rodriguez trotted out of the room. Memories from past submarines told him to climb a ladder, but the central nervous system of the *Hawaii* spanned the middle deck. A photo-optics mast and monitor system had replaced the old-world, hull-penetrating periscope, freeing the control room to move to a wider, mid-deck location.

The design took getting used to, Rodriguez reflected as he entered the spacious control room.

A jogger, Rodriguez considered the mind and the body as one. Allowing one to fall into disrepair dragged the other into atrophy, he had thought—until he met Richard Jones, his executive officer.

Jones wore coke-bottle glasses and filled his blue cotton jumpsuit from neck to thigh with one, smooth, convex contour that defied gravity and reminded Rodriguez of a Dr. Seuss character. But Jones was the smartest man Rodriguez had met, and his intellect kept him in the navy despite failure to meet height, weight, and physical training requirements.

The mass of Jones' body made the portly chief petty officer beside him appear normal. Rodriguez felt like a stick as he stepped between them.

"What do you have, executive officer?" he asked.

"Maybe another *Romeo*, sir. We don't know yet."

Rodriguez glanced at the monitor that showed raw sonar data. Fifty-hertz lines representing an electric generator and several lines at the higher frequencies of a diesel engine had appeared on the same bearing.

"We've got the lower frequencies on the towed array and contour array," Jones said. "We picked up the higher frequency lines on the sphere. We've solved the range."

Rodriguez read the screen. Five thousand yards—two and a half-nautical miles.

"And we just picked him up?" he asked.

"Yes, sir," the chief said.

Chief Petty Officer Jerome Bartlett's mustache wiggled while he spoke. He continued.

"We might have run right under him if he didn't just fire up his diesel. We're just below the acoustic layer, so we should hear him better when he goes deep again."

"He might hear us, too, and his hands aren't tied by rules of engagement. Back us off, executive officer," Rodriguez said. "Let's track this guy as long as we can."

If the bureaucrats had any balls, Rodriguez thought, *I'd shoot and let a salvage team identify him later.*

*

The *Hawaii* had spiraled four miles away from the snorkeling submarine. Rodriguez reclined in his chair on the elevated conn.

In front of him, Jones and Bartlett integrated data into a useful tactical scenario. To his left, monitors and control stations for managing tactical data and weapons lined the side of the hull. In silence, a handful of men studied those screens. To his right, a team of sonar operators sifted through raw acoustic sound.

Jones spoke over his shoulder.

"Sir, he's secured snorkeling," he said.

Rodriguez called up the frequency data on his monitor. The lines began to shrink and collapse into history. He yelled across the room.

"Any hull popping?" he asked.

A chief petty officer seated with the sonar team pushed a headset behind his ear, stood, and shook his head.

"No, sir," he said. "It could be the acoustic layer, or it could be that he's got real solid hull construction. Maybe he hasn't gotten deep enough to hear his hull compressing yet."

"Keep listening," Rodriguez said.

I've got a Kilo, he thought. *Damn! Why won't the bureaucrats let me shoot?*

"We've got some hull popping," the far away sonar chief said. "Not much, but enough. He's coming down—passing through the surface layer. Should be in the same acoustic layer as us soon."

"Rig ship for ultra-quiet operations," Rodriguez said. "Make turns for four knots."

Tense, silent moments passed. Rodriguez flipped through screens showing acoustic data, but nothing appeared.

Quiet bastard, Rodriguez thought.

"More hull popping," the sonar chief said.

"Let's get some sustainable data."

More silence.

"Got him!" the sonar chief said. "We hear rudder swath. And we've got their screws. Contact Sierra-eleven is running one five-bladed screw, making twenty RPM. We won't know what speed that equates to until we identify ship class. Tracking on the chin array."

"Just the chin?" Rodriguez asked. "We can't hear anything on the other sonar arrays?"

Jones turned with alacrity that seemed impossible for his mass.

"They're deep, sir," Jones said. "Probably deeper than we are, and we're hearing them from below on the chin. Also, the harmonic of their screw is at a high enough frequency to be optimized on the chin array."

"Deeper than us?" Rodriguez said as he stood and huddled with Jones and Bartlett.

"Five blades don't correlate to a *Kilo*," he said.

Jones and Bartlett shook their heads.

"And Chinese standard operating procedure doesn't have any of their submarines operating below six hundred feet."

More shaking heads.

"What the hell are we tracking?"

"Sir," the sonar chief said.

Rodriguez glanced over Jones.

"Go ahead," he said.

"We just heard a trim pump start. Classifying now. It's not correlating to anything Chinese. Nothing."

Rodriguez tried to fathom the identity.

"*Agosta* class, sir," the sonar chief said. "The new one—*Agosta90B* to be exact."

"The Taiwanese have one, and a Pakistani hull was located in a Chinese dry dock a couple days ago, sir," Jones said. "It has to be one of the two."

"I concur," Rodriguez said. "But we don't know if he's friend or neutral. Or worse."

He stepped back to the elevated conn.

"Attention in the control room," he said. "We will trail Sierra-eleven, an *Agosta* class submarine."

"Trail?" Jones asked. "Beyond our patrol area, sir?"

Good question, Rodriguez thought. *That's my concern.*

The features on Jones' face sagged as he fell into a stupor. Rodriguez had developed the patience to wait for the stupor's results. If he were doing anything stupid, Jones would figure it out during his semi-autistic analysis.

"You think it pushes the envelope on our orders?"

"We should verify when possible," Jones said, "but I believe it's within the spirit of our orders, sir."

"Let's do it then," Rodriguez said, "but don't forget—this *Agosta* may shoot first and ask questions later."

CHAPTER FIFTEEN

OLIVIA TIPPED BACK A CAFÉ crème and inhaled the cool evening air. Her shoulders ached from riding.

She was dining at a local café hidden from tourists, and traffic on the street was sparse. On the other side of the patio railing, Jake's black Ninja reclined against its kickstand next to her blue one. Color-coded jackets and helmets rested on the handlebars.

"Thanks for the time to prepare," she said.

"I haven't ridden in months myself," Jake said. "It was a good idea to practice tight turns around here and getting on and off the *autoroutes*."

"It was fun tooling around here with you for a day," she said.

"You almost laid it down turning off the bridge."

"I learned not to watch the scenery, no matter how pretty the Rhône is. I need to watch the road."

Jake left euro bills on the table.

"Look," he said, "about the racing part of this. I wasn't serious. There's no hurry."

"Bullshit," she said. "If it weren't for me slowing you down, you'd be breaking the sound barrier."

"Maybe, but I like it better having you with me."

She walked to her motorcycle and slipped on her protective gear.

"I can keep up with you," she said.

"We'll see."

"Eight o'clock tomorrow?" she asked.

"I would like to see if we can have lunch in Lyon. Maybe stay the day," he said, "depending on how we feel."

"See you tomorrow."

Olivia turned the ignition key and heard the rocket rumble. Her bones vibrated. She released the clutch and felt her arms snap taut.

With a rekindled command of large motorcycles, she navigated the streets to her apartment, locked the bike, and worked her door open. Within minutes, she was asleep.

*

Olivia dreamt.

As with prior episodes of the recurring nightmare, pain swelled in her skull.

A knife scratched her throat. The slave trafficker was on her, and she felt the burning and throbbing that her subconscious forced her to relive.

She rose above herself and asked the naked CIA officer on the Parisian pimp's couch where her pimp was. For the first time in the series of recurring dreams, the rape victim pointed.

His face bruised and blood trickling from his mouth, the Parisian pimp knelt before the trafficker's henchmen. The pimp looked at her.

"How did this happen?" he asked.

"Jean-Claude?" she asked.

"I wish I had known your real name."

"Olivia," she said.

A henchman sliced the pimp's throat open.

Olivia awoke, covered in cool sweat. Her alarm clock indicated that it was three o'clock in the morning.

"That felt too real!" she said.

Jean-Claude had been killed during her rape, but Olivia had never seen the body. She wondered if the dream was based upon a repressed memory and stepped into the shower to clear her mind. Propping the hand-held showerhead on a latch Jake had constructed for her from wire hangars, she let hot water beat down upon her.

If that was part memory, she thought, *why now?*

Fearing she wouldn't get back to sleep, she slid into her riding gear and took the motorcycle into the night. Atop the bridge that spanned the Rhône, she slipped the bike out of gear and idled to the west bank and into Villeneuve.

Seeking peaceful contemplation, she left the bike parked in the gravel and stepped through tall grass. When she liked her view of the river and Avignon on its far side, she sat and thought.

In her tranquility, she explored her mind to sort memory from subconscious conjecture. When a question—one that needed answering—took center stage, she picked up her cell phone. Tommy was on watch.

"Where are you?" he asked. "I don't like when you run off like that. I've been trying to call you."

"I had my phone off. I needed time alone."

"When are you coming back?"

"After I talk to Rickets," she said.

"Rickets? Now?"

She wasn't in the mood for explaining herself.

"Set it up."

She heard the clicking of switching relays.

"You're secure with Director Rickets," Tommy said. "Hurry back so Robert doesn't put my ass in a sling."

"It's nearly four in the morning there," Rickets said. "What's wrong?"

"Jerry," she said, "I think I remember."

"Remember what?"

"Paris. How Jean-Claude died," she said.

"You called me on a secure line in the middle of the night to tell me how a pimp died?"

"I think I'm starting to reconstruct my memory. Maybe getting close to Slate is allowing me to unlock memories."

"That's a dangerous place to tread," he said.

She had expected more enthusiasm and frowned.

"What's dangerous? My memories or getting close to Slate?"

"Both. Getting close to Jean-Claude blinded you and nearly got you killed," he said.

"I'm not sure if I was dreaming, but it was as clear as a memory. Jean-Claude was on his knees and looking right at me when Marko's guys killed him."

"You're mixing memory and emotion. You should ignore those memories until we can get you to a psychologist to reconstruct them properly."

She replayed the last moments of the Parisian pimp's life. A chill ran through her as she relived her emotions. Through her fear and pain, she remembered having pitied Jean-Claude during his dying moments.

"Jerry," she said, "I remember the smell of sweat, the aching in my jaw, the pool of blood running from the brunette whore's throat. What's weird is that I remember having pitied him. If he had turned on me, don't you think I would have felt something different?"

"You're under a lot of stress. You're not seeing things clearly."

"No, Jerry. I'm just starting to see my past enough to question it. Are we sure he compromised my cover?"

"Who else could it have been?"

"I just don't see him turning on me. I'm starting to regain faith in my judgment, and my instincts say it wasn't him."

Rickets released a drawn out sigh.

"Well, in a way he did," he said. "He became enamored with you, and the brunette whore could tell. She got so jealous that he told her you were CIA to calm her down, but it backfired. She turned both of you over to Marko."

"That damned brunette whore blew my cover?"

"It's an ugly truth I wanted to protect you from."

"But Marko killed her," she said.

"He wouldn't let someone who turned on her master join him. Based on the reconstruction at the scene, he took care of her first."

Olivia recalculated the evidence leading to the most traumatic event of her life, but a vital piece eluded her.

Her voice fell to a hoarse whisper.

"How do you know it was her?" she asked.

"Her clientele included enough Parisian officials that she was able to probe them until she found one that knew about our operation. That led her to me."

"To you? Why?"

"She threatened to turn you over to Marko if we didn't pull you out and pay her fifty thousand euro."

Olivia's blood pressure rose.

"And you didn't call it off?"

"Look, I know what you're thinking, but I thought she was bluffing. I couldn't give up on the most filthy, prolific slave trafficker in all of Europe for her."

"How could you have sent me in there knowing she could blow my cover?"

"I agonized over that decision, and it still haunts me. But I had to make the call. I didn't think she was serious. I thought you were safe."

Olivia's throat tightened.

"You used me," she said.

"I did my job. I made the tough decision."

"With my body. It wasn't your decision to make."

"I know it was horrible, but you took down a tyrant. You spared hundreds, maybe thousands of women—girls—from lives of bondage."

"You succeeded. You were promoted. I was raped."

"You're strong enough to put it behind you, and you have a brilliant career ahead of you. I'll see to it that you receive due credit for what you've already done with Slate and Renard."

"I can't believe you used me," she said

"I'm sorry. I don't know what else to say."

"Jerry," she said, "I need to know … Jean-Claude. Did he know she had threatened you?"

"I'm sure he didn't. He was—I hate to say it for a pimp—but he was honest."

She watched moonlight shimmer on the Rhône and reflected that she was a stalwart judge of character. She would never doubt her instincts again, she decided.

"You lied," she said. "My instincts with Jean-Claude were right."

"Look," Rickets said, "you're understandably distraught. I'll have Robert—"

She hung up, hurled the phone into the river, and screamed at the top of her lungs.

Fighting back tears, she put her helmet on and jumped onto her bright blue Kawasaki. To drown out her sniffling, she gunned the engine. She released the clutch, ripped through the gears, and sped through the gate into the city.

She rode through the streets of Avignon toward Jake's apartment. Cobblestones shook her arms as she turned toward his garage. She parked on the street, dropped her helmet, and trotted to his door.

Her fist hit his door in frantic repetition until it creaked open. His hair disheveled and his face puffy with sleep, Jake greeted her in a raspy voice.

"Olivia," he said, "what's wrong, honey?"

She wanted to say something without compromising her cover to let him know how much she needed someone to trust, but she couldn't find the words.

She collapsed in his arms and cried.

CHAPTER SIXTEEN

Jake helped Olivia to a chair.

"I'll get you some tissues," he said.

Expecting a quivering mess upon his return from his basement bathroom, Jake instead found Olivia pacing.

"You still want these?" he asked.

She grabbed the tissue box, blew her nose, and lowered the box to an end table.

"I need you to trust me," she said.

"I'll do what I can."

"We need to get out of here."

"We're leaving in three hours," he said.

"I mean now."

"Why?" he asked.

"That's where I need you to trust me."

"Only if you tell me what's going on."

She murmured to herself, and Jake started to worry.

"I just have a bad feeling about staying in Avignon tonight," she said. "Can we just hit the road?"

"Why were you crying?"

"Panic attack," she said. "I've been having them for a while. Can we go?"

"You're too strong to freak out for no reason. Tell me what's wrong."

She sighed, slid her arms around his neck, and tilted her head into his chest.

"If we leave now, we can watch the sun rise on our way to Lyon," she said. "That would be so romantic."

"Don't play games with me."

"Fine," she said. "Can you just trust me then? I've had an emotional night, and I want to leave now. Isn't that enough for you?"

"Okay," Jake said. "My stuff's already packed on my bike. Do we need to go by your place?"

"No. Let's go."

*

A black gas tank swallowed the glow from Olivia's brake light. Jake inhaled the scent of gasoline and rubber and lifted his gear shifter with his toe. Coasting towards the intersection, he saw the red glow intensify and stood on his brake lever.

He protested into his wireless helmet-to-helmet communications system.

"Why'd you stop?"

"Cops at the gate," Olivia said.

"It's a walled city," Jake said. "They hang out at gates, or would you rather have them looking for bad guys tunneling in and out?"

She dipped her helmet, and her body slumped.

"It's a check point," she said. "I'm sure they're set at every gate tonight."

Jake could no longer tolerate her irrationality. He parked his bike, slipped his helmet off, and stepped to Olivia. He yanked her arm.

"All of a sudden you bawl your eyes out, and now you're afraid of cops. What the hell's going on?"

As she removed her helmet, a tear dripped from her chin and splashed on the gas tank.

"Crying isn't going to work anymore," he said. "If you don't start talking, I'll drag you to those cops."

She raised her head. Her face was red and her eyes filled with water.

"They'd arrest you on the spot," she said.

"Why me?"

"Because I'm with the CIA."

Confusion turned to primal fear as he sensed his past catching up with him. He let go of her and engaged his survival instincts. He was apprehensive but cool.

"So you work for the CIA? How does that get me arrested?"

"Because you're not Jake Savin. You're Lieutenant Jacob Slate, responsible for the hijacking of the USS *Colorado*. I know everything. The *Tai Chiang*, the *Miami*, and now the *Hamza*. And because I lost my cool, I'm sure they're going to bring you in as soon as they can."

Jake knew she was unarmed but backed away as if she could strike with venom.

"I knew you were too good to be true," he said. "Pierre warned me, but I didn't believe him."

"I'm not a complete lie," she said. "Not everything."

"What do I believe?"

"I want to help you."

"Bullshit."

She raised her voice.

"If I didn't want to help you, you'd already be in a brig awaiting your Court Martial."

"Okay, fine. Let's say you got me by the balls, and you're my only chance of freedom. Why would you help me?"

"Because I think you're worth it," she said.

For lack of a better option, he had to believe her.

"Pierre and I have pre-arranged escape scenarios," he said. "I have some body armor and non-lethal weapons in my basement. We put on the armor, suit up, and—"

"I didn't say I was going with you," she said.

"You just said you have no one else. And from the way you're behaving, it sounds like your career is over."

"There's a difference between having no career and being thrown in jail for abetting a fugitive."

"You can risk an adventure with me or go back to whatever life you had. You make the call."

Again her head dropped, and he sensed she was holding back tears. Instinct told him to hurry, but he let her struggle through her decision.

She raised her head.

"You can't go back to your apartment," she said. "The cops I saw at the gate had riot gear to keep you in the city. That means the local police are being mobilized, and your place is unsafe by now."

"I have ways to sneak in. You know my past. I live where I live for a reason. We can get in and out unnoticed. There are tunnels and basements."

"No," she said. "I have a better idea. I'll help you, and I'll go with you, but you have to trust me."

"Doesn't sound like I have much choice."

"You're more valuable alive than dead. I'm pretty sure the cops don't have orders to kill."

"Oh yeah?" he asked. "How sure?"

"Sure enough to ride in front of you. Get on your bike, turn off your lights, and snuggle up to my tailpipe."

She strapped her helmet to the back of her seat, unzipped her bright blue jacket, and fiddled with her bra.

"I figure when the cops see a hot chick on a bike with her hair in the breeze, they'll hesitate. Then I'll flash the cleavage. That always buys extra time."

"They probably know you're coming."

"So what? They're still men, right?"

Jake slipped on his helmet and followed Olivia around the corner onto Rue St-Michel, the main road out of the south gate. Fifty yards ahead he saw two police cars squeezing traffic through the gate to one lane.

Two cops aimed a flashlight into a Renault hatchback and waved the car through. Two more cops stood on the stone arch's other side. A fifth cop, the evident leader, stood beside stacked riot gear.

Her hair fluttering in the breeze, Olivia pulled away. Jake accelerated and drafted her. Looking ahead, he saw the cops grow agitated. The leader chattered into a two-way radio while pointing at the riot gear. The other four flipped helmet visors over their faces. Two lifted riot shields and blocked the entrance.

The leader illuminated a blinding light. Jake squinted and heard the leader's voice over a megaphone.

"Stop for identification."

I hope you know what you're doing, he thought.

Olivia arched her back, shook her hair in the breeze, and reached for her chest. The stupefied cops lowered their shields and ogled. The leader barked and the shields rose again. The other two cops reached for their holsters.

Jake heard a belching drone, a squealing tire, and the whine of Olivia's engine as she charged the blockade. Blue in the darkness, her exhaust smoke wafted over him. He gunned his engine to catch up to her, but she was already at the gate.

The riot shields parted and let her pass, and Jake thought he might get through unharmed.

"You are ordered to stop!" the leader said.

Jake pulled back on the Ninja's throttle and let it catapult him through the blockade, but he met a different fate than Olivia.

The riot shields converged and hammered his shoulders. The first shield knocked him sideways, and the second knocked him backward. He flipped back over the seat as the Kawasaki leapt into the street, spat sparks, and ground to a stop.

Jake rolled and landed inches from the bike. He struggled to his elbow and growled in pain. He reached for the handlebars, but the bike idled on its side.

Ignoring the throbbing in his ribs, he fought to his knees. As he tried to stand, he noticed the two cops he had rammed lying on the ground, but two more appeared in front of him. One held a Taser, and the other aimed a sort of rifle that he didn't recognize until it recoiled.

He heard the aerosol burst and smelled the pungent, burning spice. A second and a third ball hit him in the neck, exploded upon impact, and pepper spray wafted under his helmet. Despite searing pain in his ribs, he needed to breathe. Grimacing in agony, he lifted his arms to his helmet, removed it, and dropped it.

The Taser leads punched his kidney, and half his body convulsed under the electric current. Protected by the riding jacket, he had escaped skin-to-lead contact and was able to move one arm. As his vision blurred under uncontrolled tearing, he reached to rip off a wire.

A burst of bright blue flashed across his face, the wires tore away, and he stumbled as eddies of electric current subsided within him.

Olivia's engine howled, and she screamed twice as she struck each cop. Jake could no longer see, but he heard her tire squeal in a rapid turnabout. Mucous ran down his nose, and he reached for his throat. Someone grabbed his arm, and he prayed it wasn't a cop.

"Get on!" Olivia said.

Jake straddled her bike and wrapped his arms around her waist. He heard her pop the clutch shut and gun the engine.

A hand grabbed his shoulder, the bike accelerated, and the hand slipped off.

Jake felt Olivia leaning through a turn. He leaned with her but turned away from the hair whipping his face as she accelerated.

Tears streamed down his face, and he swallowed mucous to keep his airways open. He shut his eyes tight, held Olivia, and realized that he had to trust her if he wanted to remain a free man.

CHAPTER SEVENTEEN

Cued by the bike's vibrations and the strands of hair that had become bullwhips, Jake gauged the Kawasaki's speed at more than one hundred and twenty miles per hour. He buried his face in Olivia's back.

Confident they had outpaced any pursuit, he tapped her thigh and yelled for her to stop.

The engine growled as Olivia downshifted. The bike veered to the side of the *autoroute* and stopped. Jake elongated and twisted his torso to work out soreness.

"Ouch," he said.

"Don't move," Olivia said.

Her fingers caressed his face but felt like ice picks.

"Your face is red. You're going to be miserable for at least an hour," she said. "Can you make it?"

"Make it where?" he asked.

"The Italian border. I don't know. I'm kind of making this up as we go."

He opened his eyes and saw red hair and the bright blue of her jacket. His eyes stung, and he closed them.

"You can really ride," he said.

"When I have to."

"Are you afraid?" he asked.

"I just threw my life away, and I don't know where the hell I'm going."

"You're going with me, right?" Jake asked.

"I have nowhere else now."

"What's the road look like?" he asked.

"Clear. The police in Avignon don't have anything that moves as fast as us, but I'm sure they're coming."

"We can outrun Avignon police. It's the rest of the world that scares me."

"There'll be checkpoints on the *autoroutes*," she said. "Every cop in Provence will be watching for us, and I bet a search helicopter is taking off from Nîmes right now. But if I push it, we can go through the Luberon region. The tree cover will make it harder for an airborne search to find us. We could reach the border in three hours."

Jake rubbed his eyes.

"I like your style," he said. "But I told you Pierre and I had escape plans. When you have a past like ours, you'd be stupid not to. I assume Pierre's place isn't safe?"

"It's under surveillance."

"That rules out escape plans alpha through charlie. We'll have to jump ahead to escape plan delta. We're on A-7, right?"

"Yeah."

"How far from Cavaillon?"

"I saw a marker a minute ago that said ten kilometers. Is that where we're going?"

"Not quite. Almost."

Jake groped for his phone, tugged it from his pocket, and handed it to Olivia.

"Dial 'Alain LeClerc' from the stored numbers."

"It's ringing," she said.

She placed the phone in his hand and he pressed it to his ear. He heard a groggy voice.

"*Allo?*" the man asked.

"The fox is trapped in the chicken coup," Jake said.

"*Mon Dieu*," the man said. "Does he want to leave?"

"Yes," Jake said.

"How many?"

"Two."

"Only two?" the man asked.

"The rest are already safe," Jake said.

"Urgency?"

"Immediate. We'll be there in minutes."

"All is prepared," the man said. "It always has been."

Jake slid the phone back in his pants.

"Who was that?" Olivia asked.

"Pierre's brother-in-law."

"Marie's brother?"

"No. From his first wife. Long story," Jake said. "Let's make best speed towards Cavaillon. After the exit, call out street names, and I'll tell you where to turn. We're looking for a sunflower farm."

*

As the bike slowed, Jake squinted at incandescent lights outlining the silhouette of a large structure. Engines whirred and propeller blades whipped the moist air.

"Straight to the airplane," he said.

Its twin engines droning like beehives, a blur of white taxied out of the hangar. The bike stopped, and Olivia grabbed Jake's hand. She guided him to the airplane and opened the passenger door.

"Hide the bike," Jake said.

He climbed into the passenger seat and smelled the stale scent of plastic and vinyl.

"Alain?" Jake said.

"Yes, of course," Alain LeClerc said.

"I can't see very well," Jake said. "Pepper spray."

"I noticed a stench."

The door slammed and Olivia jumped into the backseat.

"The bike's in the hangar," she said. "You should have someone hide it better once we're airborne. We need to hurry. I think I saw a cop turning off the *autoroute* behind us, but I can't be sure."

"And where are we going?" LeClerc asked.

"Unless Pierre has something to say," Jake said, "we make for Tuscany."

"I have been trying to call him since the moment you woke me. It concerns me that I cannot reach him."

"He's half way across the world," Jake said. "Can we just get airborne?"

"As you wish."

Its lights revealing a lane of hard dirt carved in a sea of grass, the plane accelerated and lifted into the darkness. No one spoke until LeClerc leveled at a low cruising altitude.

"I'm heading towards Italy," he said.

"Good," Jake said. "I'll see if I can get hold of Pierre."

His vision clearing, Jake dialed the number to Renard's global account, but Olivia grabbed his hand.

"I wouldn't use that yet," she said.

"Why not?"

"Your calls are being eavesdropped."

"How?" he asked. "I have 256 bit encryption on a digital GSM standard."

"We set up a false base station in Avignon to intercept your calls," she said. "That lets us unravel the encryption algorithm. I'd wait until we're farther away."

"You didn't stop me from calling Alain."

"We had no choice," she said.

"Then I am implicated in whatever trouble you've found your way into," LeClerc said.

"Don't worry," Jake said. "By the time you could tell anyone anything you know about us, we'll be long gone."

"Would my phone be monitored?" LeClerc asked.

"I doubt it," Olivia said. "Not yet. We caught people off guard. The planned take down was still days away."

LeClerc handed Jake his phone. Jake dialed Renard's number but heard only a recorded voicemail.

"Escape plan delta is in effect," he said and hung up.

"Thank you," LeClerc said.

"For what?" Jake asked.

"That message just secured my bonus," LeClerc said. "By the way, I didn't catch your name, miss."

"Better that you don't know a damn thing about her," Jake said. "Let me try something."

Jake scrolled down numbers on his phone until he found Henri's. He punched it into LeClerc's phone and listened.

"*Allo*," Henri said.

"Sweet!" Jake said. "I was afraid you were already at sea. Assume we're being monitored. Tell the boss that escape plan delta is in effect and to call me at this number. Don't say it, but do you have it?"

"*Putain!*" Henri said. "Yes, I see your number. I will have him dial that number within minutes."

While waiting for Renard, Jake kept the phone in his lap and looked for a topic to ratchet down the tension.

"Alain used to fly Mirages in *la Marine Française*."

"I always loved flying," Alain said. "What I wouldn't give for a Mirage, or any jet for that matter. As you can see, my Cessna lacks speed."

"How did you meet Pierre?" Olivia asked.

"*Aspirants* at *l'Ecole Navale*," he said "Class of Nineteen Eighty Two."

"Jake mentioned you were related."

"He married my sister, but my sister and nephew were killed by a drunk driver. It was horrible for me, but it nearly destroyed Pierre. It is good to see him remarried to Marie and that he has a new son. I was beginning to fear that he'd take his misery to the grave."

Jake's vision became clearer. He noticed gray stubble caking LeClerc's chin, but with his slicked-back silver hair and burgundy turtleneck sweater covering his beige dress shirt, he looked dignified.

LeClerc's phone rang and Jake answered.

"Yes?" he asked.

"So," Renard said, "I hear aircraft engines. That's a good sign, given that we have set an escape plan into motion."

"I'm heading to safe haven per plan delta."

Although he assumed no one was eavesdropping, Jake avoided verbalizing clues that the safe haven was a villa in Tuscany.

"We should discuss the nature of your sudden egress," Renard said. "Maybe we should reconsider your destination."

"Why?"

"Because safe haven may not be so safe."

"You said it was untraceable to either of us. A quiet place across a national border in the middle of nowhere."

"It's safe if you can get there unnoticed," Renard said, "but tell me who is searching for you."

Jake sighed and felt like an idiot.

"The CIA," he said. "You were right about Olivia. She played me from the beginning."

"Damn!"

Jake rubbed his forehead.

"I'm only human. And you met her. She's perfect."

"How did you find out?" Renard asked.

"She confessed. Long story. I'm not even sure yet why she's with me."

"*Merde de l'eau!* She is with you?"

"Helped me bust out of Avignon. I'd be in custody now if it weren't for her."

"This is bizarre. I don't—"

Olivia yanked the phone from Jake.

"My name is Olivia McDonald, and every piece of public information about me up until my graduation from Yale's PhD program is true. After that I entered the CIA, and I know your complete history starting with your failed attempt to steal Russian nuclear warheads, your failed attempt to steal the *Colorado*'s warheads, and your operation of commanding the Taiwanese submarine *Hai Lang*. You're probably standing on it right now."

Jake overheard Renard's reply.

"I don't know which is worse—that you know everything about me or that you summarize my life as if it were a complete and utter failure," he said. "As for you, I assume you are now a fugitive. If you are indeed with Jake, then the closer you are to me, the farther you are from the grasp of the CIA."

Olivia's eyes fluttered over Jake with concern.

"You just want me to make sure he joins you."

"Damn it, woman, I'm surrounded by old men and novices. Jake is a genius with experience, and he's cool under fire. I need him."

Jake took the phone.

"I'll join you," he said.

There was silence.

"I said I'm with you," Jake said.

"Finally. You've made the right decision, *mon ami*."

"How do I get there?" Jake asked.

"I expect to make the arrangements shortly, but I suspect your first stop will be the naval base at Algiers."

"Algiers?"

"Indeed," Renard said. "One of Admiral Khan's greatest threats is the Indian *Kilo* class submarine. If you were he, would you not befriend a fellow Moslem naval commander who has *Kilos* in his own fleet?"

"So we have an ally across the Mediterranean."

"More a professional acquaintance," Renard said. "This will not be free. I will split the cost with you, but a ticket for two from Algiers to Karachi via military transport may cost seven figures."

A million euro would only dent Jake's holdings.

"Set it up," Jake said.

"Soon, my friend. I will also electronically send technical manuals. Disks should be burned for you before you arrive in Algiers. You need to begin studying."

"It will give me something to do during my travel. What am I studying? Diesel submarine tactics?

"That, of course," Renard said. "But I need you to master the Subtics combat system."

"Can do. Anything else?"

"The Taiwanese have employed an unmanned vehicle in the *Hai Lang*. They've mastered unmanned technology and have developed a torpedo tube-launched rover. Ye, the submarine's official commanding officer, wants to use it, but I don't trust robots. See if you can make sense of the system."

"Anything else?"

Renard's voice fell to a whisper.

"What exactly did Olivia do to assist with your escape?" he asked.

"I couldn't see well, but I think she swept two cops with a leg whip. It was some sweet riding."

Jake glanced at Olivia. She shrugged and smiled.

"More or less," she said.

"Very well," Renard said. "It sounds legitimate, but think it all through carefully when your head is clear. If she were able to fool you to this point, what is to keep her from continuing? Your entire escape may be a charade to earn your deeper confidence."

"For what?" Jake asked.

"I have no idea," Renard said.

Jake looked at Olivia. She was staring through a window, and the rising sun cast a shadow from her sleek jaw to the supple flesh of her neck. He thought she looked beautiful but remembered that nature employed visual allure to trap prey.

"Anything else?" he asked.

"Let me speak to Alain," Renard said.

Sunlight creeping over the horizon bathed LeClerc as he raised a hand from the control yoke and placed the phone to his ear. He exchanged quick words with Renard.

"Algiers is our new destination," LeClerc said while lowering the phone, "and I am a very rich man."

*

Over blue water, Jake's thoughts melded with the drone of the twin turbo propeller engines. He scanned the innards of the Cessna, and a pile of tightly wrapped canvas bundles gave him an idea.

"How much does a plane like this go for?" he asked.

"I could probably get nearly four hundred euro," LeClerc said. "Why?"

"How long ago were those packed?" he asked.

"The parachutes? I don't like where this is going."

"How long ago?"

"Three weeks," LeClerc said. "Pierre insisted I kept them at the ready as part of earning my stipend."

Thankful he didn't have to use the parachutes per 'plan echo', Jake wondered if LeClerc were willing.

"One million euro," Jake said, "should cover your expense and troubles if you ditch this thing in the Med after you drop us off in Algiers."

"Easy for you to say."

"You ditch close to shore—over a fishing haven or shipping lane—and swim in or wait for a vessel to pick you up. We'll ask Pierre's contact in Algiers to make sure a patrol craft comes and gets you. Hell, you'll even have a phone and your coordinates. Every sea captain in Algeria speaks French, I'm sure."

"Why?" LeClerc asked. "What advantage is gained?"

"Covers everyone's ass. If you get questioned, say I made you jump. No one in Algiers has an airplane to hide, and the trail leading to my butt gets colder."

"It could work," LeClerc said.

"Can you do it?" Jake asked.

"I ditched a damaged Mirage in the North Sea short of a carrier at night. Comparatively, this will be a joy."

CHAPTER EIGHTEEN

THE HALF-NIGHT OF SLUMBER caught up to Jake as he reclined in his seat. He wanted to sleep but found the three rows of passenger chairs in the idling Algerian C-130 cargo aircraft uncomfortable. Olivia dozed by his side.

Jake glanced over his shoulder. Web nets stretched over aluminum bars—uncomfortable but efficient seating for unfortunate souls subject to military mass transit—lined the fuselage. They were empty. Except for the pilot and co-pilot, Jake and Olivia were alone.

A lithe man Jake's age tossed his military cap aside and threw his arm over the back of his pilot's chair. Though the sky was overcast, the pilot wore sunglasses and seemed content to keep them on for fashion's sake.

Airedales, Jake thought. *Arrogant across the world.*

Through the cockpit door, the pilot addressed Jake.

"You must be important," he said in French. "This aircraft was scheduled for paratrooper training today."

Jake realized the depths of his paranoia as he found himself scanning the cockpit for firearms. A pistol hung from the pilot's waist holster, but Jake conceded that he would be at the mercy of Algerian military forces until he landed in Karachi.

"Me? Important?" Jake asked. "Maybe, but I'm guessing you were instructed not to ask."

The pilot smiled, stood, and stepped into the small four-row passenger seating area. He looked ready to offer a retort, but footsteps and clunking drew his attention to the external door. The pilot's body straightened with as much respect for rank as Jake figured the man could muster.

"Colonel," he said.

The plane's new occupant nodded at the pilot. Jake felt an urge to stand but the potbellied lieutenant colonel lowered a suitcase onto his lap before he could react. His thick mustache wiggled across his pock-marked face as he spoke, and his breath stank of unfiltered cigarettes.

"The disks inside this case were just created for you," the lieutenant colonel said. "My orders were to bring them to you—personally."

As the lieutenant colonel dropped a key in Jake's hand, more men clamored into the aircraft. Trim and muscular, they wore sandy-colored desert combat fatigues. One of them lowered a computer case to the aisle.

"Two laptops and power cords," he said.

Another man placed a third laptop on the floor.

"In case one of the other's fail," the lieutenant colonel said. "It appears that you will both have busy flights."

"Thanks," Jake said.

The lieutenant colonel nodded and started off, but the other men—six by Jake's count—moved to the cargo net seats.

"What about them?" Jake asked.

The lieutenant colonel drew his military cap low over his brow.

"For your security."

*

As the Algerian cargo plane leveled at a cruising altitude, Jake examined the contents of his suitcase. Two-dozen compact disks lined the case. Each had a number on it, and the first also had a message typed on it in French.

"Read me first," it said.

Jake closed the case and placed it on the seat beside him. As he rested a computer on his lap and waited for it to boot, he sensed Olivia staring at him.

"What makes you think you're privy to any of this?"

"They gave me a laptop, too, didn't they?" she asked.

"Let's get something straight," he said. "I appreciate you helping me escape, but remember who you are."

"I rescued you at my own risk," she said. "And if you figure out who I am now, let me know."

As the computer came to life, Jake realized his world had crumbled on the other side of the Mediterranean. He distracted himself from defeatist thoughts by focusing on the screen.

The first disk contained a solitary text file that revealed a directory of the remaining disks—a catalogue of the *Hai Lang's* systems. But two disks stood out. They contained information about the captain and certain crew members of the Pakistani submarine, *Hamza*. Notes in parentheses stated that those disks were for his 'new friend'.

The last line in the directory was a personal note.

"Study well, *mon ami*. Pierre."

Jake reached into the case for the two disks created for Olivia and tossed them across the aisle into her lap.

"Knock yourself out," he said and waited for a snide retort, but she spun her computer onto her lap and jammed the first disk into the machine.

One of the security escorts from the back of the craft approached. He carried a coffee pot and plastic cups.

"We all must stay awake," he said.

Jake thanked the soldier, took a cup, and stashed a few cubes of sugar on his laptop keyboard. Cream did not appear to be an option. He glanced at Olivia, but her laptop consumed her.

"I'll take both cups," Jake said.

"Feel free to get all you need," the soldier said.

Jake expected the soldier to return to his comrades in the back of the craft, but he marched forward. He whistled, and another soldier joined him in the cockpit.

To keep us from trying something stupid like a hijack, Jake thought. *I'm not that nuts—am I?*

Sinking into his chair, Jake let the caffeine tickle him back to life. He read, absorbing the technology of the *Hai Lang*. Expecting a solid machine, Jake learned that the *Agosta90B* ranked among the most capable diesel submarines in the world.

The *Hai Lang* was the second ship to carry the French-designed MESMA—Module-Energy, Sub-Marine, Autonomous—ethanol-liquid oxygen propulsion plant. Jake had heard of various AIP—air independent propulsion—modules being applied to diesel-powered submarines.

By permitting small, inexpensive, and quiet diesel submarines to remain submerged for extended periods, AIP marked a strategic shift in modern submarine warfare. Jake remembered studying tactics designed to defeat diesels by outlasting them and forcing them to come shallow, gulp for air through their snorkel masts, and run their diesel engines to recharge their batteries.

Before AIP, the longest most diesels could hope to run submerged on their batteries was a week—and that at a snail's pace. After a week, propulsion load, shipboard systems, and atmosphere cleansing drained the battery.

Jake remembered articles about German and Scandinavian shipbuilders implementing various AIP systems, such as the Sterling engine and the fuel cell. The French, however, had developed an underwater bomb made of rocket fuel. As Jake studied the MESMA bomb, he had mixed emotions.

It could extend the underwater submergence of an *Agosta* to three weeks, but speed would be restricted to four knots—adequate for patrolling coastal waters or for a short-range submerged transit.

In exchange for MESMA, the ship carried thirty extra tons, generated a heat signature that could be detected by infrared if sailing shallow as fuel burned at over a thousand degrees Fahrenheit, and it carried the risk of volatile fluids. It also discharged expended gases that could be detected by the proper waterborne sensor. Jake considered a reactor less dangerous.

Apart from its unique fuels, MESMA ran a simple Rankine cycle heat engine, making steam to turn a turbine and generate electricity. Jake judged it complicated, underpowered, but tactically relevant.

Comfortable with the basics of MESMA, he studied a peculiar modification the Taiwanese had added to the *Hai Lang*. Skilled with unmanned vehicles, Taiwanese engineers had designed an unmanned probe that fit the dimensions of a torpedo. The unmanned 'drone' could be controlled via a torpedo-like guidance wire, and it could search the area around the *Hai Lang* with active and passive sonar.

Fascinating, Jake thought. *Ingenuity at work.*

Jake saw no signs of it having been tested yet, and he was disappointed to learn that the drone was disposable because the Taiwanese had yet to solve the problem of recovering one once used. He decided that if he could use a drone, he'd have to use them judiciously, but the theory looked promising.

He let his mind wander and explore the possibilities of an unmanned drone, teased himself with memories of the Olivia he knew twelve hours earlier, and fell asleep.

*

He awoke and saw Olivia closing a lavatory door. She made eye contact and walked to him.

"I was raped," she said.

"What?" Jake said. "Where'd that come from?"

"That's how I got HIV. Blown cover. I took a slave trafficker off the streets, but I paid for it."

"Okay."

Her fingers dug into the vinyl of the headrest on the empty seat in front of him.

"I know how you got it, you know," she said.

"Don't remind me," Jake said. "In fact, don't remind me that you know everything about me."

"After you got it," she said, "everything you believed in and everyone you trusted fell apart."

Jake squirmed and looked at his screen. Although the *Hai Lang's* main electric motors presented a dull subject, he found them more comfortable than Olivia's topic. He hoped she'd go away, but she lingered.

"It's nice that I can tell you the truth," she said.

Jake watched her knuckles turn white on the headrest.

"I found out last night that someone on my own team knew my cover was blown," she said.

"Was that why you came by my apartment?"

"Yeah," she said. "Now I know how you felt. All of a sudden, everything I believed in and everyone I trusted fell apart, too. You're the only one who understands."

Fatigue and frustration drained her. She sighed.

"Can I sit next to you?" she asked.

He cleared scattered disks and stood. While she gathered her belongings, he went to the lavatory and found her in the seat beside his upon his return.

He sat and let her rest her head against his shoulder. Before Jake could get halfway through a diagram of the Subtics tactical systems, she had fallen asleep.

Careful to avoid stirring her, he twisted to look at her. She was beautiful and at peace.

CHAPTER NINETEEN

OLIVIA HAD AWOKEN HOURS EARLIER and had continued studying. Information about Pakistani Navy Commander Hamid Hayat from Pakistan's Directorate for Inter-Services Intelligence had begun to etch lines across her brow.

The intelligence she had gathered from Jake and Renard showed half the picture. The data in Hayat's dossier revealed more—the paradox of a man who once studied secular government at Harvard's Kennedy School of Government but who now sought fundamentalist Islamic backing.

She fathomed a multitude of possible scenarios that Hayat could be orchestrating, but she needed more information to resolve his intent. Filling in the gaps with assumptions, she agreed with Pakistani intelligence. Hayat would cripple the Indian fleet and beget a war that would bring a fundamentalist regime to power in Islamabad.

The C-130 banked and dipped, bringing the sun's reflection in the Arabian Sea into her view.

The plane flew over P-3C Orion maritime patrol aircraft parked outside of Spartan hangars and touched down. Olivia grabbed her new laptop and case and followed Jake through the door. The men who had been her flight crew and escorts bid reserved farewells and watched in confusion as their peculiar cargo deplaned.

On the tarmac, a Lincoln Town Car with the green and white Pakistani national flag over one headlight and an Admiral's standard over the other overtook a refueling truck. It stopped, and a short man in an Admiral's uniform emerged, followed by a taller and younger man in a junior officer's uniform.

The admiral spoke, and the younger man marched up the steps into the plane. Seeing no armed men, Olivia assumed that she was on a secure installation and that the Pakistani Admiral trusted the Algerians.

Showing no concern with abandoning his junior associate, the admiral extended his hand towards his car.

"Please, get in," he said in accented French.

Olivia followed Jake into the car.

"I am Admiral Sardar Khan, Chief of Staff, Pakistani naval forces."

The trio exchanged handshakes. Olivia felt unsure if she were forgetting to curtsy or carry out some other inane act of diplomacy, but Khan seemed too businesslike to care.

"It's a pleasure to meet you, finally," Jake said.

"And you. Pierre mentioned you on his last visit."

"Do you know where he, is?" Jake asked.

"He is performing exercises in local Taiwanese waters. You cannot reach him. But I can give you these for your travels. I insist."

Khan pointed out two global Iridium phone and battery packs.

"Thanks," Jake said.

"No need for thanks," Khan said. "They are self-serving. Added motivation to ensure that you stay in contact once at sea. I assume you both know of my problem with the *Hamza*?"

"Yeah," Jake said. "We both do."

Jake glared at her, still appearing to harbor a grievance for having been duped.

"I am aware of Miss McDonald's history," Khan said, "and since my relations with the American CIA have proven dubious, I hesitated to share classified data with her. However, Pierre assured me that she will not be sharing further news of our affairs with her former employer."

A pit formed in Olivia's stomach.

Renard is vouching for me, she thought.

She had been so engrossed during her flight that she forgot that her studies had dragged her into Renard's standard recipe for attracting recruits. By stumbling into the acceptance of his gift—Hayat's restricted data—Olivia realized that she would have to be wary of any urges to return favors to the Frenchman.

"I won't share this with the CIA," she said.

"That is good," Khan said. "If the CIA knew what you know, they would only have pressure applied where it need not be applied. They would enable the mishandling of a delicate internal affair."

Olivia realized that her unique position made her the powerbroker for knowledge about Hamid Hayat. Decency demanded that she arm Khan with his fair share.

"You're right about the *Hamza*," she said.

"How so?"

"We have a satellite photograph of it refitting in a Chinese dock outside of Ningbo. That hints strongly at the potential for tactical nuclear weapons."

Khan's face turned ashen.

"If that is true, I must admit that a selfish, childlike voice within my soul wishes Hayat success."

Olivia frowned.

"He is doing what many silently dream about but think better of when of sound mind," Khan said. "And I must act of sound mind. He must be destroyed. I am now more certain of it than ever, and you have given me great relief in my decision to share his dossier with you."

"Shit," Jake said. "What's he going to do? Is he coming after America?"

"Possible, but not likely," Olivia said. "Pakistani intel drew the same conclusion I did. He's probably going after the Indian fleet. For symbolic effect, he might even try to time an attack to take out one or two Indian carriers in a high-profile location."

"I need to reposition my forces," Khan said. "When did he leave Ningbo?"

"Three days ago," she said.

"I have time. If he moves slowly to conserve fuel and remain silent, I can engage him at the Straits of Malacca."

"Makes sense," Jake said. "It's a global chokepoint."

"I will still want Pierre to search for him before he gets that far," Khan said, "but you've helped the nation immensely with this news, Miss McDonald."

"You want Pierre to do what?" Jake asked.

"I see that he did not tell you."

"I thought we were going to beat back a few Chinese *Kilos* and be done with it, not that that's an easy task. Now you're saying we've got to hunt down a renegade?"

"Perhaps I should have said nothing," Khan said. "These phones, you can try them tomorrow. Pierre should be back from his exercises after sunrise. You can talk to him personally then."

"I'll wait to see him in person," Jake said.

"Fine," Khan said. "I've reserved rooms in our officers' quarters for you to rest. Pierre's chartered jet is on the tarmac, however, should you wish to leave now. It is comfortable and permits sleeping."

Olivia exchanged a glance with Jake.

"I'd like to spend a night on a bed that's not moving," he said. "That will soon be hard to come by."

*

The next morning, Olivia's clothes from the prior day had appeared outside her door, laundered. When she slid them on, she felt invigorated.

Unsure if she were making the right choice, she stepped aboard the Gulfstream jet with Jake. The floor was covered in plush beige carpet, and the seats were comfortable leather. She continued her study of Hayat.

After several hours of study, she sought a distraction, but Jake looked engrossed in his technical studies, and the pilot and copilot had locked the door to the small cockpit.

What the hell, she thought. *Let's have some fun.*

She reached into Jake's pocket and pulled out his cell phone.

"Hey," he said.

"Watch this," she said.

She dialed and waited.

"You think it's going to work," he asked.

"We're close enough to civilization that it might."

A voice on the line sounded surprised.

"Hello," a man said. "Who is this?"

"Uncle Robert," she said. "You don't recognize me?"

"On his phone? For added drama? What the hell are you doing? Are you safe?"

"You still have your hundred percent track record of no injured officers on your watch. I might lose this connection soon, so get Rickets on the line quickly."

"Right."

She waited until she heard Rickets' voice.

"You like calling me at odd hours," Rickets said. "Where are you?"

"Heading toward Keelung."

"Whose side are you on?" Rickets asked.

"Mine."

"Careful answer," he said. "If you want to come back, I can make it happen. We can work something out with Taipei to get Slate, and I can cover for what you're doing now. We can still both claim victory on this mission. No one has to get hurt or embarrassed."

"That might sound tempting if I could believe you."

"I lost nights of sleep over what happened to you. I didn't want you to get hurt by the truth, but now that you know, I have to admit that I feel better about it. That secret between us was killing me."

"As long as you feel better."

"That's not what I meant," he said. "I'm trying to tell you I've come clean with you on everything. I want your trust back. I want you back."

"You want my trust? Then you dig up everything you can about Commander Hayat from his time in America. I mean Harvard, the naval submarine school, and everything else you have. Tell me where he shopped, what he ate, who he hung out with. You have that waiting for me pierside at the *Hai Lang*, and I'll think about trusting you."

She expected him to tell her off.

"I'll see what I can do," he said.

Rickets was either bluffing or bending over backwards to win her approval. Either way, she played it.

"And I want you to leave Jake alone."

"I can't promise that," he said. "He still stole a Trident Missile submarine."

"Yeah," she said. "And now I understand why."

CHAPTER NINETEEN

THE GULFSTREAM LANDED ON A runway at Keelung naval base. As she descended toward the tarmac, Olivia thought the upscale executive jet seemed juxtaposed with the P-3 Orion anti-submarine aircraft and the F-16 attack jets.

A stark white van rolled to a stop, and its solitary occupant stepped through the driver's side door. The lithe, silver-haired man slid a lighter under a cigarette.

"You were expecting another Admiral in a luxury vehicle?" he asked.

"Shit, Pierre," Jake said. "I'm surprised you remember how to drive."

"I wanted time alone with both of you," Renard said. "I fear we will have little privacy in the near future."

Jake marched to Renard and threw an arm over his shoulder.

"It's good to see you," Jake said.

"And you, my friend. I feared you might not join me."

"Ran into a little girl trouble."

"I would say more than a little," Renard said. "I don't know whether to thank you or to cast you away."

"Why'd you have Khan give me the data on Hayat?" Olivia asked. "What do you want from me?"

"A little courtesy, perhaps," Renard said. "You are in no position to be asking questions."

"I've earned the right by bringing him to you."

She looked at Jake, but he lowered his head and brushed by her to grab their luggage.

"You studied to be an analyst, yet you wound up in the field," Renard said. "Why?"

The question caught her off guard.

"Apparently, when men look at me, their penis-brain interlock kicks in. The CIA likes women who can toy with men. Plus, I'm kind of smart and pretty handy with small arms."

"But you are too smart to waste your time with simple seduction," Renard said. "Each time you wiggle your breasts to dislodge a man's brain from his central nervous system, you sense that your analytical skills are atrophying."

Renard had a point, she realized. When her father had died, she abandoned her desire to serve as a criminal psychologist, but she wondered if the seduction of the CIA had deflated her true passion of psycho-analysis.

"So what's next for me?" she asked.

"I want your services as an analyst."

"I figured that out already. What do you want me to resolve?"

Renard blew smoke.

"If I can finish affairs on this island according to the plan I've outlined for the Taiwanese, Hayat is my next target. I want to understand my adversary. Who is he, what is his agenda, and where is he going?"

"I was afraid that's what you wanted. I went through as much as I could on the plane rides, but there's nothing sticking out. Unless I get more data, I agree with your friend Khan that he's heading for India."

"Very well," Renard said. "Jake and I have a large enough task in front of us already. Perhaps you'll have more for us upon our return. I've arranged for the best accommodations within the confines of the naval base. I didn't want the CIA coming for—"

"How come I can't come with you?" she asked.

"A submarine is no place for a woman," Renard said.

Jake closed the van's back doors and frowned.

"Chauvinist," he said.

"It's not a matter of ability or social grace," Renard said. "It's a matter of keeping twenty-three men focused on their duties without the distraction of her curves."

"Twenty-three men?" she asked. "The *Agosta90B* requires thirty-six for a full crew."

Renard raised an eyebrow.

"I did my homework," she said. "You need an extra pair of hands. I can cook, clean things, and steer the damn thing for you."

"I don't need the extra hands for a short-duration mission," Renard said. "The manning requirements are only for extended operations."

"But you'll want me eventually, if you're going to go after Hayat. May as well start my onboard training now."

Jake chuckled and slapped Pierre on the shoulder.

"*Touché, mon ami,*" Jake said.

"You're just giddy because you think I'm going to let you take your girlfriend with you," Renard said.

"My what?" Jake asked.

"Young lady," Renard said. "This is battle. Men will die, and I cannot guarantee your safety. Are you ready to face death?"

"I can take care of myself."

"So be it, then" Renard said. "I will have Henri issue you the baggiest jumpsuits he can find. You will wear no makeup and no perfume, and you will hide your hair under a ball cap at all times."

She smirked as she passed by him and sat in the van.

"Don't worry, Pierre," she said. "I won't tell Marie you have a crush on me."

"I don't—*merde!*"

*

Jake squinted as the waterfront came into view. With most Taiwanese assets in constant action, few warships lined the piers. He saw a few aging patrol boats and a hand-me-down ex-American frigate with ripped and contorted metal frayed over its bow.

"Five-inch shell from a Chinese destroyer," Renard said. "Our submarine is just beyond."

Jake hadn't seen the *Hai Lang's* sail cresting over the pier opposite the damaged frigate.

"Where? Behind the thimble?" he asked.

"Not all submarines are larger than cruisers," Renard said. "That reminds me. You remember the masses of water required to trim the *Colorado*?"

"Yeah."

"Divide by ten. That is the approximate size ratio between the Trident and the *Agosta*. If giving orders, divide by roughly two again, because you'll be dealing with kilograms instead of pounds."

"I'm walking into hell," Jake said.

"Don't worry," Renard said. "The ship is quite automated and nearly self-trimming. And Henri made a career on the *Agostas* back in our good old days."

Renard parked and grabbed a laptop case. Jake chuckled when Olivia snatched her laptop back from the Frenchman's shoulder.

"I can carry my own stuff," she said.

Renard led them across the metal girder brow to the back of the submarine. Setting foot on the submarine, Jake felt out of place. On the *Colorado*, the brow had angled up towards the submarine's tall back, but after descending to the *Hai Lang*, he could see under the pier and into the damaged frigate's anchor well across the pier.

A man in a commander's uniform stood behind the sail.

"Commander Ye," Renard said. "Let me introduce you to our new crew members."

Ye's eyebrows rose as he fought to keep his neck from snapping and staring at Olivia's curves.

"Yes, I know she's a woman," Renard said. "But she has skills that we'll need—eventually. I'll have Henri set her up in my stateroom for privacy. Jake and I will share the executive officer's quarters, and you, my new friend, I must ask you to join your men in officer's berthing."

"Demotion upon demotion," Ye said. "Just as long as I continue to learn from the masters—and survive this."

"You are too humble," Renard said and puffed a cloud of smoke.

"During our latest exercises," he said. "Commander Ye became the first Taiwanese submarine officer to launch an exercise weapon at a submerged target without the use of active sonar. A quick learner."

"What did you shoot at?" Jake asked.

"Underwater unmanned search vehicles," Ye said. "It was all we had."

Jake shook hands with Ye.

"Are stores loaded? Fuels?" Renard asked.

"Yes, and weapons, too. Three Excocets, ten torpedoes, and one drone."

"I wish you'd throw that drone over the side and make room for another weapon," Renard said.

"I'm sure—"

"Yes, Commander Ye, I agreed to carry a drone. I cannot fathom how it will help us, but since your engineering support teams bothered to develop it, we may as well see if an opportunity for its use will present itself."

*

Jake stepped down a ladder into a room lined with long cylinders he recognized as torpedoes. Three Taiwanese sailors in blue jumpsuits and a Frenchman watched a semi-cylindrical rack swing a weapon across the passageway.

Olivia landed behind him and started towards the moving mass. She seemed mesmerized by the jungle of hydraulic pipes and armaments.

Jake scrunched her shirt and pulled her back.

"What?" she asked. "I just wanted to see."

"Until you know what the hell you're doing," Jake said, "keep away from all moving things. There are more ways to die on a submarine than you can—"

"Stop!" the Frenchman said.

A sailor near a control console released a joystick. A servomotor hummed, a hydraulic valve clicked shut, and ram arms glistening with lubrication oil glided to a standstill.

"Check that—what is the word?" the Frenchman asked.

"Strap," Jake said.

The Frenchman turned. He would have made a portly American, but for a Frenchman he was obese. Jake had found him to be a heavy beer drinker while trying to keep pace one night at Pierre's estate.

"*Bonjour*, Jake," he said. "And thank you. Yes, 'strap' is the word."

The portly Frenchman nodded as two Taiwanese sailors tightened a strap holding the torpedo to the rack. The servomotor hummed again, and the rams slid the rack toward the outboard section of the hull.

Jake turned to Ye to ask about the interface between the Subtics system and the weapons, but he saw his reflection in Ye's polished shoes.

Halfway up the ladder, Ye was engaged in conversation with someone standing over the hatch. He nodded, waved, and slid down the ladder.

"I've been summoned to squadron headquarters," Ye said. "Mister Slate, please feel free to explore. I trust you have enough experience to keep out of trouble, and I'll have a technician join you as soon as possible to answer your questions. Henri has been tasked with your berthing accommodations. You'll have to excuse me."

Ye clamored up the ladder and disappeared into the sunlight. Jake grabbed Olivia's arm.

"Stay close to me, and don't touch anything."

He led her aft and slapped his palm against a ring of machined metal. Having mastered the technique of passing through an ovular hatch that was too small for the human body's normal carriage, Jake exhaled, tucked his knee to his chest, and lowered his torso in a smooth move.

He kicked his leg forward and drew his weight over it without breaking stride. His final maneuver of the graceful display was snapping his palm off the ring and whipping his arm back to his side.

Impressed he had remembered a vital intra-submarine walking skill, Jake looked at the plastic-covered batteries on either side of the forward battery compartment. As an afterthought, he called to Olivia.

"Be careful going through the hatch," he said.

No response.

He looked and didn't know whether to laugh or offer sympathy to the sad creature holding her hand to her forehead. As blood started to flow between her fingers, he steadied her as she sat on the hatch frame.

"Ouch," she said.

It seemed more a cry for sympathy than an exclamation.

"Let me see," he said and moved her hand.

A two-inch gash bled, and the flesh over her brow was turning violet. Jake kicked off his Rockports and yanked off his socks. After sliding his bare feet back into his shoes, he put a sock to Olivia's head. He scanned the area for droplets but saw no blood.

"You have to watch your blood," he said.

"I know," she said. "But it hurts."

"I've seen worse," Jake said.

"Really?" she asked.

"No. That's a trophy hatch-gash. But that should teach you not to head-butt hatch frames."

"Not funny."

"I know. Let's get you to Henri. I'm sure he can find you a corpsman—if a ship this small has one."

She held the sock to her head as he nudged her in front of him and cupped her shoulders. Tentative, she walked as if in a snake garden. Jake guided her aft.

Out of habit, he studied the hydrogen meter to be certain that the chemical byproduct of acid and lead had not accumulated to dangerous levels, but from his in-flight studies, he knew the state of the art water-cooled batteries posed minimal threat.

"This time, duck real hard," he said.

He supported her through a hatch into the forward auxiliary machinery room. Solids state conversion modules transformed the battery's high DC voltage to the lower DC and AC voltages needed to run the operations room displays and navigation equipment.

Another hatch led to the after battery compartment, and yet another crawl through one of Olivia's ovular nemeses opened to the galley.

A Taiwanese sailor in officer whites stared at them.

"Hello," Jake said. "We seem to be surprising everyone today. You speak English, I hope."

The officer, a handsome and well-proportioned young man with tanned skin, extended a hand.

"Lieutenant Sean Wu," he said.

"Sean?" Jake asked and accepted the hand.

"That's my western name. I needed it for my year abroad at UCLA. It's easier."

Jake pointed at Olivia's head.

"You got any ice? Maybe a towel, too?" he asked.

"You caught me rummaging through here for a snack," Wu said. "But I got you covered."

Wu grabbed a clean rag from a metal counter and reached into a freezer. He withdrew a handful of ice and wrapped it in the rag.

"Thanks," Jake said, but Wu ignored his outstretched hand and moved the rag towards Olivia's forehead.

"Stop!" Jake said and grabbed his arm.

Wu glared at Jake.

"She's HIV positive. We both are. You might want me to handle this."

"Thanks for the warning," Wu said. "Let's get you to the medical cabinet."

Wu led Olivia through a passageway and sat her down in a small alcove. A bandage appeared in his hands and he handed it to Jake to place over Olivia's forehead.

Jake heard someone enter the compartment. After taping the gauze to Olivia's skin, he turned with the care of a submarine veteran. His nose passed so close to a fire extinguisher nozzle that he smelled plastic and dust.

"Is she okay?" Commander Ye asked.

"Yeah," Jake said. "She's fine, but you may want to get rid of these socks. I used one to absorb the blood. She's HIV positive."

Ye snapped an order in Mandarin. Wu slipped a latex glove over his hand, pinched the socks between his thumb and finger, and stepped away.

"I feel like an idiot," Olivia said.

Ye extended a stack of compact disk cases wrapped in rubber bands.

"From squadron command," Ye said. "The acting Defense Minister himself tasked me to deliver them."

Olivia accepted the disks.

"Make yourselves comfortable," Ye said. "Your laptops are in the commanding officer's quarters."

Jake shrugged.

"I'll show where that is on my way back up."

Jake followed Ye through a hatch and up a ladder to the ship's upper of two decks. He lost his balance for a moment but recovered.

"Was that a wave—this deep in the harbor?" Jake asked. "I thought we just rolled."

"A little," Ye said. "The tugs can be rough."

"Tugs?"

"Yes," Ye said. "Did Mister Renard not tell you we were getting underway as soon as you were aboard?"

Jake reached the top of the ladder and had to brace himself against a bulkhead. His life had become a chain of surprises.

"Where are we going?" he asked.

"Three-ship operation with us as the primary attack platform," Ye said. "We're off to change the tides of war."

CHAPTER TWENTY

Jake helped Olivia into a Spartan vinyl seat and placed her laptop on a fold-out desk.

"The operations room is straight ahead," Ye said. "I must go."

Jake closed the door to the commanding officer's quarters and knelt in front of Olivia. A purple stain blotted the outer layer of the gauze on her head.

"I'll be fine," she said. "It's just a cut."

"You don't look fine."

"Everything's just happening so fast," she said.

Jake noticed a ball cap on the desk. He reached for it and slid it on her head. It was too wide until she stuffed her hair underneath it.

The cap had two large-font Mandarin characters embroidered over a handful of smaller ones.

"It says 'Hai Lang'," she said. "That means 'Sea Wolf'. All Taiwanese submarines are named after the sea and a land-based predator—if you count dragons in that."

"At least you're starting to look less feminine," Jake said. "The bandage is a nice touch, but a pair of baggy coveralls should finish you off nicely."

She ignored him and slid a disk into the laptop. Her eyes sparkled as she read.

"Wow," she said. "Rickets came through. I've got data on Hayat from A to Z. This is amazing."

"Fine, I guess," Jake said. "But I've got bigger problems at the moment. If I know Pierre, we're taking on half the Chinese fleet by ourselves today."

Olivia kept her nose angled toward the laptop. Jake opened the door and stepped out.

"See you," Jake said.

She tapped the keyboard. He closed the door and left her to her own world.

Jake marched forward through a room with equipment that looked like controls and modules for radio and satellite communications. He ducked through an ovular hatch into the *Hai Lang's* operations room.

Six dual-stacked Subtics monitors spanned the left side of the room. He recognized one of the three men who filled half of the seats as Antoine Remy, Renard's sonar expert. Short with a wide nose, Remy wore a sonar headset that made his head appear extra-wide. He reminded Jake of a toad.

Remy waved his hand but didn't smile. The pre-battle atmosphere in the room was too businesslike for levity.

"Hello, Jake," he said and turned back to his monitor.

The Taiwanese sailor seated beside Remy pointed and said words inaudible to Jake, and then he turned to another Taiwanese sailor. Jake surmised that the middle sailor was correlating sonar data with radar contacts as the ship navigated the channel.

Ahead, a single Taiwanese sailor sat at the front of the room jiggling a joystick that controlled the rudder. The seat beside him at the ship's control panel was empty, and Jake realized that it would remain empty until someone needed to control ballast, stern planes, and bow planes once the *Hai Lang* submerged.

To Jake's right, Renard stooped with his face in the periscope optics. His feet traced a semi-circle until the optics pointed backwards. A Marlboro wiggled in the corner of his mouth as he talked.

"Channel entrance range, mark," Renard said.

The middle sailor at the Subtics monitors shouted in accented but confident English.

"Good fix," he said. "Are we on track?"

Leaning over a horizontal screen to Renard's right, one of the final two men in the room, a short Taiwanese sailor with a slumped body and thick glasses, tapped a magnetic pen against the electronic navigation chart. He stiffened his fingers over the chart and slanted his arm. Standing opposite the sailor, Lieutenant Sean Wu nodded.

"We're twenty yards too far to the right," Wu said. "We need to come left. Recommend five degrees rudder."

Renard peeled his eye from the periscope and reached above his head for a microphone.

"Jake," he said. "We won't need you until we're submerged. I want you to study the battle plan. Over there."

Renard aimed the microphone at the farthest Subtics monitor and then raised it to his lips.

"Does five degrees left rudder look good from up there?" Renard asked.

Commander Ye's voice crackled from a speaker.

"Yes," Ye said. "Helm, left five degrees rudder, steady course zero-four-nine."

Aside the ship's control station, Jake saw sunlight peeking through an open hatch. He walked to it and glanced up at Ye's shoes twenty feet above in the bridge.

"I thought you were in command?" Jake asked.

Renard kept his face to the optics.

"Consider Commander Ye a pilot for now," Renard said. "Don't worry, this ship is ours to fight."

Jake sat at the forward-most Subtics dual-stacked monitor and console station. Two seats away, a sailor turned to him and frowned.

"Hello," Jake said.

"Don't waste your time," the middle Taiwanese sailor said. "Petty Officer Zhu's English is the worst on ship. Maybe the worst on the island. But he's very good with the fire control system."

"Thanks," Jake said.

Jake had studied the Subtics system during his flights but needed to familiarize himself with it. Exploring, he tapped buttons.

Images and icons flew by his screen, and the system reminded him of the early stand-alone submarine tactical systems the United States Navy had introduced in the early nineties. The difference, he had read, was that Subtics was generations ahead in automation and integration.

The system allowed operators to read and operate all of the *Hai Lang*'s sensors and resources for detection, tactical data processing, navigation, external communications and weapon launching.

Where sailors of Jake's past had to use manual intervention between each step, Subtics integrated the work. Aboard the *Hai Lang*, he expected less fumbling with placards, less fiddling with plastic trigonometric wheels, and less artistic work in the penciling of curvilinear sound propagation lines. As he scrolled through screens, Jake felt at one with the system.

He wondered if the Chinese sailors aboard the new *Kilo* class submarines had equivalent data processing, and he wondered which ship held the acoustic advantage. Data processing was irrelevant if there was nothing to process.

In submarine warfare, that meant sound and the acoustic advantage—who would hear whom first.

Jake found a screen that showed the decibel level of sounds emanated from the *Hai Lang* over all directions and multiple frequencies. He memorized which combinations of machinery operation created the least noise.

No reactor plant, he thought. *Just run at a snail's pace on the cruising motors, and we're a silent ghost.*

Next, he flipped to the best estimate of the sound profile of Chinese *Kilo* class submarines.

And we're going to battle against ghosts, he thought.

Tapping the keyboard at his console, Jake called up a new view. A blue inverted triangle represented the *Hai Lang*. It overlay dozens of smaller blue inverted triangles. Jake threw his voice over his shoulder.

"What are the little blue triangles?" he asked.

The English speaking Taiwanese sailor seated at the monitors leaned back and glanced at Jake's screen.

"Mines," he said.

"Mines?"

"Anti-submarine mines. They only attack targets below fifteen meters. That's why we transit on the surface."

"We have air superiority to the twelve mile international water boundary," Renard said. "We are at risk on the surface beyond that distance. We'll dive eight miles from shore and slip into international waters."

Tapping again, Jake called up a two-dimensional overhead view of a planned battle scene. He advanced it over time and watched Renard's intentions unfold.

"Shit, Pierre," he said. "I can't tell if this is the most brilliant or most stupid battle plan I've seen."

Renard's voice echoed off the periscope.

"I've made a few assumptions about the Chinese doctrine of submerged battle and have placed some faith in Taiwanese technology, but it's a sound plan."

"What if it isn't?"

"That's the chance we take," Renard said. "And after two days of arguing with a room full of Admirals to make them buy into it, I'd rather face the Chinese than try to have it changed. But if you see a flaw—"

"No," Jake said. "No flaws. I just hope this little submarine can do everything it was built for."

CHAPTER TWENTY-ONE

Hayat gulped bismuth fluid to ease his queasiness, and the increased codeine dosage kept his pain in check. As his body crumbled under the scourge of cancer, he understood that medication alone would fail to ease his passing. He drew strength from daily prayer.

The mind, body, and spirit are one, he thought. *How smart I thought I was. I shunned Him, and I will pay with my life. But he lets me draw strength from His love, and I will rejoice with Him in the afterlife.*

"Captain?" the middle-aged corpsman said.

Hayat returned the bismuth bottle to a tray.

"Yes?"

"The men suspect that you are ill, sir."

"Of course they do," Hayat said. "They are observant, and there are clues we cannot avoid. You are here, a man with far more medical training than a common corpsman."

"I was assigned to this patrol because of its duration. Men may need treatment that a less experienced corpsman cannot give, and we are far from home. I'm more concerned that they have taken glances in my medical locker. They see the stores of bismuth fluid and codeine."

"Then let them speculate," Hayat said. "It is better than admitting that their captain is dying."

The corpsman extended a bottle of codeine and tipped two pills into Hayat's hand.

"I must also be direct about the crew's doubts concerning Lieutenant Commander Raja," the corpsman said. "The junior officers and the senior enlisted see that Raja's experience is less than the average executive officer."

Hayat dumped the pills into his mouth and washed it down with bitter tea.

"Indeed he is junior," he said. "He has little more experience than Lieutenant Walid. But certain ranking officers recommended him, and I saw potential. I am pleased with his progress and confident he could lead this ship. You have ways to relay my confidence in him to the crew, do you not?"

"Yes, sir," the corpsman said. "They know that I have privileged information about you. I will make it known that your confidence in Raja is not feigned."

"Very well. You are dismissed."

The corpsman shut the door behind him, and Hayat reached for a rolled carpet. Before unfurling it onto the deck, he noted the *Hamza's* course on a digital repeater and calculated the bearing towards Mecca.

As he knelt to affirm his faith and draw strength, his phone jingled.

"Captain," he said.

"Raja, sir. We've detected a possible submarine."

Hayat returned the phone to its cradle, and a sting coursed the length of his spine as he stood. Bracing himself against his doorframe, he waited for the pain to subside and his head to clear.

He left his stateroom and followed the passageway into the operations center. Raja leaned over the nearest Subtics monitor.

"Transients," Raja said. "Flowing water followed by multiple valve operation. Bearing two-seven-five."

"That's almost directly behind us."

"Yes, sir," Raja said. "We heard it on the after section of the towed array sonar."

"The bearing is difficult to calculate at that angle," Hayat said. "It could be ten degrees either way."

"Shall I commence a break-trail maneuver?"

Hayat raised his palm.

"Do not be hasty. No need to attract attention."

Raja stood and approached within whispering range.

"Sir, are you willing to take no action?"

"If it is a submarine or any combatant with hostile intent, it would already have killed us."

"And if we are being followed, sir? The mission could be at risk."

"We have nearly two months and ten thousand miles to travel," Hayat said. "If we are being trailed, I doubt our adversary has the food stores, patrol authority, or patience to follow us to our end."

Raja straightened.

"You mean to do nothing, sir?"

"We do not have the fuel or time to waste."

"We could attack, sir. Rid ourselves of the concern."

His confidence is growing, Hayat thought. *I must temper it with wisdom.*

"Attack a three-minute old transient with an uncertain bearing? We may as well shoot a torpedo into oblivion."

"We can turn and optimize our sensors against it."

"You would create flow noise and rudder swath while in the sites of an alerted adversary," Hayat said.

Raja leaned back into whispering range.

"I begin to sense fear in the men, sir," Raja said.

"This is a long and slow journey into the teeth of the enemy," Hayat said. "It is natural to be scared. We faced our fear once before and overcame our adversary in battle. And so we shall again. Maintain course and speed."

*

Over ten seconds, Commander Rodriguez had felt the rise, fall, and resurgence of fear cascade through him. A shriek over the hiss of water had announced a flooding casualty over the ship's emergency circuit. The inrush from the buoy and countermeasure launch tube had compelled Rodriguez to spring from his seat and contemplate a critical decision.

He had thought of emergency blowing to the surface—releasing high-pressure air into the *Hawaii's* ballast tanks in a contained explosion. It would have revealed his position to the *Agosta*, condemning him to a potential torpedo attack. Stretching the limits of his patience as the early seconds of the flooding unfolded, he had waited.

The report had finally come.

The flooding is stopped.

One of Rodriguez' sailors had tripped the flood control valve system for the backup valves that stopped the flooding.

Thankful his patience had precluded him from blowing to the surface, Rodriguez exhaled. But his moment of relief was short.

He had darted to the row of sonar monitors to stare over the shoulders of his acoustic experts. Ten seconds after his panic began, it rose again.

"We just made noise," he said. "Watch for signs of counterdetection. Listen for signs of weapon launch."

Rodriguez thought of kicking the *Hawaii* into high gear and evading. He could break away and come back, but he didn't want to risk losing the *Agosta*. Again, he exercised patience and confidence in his ship and crew.

Over tense minutes, the *Agosta* gave no indication of having heard the *Hawaii*. Rodriguez stepped to a fire control display.

"Still at seven knots?" he asked.

"Yes, sir," Chief Bartlett said. "And still on course zero-eight-three. He didn't flinch, sir. Wish I could say the same. I think I wet myself."

Rodriguez returned to his captain's chair and waited. A minute later, his obese executive officer led a leather-faced chief petty officer into the control room.

"It looks like a gasket blew in the control valve that locks the breach door," Jones said. "When they opened the muzzle door to launch the communications buoy, the breach popped open. The water knocked Davis half way across the compartment, but Martin was able to get to the flood control valves."

"Davis is okay?" Rodriguez asked.

"He swallowed half the ocean, but the corpsman thinks he'll be fine."

"The buoy?"

"Stuck in the launcher."

"Then nobody knows we're trailing this *Agosta* yet. I wanted to get a message off with a buoy, but it looks like we're going to have to bite the bullet and go to periscope depth to communicate."

"We can fix the control valve, sir," the leather-face chief said. "If the problem is what I think it is, we just need to replace the gasket. I can't guarantee that it won't rupture again until we have more time to troubleshoot the whole system, but repairs to get it working again won't take long. It's just a matter of making a lot of noise."

"How long do you need?"

"Six to twelve hours. We need to isolate hydraulics to the valve, and it's got some small innards. Takes a little skill to take apart and put back together."

"That's too long," Rodriguez said.

"What if you removed the control valve, repaired it offline in the engine room where everything is soundproofed, and then put it back?" Jones asked. "It would take longer overall, but you'd only make noise removing and reinstalling it."

"We'd have to disengage this *Agosta* twice, but at the speed it's moving, we could reacquire him," Rodriguez said.

"I'm pretty sure my guys can fix it like the executive officer says, sir," the chief said.

"Okay," Rodriguez said. "Map out the isolation boundary and get the system isolated. Try to be ready to work at the beginning of the next watch section."

The chief stepped away.

"The *Agosta* didn't make a peep," Rodrgiuez said. "Either he didn't hear us, or he didn't care."

"He's now well beyond the Chinese exclusion zone," Jones said. "He's going somewhere. You were right to follow him, sir."

"I want to think he's transiting somewhere, but he's moving so slow. Seven knots doesn't get you anywhere fast. That ship was designed for ten knots transit."

"But the slower you go, the less you have to snorkel."

"Relevant if you're remaining hidden," Rodriguez said. "And it extends range, if you're concerned about fuel."

Jones slipped into another thought stupor.

"Sir," he said after emerging from thought. "I'll double check, but I suspect that an *Agosta* has food stores for about sixty days. I think that's the longest recorded *Agosta* patrol."

Jones slid back into his stupor.

"Go on," Rodriguez said.

"Sixty days, seven knots, leaving roughly from the northern tip of Taiwan, and traveling on course zero-eight-five," Jones said. "That's a great circle route to …"

His stomach brushing the seated Chief Bartlett aside, Jones stooped over a fire control monitor and fiddled with a trackball and buttons.

"… plus or minus a couple hundred miles either way," Jones said, "if this *Agosta* maintains course and speed, he'll arrive in the Hawaii operation areas with about a week's left of food and fuel remaining."

"Then maybe disengaging and going to periscope depth isn't such a bad idea," Rodriguez said. "We may need to do some two-way communications to figure out who this guy is—and see if anyone wants to tell us what to do about him."

CHAPTER TWENTY-TWO

Knowing he would face battle today, Jake had slept fitfully during the night. The *Hai Lang* was submerged, twenty-five miles northeast of Keelung.

He sat at Renard's right—the traditional chair of the executive officer—between the two Frenchmen in the wardroom. Claude LaFontaine, Renard's pick as engineering officer, sat beside him.

Jake washed down a piece of bread with an extra cup of coffee and noted that the pot traveled no further than Renard and LaFontaine. The Taiwanese officers drank tea.

"Hey Sean," Jake said. "Did you drink coffee at UCLA?"

"That stuff's nasty," Wu said.

"You must not have had a real academic load, then."

Wu laughed, but Ye, seated opposite Jake, gave the young officer a stern look.

Renard lowered his coffee cup, reached for his gold-plated Zippo lighter and a Marlboro, and lit up.

"I know you must discipline your men, Commander Ye," he said. "They are yours and will remain yours after my team and I depart."

Renard blew a cloud of smoke that billowed into the overhead and crept into the ventilation system.

"But if he's confident enough to laugh before battle, then let him laugh," Renard said. "If he's nervous and wishes to laugh, then let him laugh. I say let them behave naturally until the moment arrives. I've watched your men. They are well-trained and focused. Each will do his duty in the face of battle."

Ye nodded and glanced at a wall clock.

"It is time," he said.

Renard twisted his arm to expose his Rolex.

"Less than an hour," he said. "Let's secure morning meal and let the men putter about for bit. Battlestations in say, thirty minutes?"

Ye nodded.

"So be it," Renard said. "Good luck to us all."

*

Jake wore a cotton jumpsuit that reminded him of an American submarine uniform. He attached a wireless communication set to his web belt and slid a speaker and microphone piece over his ear.

He turned to Renard who sat behind the periscopes. Renard puffed on a cigarette and carried himself with confidence. He appeared invulnerable.

Jake had yet to share his optimism.

"Go on, man," Renard said. "Take control. I christen thee the tactical coordinator."

Jake leaned forward.

"Shit, Pierre, I don't know this submarine well."

Renard's face became hard.

"You are supremely qualified to do what you must."

"I hope so."

"You fear you are not qualified because you are Admiral Rickover's bastard son. The father of your nuclear navy trusted no machine, and he demanded that every nuclear-trained sailor know far too much about his equipment.

"If you don't know the algorithms behind each fire control program or don't know the innards of every valve ..."

Renard waved his hand at the periscope's hydraulic control valves above him.

"... you are not inept. Rickover's navy would have you believe otherwise, but in fact, the best tacticians pick and chose what they wish to know. True genius is an uncluttered mind armed with only relevant knowledge."

"I noticed that most of the stuff you sent to me to study was at a functional level. You didn't send me many design documents," Jake said.

"Precisely."

Jake started to believe.

"And you know far more than the Taiwanese," Renard said. "They've never had this technology at their disposal. Their other submarines don't even have towed array sonar systems or conformal arrays worth using."

"But this is more advanced stuff than I'm used to."

"Is it?" Renard asked. "I think not. The processing and human interface is advanced. The acoustic arrays may be more sensitive, but the theory and the employment of the data you know better than most."

"What about the hole-in-ocean sensor?"

"It is new technology," Renard said. "You read about it on the aircraft, didn't you?"

"Yeah."

"Then you know it well enough, and I submit that you know how to use the data better than anyone."

Jake found Renard's confidence contagious.

"Man your station," Renard said. "We'll get through this day, *mon ami.*"

*

Renard's confidence surprised him. All his past episodes of combat had been accidents—plans gone wrong. This, his first time choosing to enter battle, felt like the culmination of every step he had taken in his life.

A career as a submarine commander, a strategic advisor, an arms broker, and a tactical planner had led him to this point—a point he believed would find its way into the annals of history. This was his day to dedicate every shred of his existence to swaying the tide of a war in the favor of a democracy. Today was his destiny.

Even with a wife and child, even with mortal fear lurking somewhere deep inside, and even with the lives of dozens of men at stake, he searched within himself for a shred of doubt but found nothing.

He watched Jake prance behind the row of men seated at the Subtics monitors. Jake stopped, appeared to listen to his headset, and then leaned over Commander Ye's shoulder. He and Ye exchanged words, and Jake looked up.

"Ship's rigged for ultra-quiet," Jake said.

"Very well," Renard said.

He looked at his Rolex. Eight o'clock in the morning.

Time to become the hunter, he thought.

Less than a minute later, Antoine Remy raised his finger in the air. Like a tiger, Jake pounced and huddled over him.

"The helicopters are pinging," Jake said. "We're analyzing their range on the wide aperture array, but it looks like they're right on time where they need to be."

Renard glanced at a monitor as seven blue triangles appeared. Thirty miles from the *Hai Lang*, they spanned a line twenty nautical miles long.

"We have the frigate now," Jake said. "The *Kang Ding* is pinging."

Near the middle helicopter, a blue square appeared on Renard's screen. A speed-leader from the square—an estimate of the *Kang Ding's* speed—pointed toward the central inverted triangle that represented the *Hai Lang.*

According to his plan, Renard expected the *Kang Ding* to sweep zigzag lines in the ocean with an average speed of eight knots. Within the three and a half hours it would take the frigate and the helicopters to reach the *Hai Lang*, he hoped they would roust a target.

He watched a second blue square appear on his monitor in front of the one representing the *Kang Ding*.

"We can't hear it," Jake said, "but I thought I'd track the *Tai Ping*, too, as long as we know it's there."

*

Renard had cut long, slow lines back and forth across his waiting point. The helicopter, frigate, and silent stealth patrol craft task force had swept eight miles west during the first hour.

A triangle disappeared and reappeared ten minutes later as one helicopter withdrew its dipping sonar and was replaced by a refueled aircraft. The relieved helicopter headed toward the frigate to refuel, return, and relieve the next in the line. A taxing workload on the flight crew, Renard knew, but worth the effort.

Renard heard the day's first enthusiastic report.

"Helicopter five is range-gaiting," Jake said. "Shortened ping cycles. It's got something!"

"Our aspect in helicopter five's direction?"

"Optimal," Jake said. "We're broadside enough for all sensors. If that helicopter rousts him, we'll hear it."

"The frigate," Remy said. "She has stopped pinging."

"Per plan," Renard said. "The helicopter has informed the group of its discovery, and the frigate has gone quiet so that the *Tai Ping* can identify the contact. The helicopter next to number five should also attempt a passive search. Active return only finds but does not classify an enemy. They must now listen."

Jake sidestepped behind seats and conferred with Remy.

"The *Tai Ping* is on top of the contact and has started pinging," Jake said.

"That means they've identified the contact."

"But we can't," Jake said. "It's still too far—"

"High speed screws!" Remy said. "We have the submerged contact, now. It's running!"

"Designate as contact one," Jake said. "Track contact one and make every effort to classify."

"Give me an intercept course," Renard said. "Put us on its track, five miles ahead of it."

Renard waited as the Subtics system accumulated enough data to calculate the target's course and speed.

"The contact is making fourteen knots, almost due west," Jake said. "At our speed, it will take us twenty minutes to get to his track. That should work. Course zero-two-five."

"Henri," Renard said. "Left five degrees rudder, steady course zero-two-five."

Henri nodded. The young Taiwanese sailor seated beside him at the ship's control panel reached for a joystick. The deck angled into the turn.

"Since the helicopters are backing off, I assume this is no *Kilo*," Renard said. "Otherwise, they would sink it."

"I'm just starting to hear the main electric motor," Remy said. "It's a *Romeo*."

"Very well," Renard said. "This is why we're here."

"Launch transients," Remy said. "Torpedo in the water!"

Jake hunched over the French sonar technician's shoulders again.

"Looks like contact one just shot at the *Tai Ping*."

"I trust that it is a poor shot?" Renard asked. "Over the shoulder, while running—I expect it is a desperate attempt to force the *Tai Ping* to break pursuit."

"*Tai Ping* is hitting evasive maneuvers," Jake said. "Torpedo has passed aft of *Tai Ping*. The *Tai Ping* is re-engaging."

"Contact one is pinging now," Remy said. "Low frequency sonar, but short intervals. It makes no sense."

"What the hell could he be looking for?" Jake asked.

Sensing his plan unfold with perfection, Renard reclined in his chair and exhaled smoke.

"He's not looking," he said. "He's calling for help."

CHAPTER TWENTY-THREE

RENARD ARRIVED AHEAD OF THE fleeing *Romeo* and loitered. Like a wounded prey, the targeted submarine would attract attention.

Renard's monitor showed that the helicopters and frigate had reversed course, detaching to escort the Taiwanese tanker convoy through the corridor they had swept and leaving the stealth patrol craft *Tai Ping* and the submarine *Hai Lang* to hunt the Chinese submarine.

If nothing else, Renard thought, *the distraction will enable to convoy to pass.*

"Sporadic active sonar from the *Tai Ping*," Jake said.

"The *Tai Ping* holds the *Romeo* with its blue-green laser," Renard said. "That sensor is insignificant at long range but inescapable at short. The pinging is to remind the *Romeo* that the *Tai Ping* is there. It is instilling fear."

"New submerged contact!" Remy said. "Moving fast."

Jake huddled beside Remy and studied the data.

"It just raced by us," Jake said. "Another *Romeo*, running in to help his buddy. It was rattling on multiple frequencies and was deaf to the world."

"Let it go," Renard said.

Several heads turned to Renard, the most accusative glare coming from Commander Ye, seated in front of Jake where he handled weapons control.

"The *Tai Ping* can manage against two *Romeos*," Renard said. "We will not reveal our position for less than a *Kilo*."

Minutes passed in which Renard sensed the disgruntlement of the Taiwanese for his having let a *Romeo* pass unscathed. He began to doubt his decision of leniency when Remy pressed his headset to his ears, closed his eyes, and raised his finger.

"Medium-speed screws," he said. "Bearing three-five-zero. Seven blades!"

"*Kilo* class!" Renard said. "Correlate speed. Let the integrators process and give me bearing rate. We know its destination, so apply your judgment to the solution."

Jake bounced between Remy and Ye, iterating raw acoustic data towards a solution that targeted the *Kilo*.

"Range is sketchy," Jake said. "But we've got something tight enough for a good shot. Recommend you take it. Tube one is ready."

"Shoot tube one!" Renard said.

A muffled whine emanated from the torpedo room and Renard's ears popped as high-pressure air relieved into the compartment.

"Successful launch," Ye said. "Torpedo course is zero-two-five. It will turn its seeker on in three miles."

Jake appeared in front of Renard.

"Let's make it a passive shot," he said.

"Passive?" Renard asked.

"We can always make it active again, but with that *Kilo* moving—best we can tell at fifteen knots—that torpedo is going to hear him. And if we keep the active seeker off, he'll never hear it coming. No evasion."

"Indeed," Renard said. "Do it then."

Jake hunched over Ye.

"Seeker is commanded to perform passive search, optimized for the *Kilo's* screws," Ye said.

Two minutes later, the torpedo's speed leader shortened on Renard's display.

"Torpedo has slowed. Torpedo seeker is conducting passive search," Ye said.

The petty officer seated beside Ye rattled off quick words in Mandarin. Ye translated.

"Torpedo hears the *Kilo*," Ye said.

Jake studied the monitor over Ye's head.

"Between our own sensors and the weapon, we've got him nailed," Jake said. "Torpedo's a mile and a half away from the target."

"Turn on the active seeker at five hundred yards," Renard said. "Just to be certain."

The weapon closed. Ye tapped his console.

"Active seeker engaged," Ye said. "Weapon switched straight into range-gaiting and is shortening its ping interval. *Kilo* is accelerating."

"Countermeasures!" Remy said.

"Guide the weapon through if needed," Renard said.

The deep rumble reverberated through the *Hai Lang's* hull. The throbbing hiss that followed indicated that vaporized water had bubbled to the surface. Renard even heard a metallic creak.

"Hull rupture," Remy said. "The *Kilo* is sinking."

Renard realized that he had defeated one of the world's most feared submarines. He also felt an uneasy sickness in having killed dozens of his submarining brethren. He sat and calmed himself, but the veins in his neck throbbed.

"Keep your wits about you men," he said. "There may be other submarines nearby. There will be plenty of time for celebration later."

A distant explosion filled the operations room with less vigor than the prior detonation.

"Explosion on the bearing of contact one, the first *Romeo*," Remy said. "Hull fracture. It's going down."

"The *Tai Ping* was weapons free as soon as it heard our warhead," Renard said. "And it wasted no time taking out an old *Romeo*."

The day is ours, Renard thought.

Silence enshrouded the room. Renard considered searching for the second *Romeo* he had heard running to the first's rescue but decided against turning himself into a potential friendly fire target for the *Tai Ping*.

He decided to clear the area when Remy stirred.

"Hull popping," Remy said.

"What?" Renard asked. "On what bearing?"

"One-three-three," Remy said. "Hull popping has stopped. I hear nothing else."

"Someone's changing depth," Jake said. "Their hull is creaking with the pressure change. If all we hear is the hull popping, it could be a slow moving *Kilo*."

"Perhaps someone is coming shallow to share the bad news with the Chinese East Sea Fleet Command," Renard said.

"We just scared the shit out of someone," Jake said. "You think we should drive towards him and check it out?"

"An *Agosta* against an alerted *Kilo* on even terms?" Renard asked. "I would consider the outcome a coin toss at best. Would you wager your life on that?"

Jake frowned.

"Hold on," he said and darted to Remy.

"Antoine," Jake said. "Any biologics—marine life—on the bearing of the hull popping?"

"Yes. A very large shrimp bed."

Jake trotted across the row of Subtics stations and sat at an empty seat. He fiddled with the console.

"Nothing yet," he said. "But I'm going to try different elevation angles."

Renard's curiosity got the better of him and he gravitated behind Jake. He inhaled cool a tobacco taste and blew smoke into the overhead.

"What's on your mind?" he asked.

"Hole-in-ocean," Jake said.

"All I see is mush," Renard said. "This system is just an experimental waste of hydrophones."

"Agreed it's shitty as a detection sensor," Jake said. "But let's see about localization."

A dark spot appeared on the screen.

"Even if that is our target, I can't shoot a torpedo at an ink dot."

Jake tapped keys.

"I'm trying to listen on the best frequency that the shrimp are putting out," Jake said. "It's broadband, but we can still optimize within the higher frequencies."

The blot on the screen became oblong and piqued Renard's interest.

"Not bad," he said.

"Let's apply a filter," Jake said.

Like photography software, the Subtics filter cleaned the image of a cylinder with rounded ends. A small rectangle atop the cylinder hinted at a submarine's sail.

"*Mon Dieu!* It looks like a submarine," Renard said.

"I'm comparing the dimensions to the scale of a *Kilo*," Jake said. "We know how many degrees of arc that acoustic silhouette spans, and we know the length of a *Kilo*. We'll have to guess at the aspect, but it looks broadside enough. A little trigonometry gives us the range. And since he's not moving, his speed is zero. You have a targeting solution."

"Thirteen miles," Renard said. "That's a strain on a torpedo's range."

"Shoot it slow," Jake said. "Conserve fuel. If this guy's really scared, he might just sit there for a while and wait to see what happens. We can slip a slow one up his tailpipe, don't you think?"

"Commander Ye," Renard said. "You can get thirteen miles out of a torpedo, and set it with passive homing, can you not?"

Ye tapped his keyboard.

"Yes," he said. "It will be a very slow moving torpedo, but the weapon in tube two is ready."

"Shoot tube two," Renard said.

*

Renard checked his Rolex. The torpedo had been running for twenty minutes.

"Torpedo maintains speed—already running at minimum. Torpedo seeker is conducting passive search," Ye said.

The petty officer seated beside Ye shook his head and mumbled a dirge. Ye translated.

"Torpedo hears nothing," Ye said.

"It's where it should be," Jake said. "The *Kilo* hasn't moved. I still have it on hole-in-ocean. It may just be too quiet."

"Fuel remaining, Commander Ye?" Renard asked.

"Seven percent."

"Damn," Renard said. "A dilemma. If our solution is off by even a mile, the torpedo could pass by and never hear it. If we go active, we alert the *Kilo* and begin a chase with almost no torpedo fuel."

Hoping for insight, he looked to Jake.

"Fifty-fifty," Jake said. "Use your instincts."

"Commence active search," Renard said.

He retreated to his captain's chair.

"Active return!" Ye said. "Torpedo has acquired and is accelerating. Fuel remaining, six percent."

"High speed screws!" Remy said. "The *Kilo* is accelerating. And there are countermeasures!"

"Bearing to the *Kilo*?" Renard asked.

"One-three-two," Remy said. "It won't change much. He's too far away, sir. We won't track the *Kilo* from here. The weapon will have to find him itself."

"Accelerate the weapon through the countermeasures," Renard said, "and recommence search."

The sailor beside Ye hunched over his screen, tapped his keyboard, and talked to Ye.

"Weapon has reacquired and is closing. We have a solution to the *Kilo*." Ye said. "It has reached fifteen knots and is still accelerating. Our weapon is at sixty-three knots, and would impact in two minutes, but it will run out of fuel sixteen seconds before impact, three hundred meters from the target."

"You assume nominal *Kilo* acceleration?" Renard asked.

"Yes."

"Target aspect?"

"I don't understand," Ye said.

Jake raced beside him, pointed at the monitor, and explained. He looked to Renard.

"Two-one-zero relative," Jake said. "He's running, but not tail to weapon. He's trying to slip left to work himself out of the torpedo seeker's acquisition field."

"Then a command detonation will have some broadside effect?" Renard asked.

"Yeah," Jake said as he ran his hand through his hair. "Shit, Pierre, that's a great idea."

"Commander Ye," Renard said. "Command-detonate the weapon at one-half percent fuel remaining."

Renard exhaled smoke as the hair on his neck stood.

If I miss, he thought, *that Kilo will come for us.*

*

The torpedo's life waned. The algorithms within its central nervous system cried out alarms. One program shrieked in machine code that fuel approached exhaustion. Another requested more time to close in on the target. The central processing unit concluded that its conflicting programs portended failure.

It asked its onboard gyroscope for an update and sent its position to its launch platform—the submarine *Hai Lang* that hosted the torpedo tube from which it had sprung. It then calculated its target's course, speed, and depth and passed the data via wire to the launch platform. The launch platform acknowledged receipt of the data but offered no resolution to the impending mission failure.

An algorithm took center stage and howled that failure via fuel exhaustion was eminent. The central processing unit relayed this to the launch platform. This time, the launch platform offered more than acknowledgment. It offered purpose.

The new purpose was to detonate before death. The launch platform assured the central processing unit that this would destroy the target and complete the mission. The torpedo armed itself and gave the launch platform a final chance to change its command. It did not.

The torpedo sent the detonation signal to its warhead.

*

Renard tensed and leapt towards Antoine Remy.

"Well, what do you hear?" he asked.

"The explosion is subsiding. I hear the *Kilo's* flow noise. It is still tracking at twenty-eight knots."

"Damn," Renard said. "We missed and are now in an equal battle."

"Wait," Remy said. "The *Kilo's* screw is slowing. The screw has stopped."

Renard had his hand on the nape of Remy's neck and noticed he was squeezing too hard. He let go.

"High-pressure air!" Remy said. "It's surfacing!"

Tension flowed from Renard. He inhaled the cool tobacco taste and relaxed. "The only thing better than sinking a Kilo," he said, "is forcing one to surface."

CHAPTER TWENTY-FOUR

Renard had taken the *Hai Lang* shallow but short of periscope depth. The ship's acoustic sensors heard helicopters encircling the crippled and surfaced *Kilo*, but they could have been Chinese, he decided.

It wasn't until he heard the sounds of the *Tai Ping* racing into audible range that he risked extending a mast.

At periscope depth, Renard raised the periscope and took an automated three-hundred and sixty degree sweep. As he studied the panoramic printout of the world above, he heard a voice hailing him over his elevated radio mast.

The words were in Mandarin, and he nodded towards Ye.

"Take that, please," he said.

Ye stood and reached for the microphone above Renard. He flipped a dial, lowered the microphone, and spoke in Mandarin. An energetic conversation ensued.

"I just told them we are alright and awaiting orders," Ye said. "They were happy to hear that."

"What news, then?" Renard asked.

"The convoy was attacked by a Chinese destroyer, but aside from one missile that escaped the *Kang Ding's* defenses and damaged a cargo hold, the convoy is unscathed and in safe waters heading towards Japan to pick up fuel."

"This is great news," Renard said. "Perhaps they offered you something more local, though?"

More Mandarin banter.

"Yes," Ye said. "The crew of the *Kilo* has abandoned ship and is being receptive to our rescue efforts."

Renard looked at his periscope's photograph.

"*Mon Dieu*," he said. "The superstructure is lined with Chinese sailors. Some look unconscious or dead. There is a foul-looking vapor rising from both escape hatches."

Renard lowered his periscope.

"We are rescuing them?" he asked.

"We sent two Chinook helicopters with infantry squadrons to storm the submarine, but we also sent a medical helicopter," Ye said. "Given the condition of the men on that submarine, there was no need for combat. It appears that you damaged one of their battery compartments and filled the ship with chlorine gas."

"We're in international waters," Renard said. "Four miles from Taiwanese waters."

Ye smiled.

"Our combat air patrol has been extended to cover the area," he said. "It is our battle space, and we've sent a tug to tow the *Kilo* back to Keelung. Our orders are to verify that this space remains ours until the tug has taken the *Kilo* into local waters.

*

Half an hour later, Renard watched through the periscope as a tug dragged the injured *Kilo* toward Keelung.

Ye monitored radio chatter and mentioned that most of the officers and senior enlisted Chinese sailors had been evacuated via helicopter before the rest of the crew. The purpose had been to remove the leadership and minimize the chance that a would-be hero would try to scuttle the *Kilo*.

No matter, Renard thought. *Taiwanese commandoes are aboard that ship with medical personal. It is ours.*

When the *Kilo* crossed into Taiwanese waters, Renard lit a fresh Marlboro.

"Shall I give you back your submarine?" he asked.

"I will take us home from here," Ye said.

*

Jake slapped Renard on the shoulder and found himself dragged into a rare hug with the Frenchman.

"That was amazing, *mon ami*!" Renard said. "Today we erased the failures of our past!"

Jake broke loose from Renard and found himself swarmed with slaps, handshakes, and smiles from the Taiwanese sailors. If they had considered him an intruder, they now considered him a champion.

Sean Wu slapped his hand so hard into a handshake that it hurt. Wu pulled him into a loose hug and released him.

"You're a rock star!" Wu said. "That was sweet!

Jake ducked out of the operations room and followed a passageway aft. He knocked on the door of the commanding officer's stateroom.

No response.

He twisted the handle and pushed the door open. Looking ghastly in the laptop computer light and backlit by a small lamp, Olivia gazed at her screen. She had made herself comfortable in the ship's only private quarters.

Jake cleared his throat, and she stirred.

"What?" she asked.

"I thought you were going to help out," he said. "Maybe steer the ship or something."

"Not yet," she said. "I don't think Pierre wants me in the operations room. I need to study Hayat's dossier anyway. You can't believe what I've learned about him. He's amazing. He's a dichotomy of—"

Jake ran his hand through his hair and pulled back moist fingers. He noticed that his body tingled and his knees felt weak from stress.

"Do you have any idea that we were just in a battle? Two, technically, I think."

She slid her legs from under her buttocks and onto the floor, wiggling in an effort to make blood flow through her extremities and yawning.

"I'm sorry," she said. "We were just where?"

Jake knelt in front of her.

"Never mind," he said. "How are you feeling?"

"Fine, I guess. A little unsure if I should be out here with you and Pierre, but I'm getting into this Hayat character. He practically turned his back on Islam."

Jake didn't care. He kissed her and refused to pull back until she accepted him. He caught her as she fell off the chair.

"Wow!" she said. "What was that for?"

"I don't know," he said. "Maybe just my way of saying I'm glad you're here."

*

Renard wasn't surprised that a black limousine awaited him on the concrete pier. As he climbed the *Hai Lang's* brow and passed beside a damaged frigate, he saw acting Defense Minister Li step out of the car.

He waved his palm at Slate and Ye.

"Let me handle 'his majesty'," he said. "I suggest you two stay on the ship for a while."

Renard swaggered towards Li. The cocky young bureaucrat smiled and extended a hand.

"The most decisive victory in years," Li said. "Quite possibly the most decisive of our naval history."

"Will you not agree then that my debt to your nation is paid in full?" Renard asked.

Li's young face became somber.

"In full?" he asked. "If you had accomplished what we had paid you to accomplish with the *Colorado*, this day would never have been necessary."

"My debts were grand," Renard said. "But so are my deeds of this day. My planning, my action in combat—you have much to claim for it."

The grin returned to Li's face.

"You have planned and executed a day beyond my wildest desires," Li said. "One *Kilo* sunken and one captured! A coup I could never have imagined. Much as you would like to deny its existence, I have a conscience. I must pardon you from all shortcomings of your past."

Li laughed and extended his arms into the sky.

"You have turned the fortunes of this war!"

"And all but solidified you the permanent role as the Defense Minister," Renard said.

"The young must replace the old."

Although Renard disliked Li, he recognized his abilities and knew he'd make a competent Defense Minister.

"There is more work to be done," Renard said, "but I am honored to have served your nation. I'm confident that Commander Ye can lead the *Hai Lang* adequately enough to—"

Li tugged at the breast of his three-piece suit.

"You don't get off that easily, Renard," he said. "I've received a call from Admiral Khan, your friend from Pakistan. You and the *Hai Lang* have more work to do."

"I'm sure Khan paid you a hefty fee to lease it."

Li reached within his suit for a cigarette and lit it.

"Enough to offset much of the overage we paid for the submarine when we bought it," Li said, "and a hefty enough sum to fund many more blockade runs."

Renard had seen Khan's request coming, but with thoughts of returning to his family, he had hoped Khan would not need him.

"How long would I have the *Hai Lang*?" he asked.

"One-month contract with an agreement to negotiate if needed longer," Li said.

"One month is how long it would take the *Hamza* to reach the Straits of Malacca from Ningbo," Renard said, "if it were conserving fuel to reach India and trying to transit submerged and undetected."

"I take it by your willingness to accept this mission that Khan has also offered you a hefty fee to command it."

Touché, Renard thought.

"When do I leave?" he asked.

"Tomorrow at dawn," Li said. "I will have waterfront support handle most of the reloads to give your crew time to celebrate their victory."

"My crew?" Renard asked. "Who are they now?"

"The same you just led," Li said. "After that victory, you should have little trouble influencing them to stay with you. During your inbound transit, I asked Ye to find extra hands for the extended operation. After today's results, I predict no lack of volunteers."

"I begin to sense the camaraderie," Renard said.

"Enjoy your liberty," Li said. "It will be short but well-deserved. If you need a bar or other establishment in the city opened for your crew, you need only call me."

Renard probed Li for his perspective of the danger he faced from the CIA.

"You know I cannot leave the protection of this base," he said. "I'm certain that the CIA has mentioned they know of my presence here."

"That offer to celebrate did not include you or your American colleagues," Li said. "The CIA has not threatened action, but you are safer behind the base's gates."

"How did the CIA approach you?" Renard asked. "About Slate, the lady, and me?"

"A CIA courier brought disks to my office and insisted that I forward it unseen and under top military security control to the lady on the *Hai Lang*."

"Did you admit to the presence of the lady?"

"I don't play charades with the CIA," Li said. "I volunteer all relevant military data with candor. It pays off with the intelligence they offer in return—selective as it is. But since I did not know about CIA officer McDonald at the time, I could not admit to it."

"You know her name and identity?" Renard asked.

"Commander Ye verified her name and presence before you deployed. As for her role in the CIA—past, present or future—I have enough evidence to speculate she is associated with them, but I don't care. If she's your version of an intelligence specialist rider on the *Hai Lang* and will help you with your mission, then I accept her presence."

"You will protect us, then?" Renard asked.

"How so?"

Renard stepped closer and could smell Li's cologne.

"I have a family with whom I wish to be reunited," he said. "I don't want to risk my life again only to be incarcerated upon my return. You have the power to hold the CIA back while I'm on your soil."

"The CIA will not bother you or your colleagues while you are on any of my bases," he said. "But I cannot offer you asylum indefinitely."

Li tossed his cigarette to the concrete and stamped it out. He ducked into the limousine and Renard called out.

"Your word, then," Renard said. "I want your word that you will protect Slate and my family upon our return to Taiwan and that you will provide us military transport to a nation of our choosing."

Li closed the door and rolled down the window.

"To a nation of *my* choosing," he said. "You will have to trust my judgment."

"Agreed," Renard said.

Li lit a cigarette and blew smoke out the window.

"Okay, Mister Renard," he said. "You have my word."

The limousine rolled away.

Their heels tapping the concrete waterfront, Ye and Slate approached.

"What was that about?" Jake asked.

Renard explained the new mission of the *Hai Lang*. Neither Jake nor Ye appeared surprised.

"I'm sure my crew will join you," Ye said and walked from the pier.

"You don't want to ask them now?" Renard asked.

"It can wait until morning," Ye said.

When Ye stepped out of earshot, Renard turned to Jake.

"I believe he's becoming confident," he said. "Almost arrogant."

"Remind you of anyone we know?" Jake asked.

"Perhaps two people we know."

Renard shared a laugh with Jake and shouted to Ye.

"Where are going, my friend?" Renard asked.

"My wife," Ye said as he yelled over his shoulder. "I will return tomorrow morning. Perhaps at eight, but maybe later. Don't bother calling."

Renard opened his mouth, but Jake cupped his shoulder.

"Let him go, Pierre," Jake said. "He's earned it."

CHAPTER TWENTY-FIVE

RENARD STOOD IN THE GRASS outside the Keelung officers' club and held Marie and his son Jacques.

"I know this is impossibly difficult for you," he said, "but there is nothing I can do. I must deploy again tomorrow. Let us enjoy dinner with our guests, and we will have private time later this evening."

When he finished talking to Marie, he joined his companions on the dining floor. Jake, Olivia, and a surprise guest, Lieutenant Sean Wu, accompanied Renard and his family.

"You have chosen the most interesting company available to you," Renard said, "but certainly you could have found more lively companionship with your shipmates."

"The married ones are with their wives," Wu said. "And the rest are getting drunk and trying to get laid. I have a serious girlfriend."

Wu slid a forkful of shrimp cocktail into his mouth and glanced around the table. He appeared to realize that no one would make a peep until he gave more detail.

"In Hawaii," he said. "She's Hawaiian. We met at UCLA. We've been dating almost three years."

"That's difficult," Renard said.

"I used to see her every month or so. The flight isn't that bad. At least it wasn't until the war. Then airline prices shot up. You pretty much need to be on executive business keeping the economy running if you plan to fly off the island."

"Indeed," Renard said. "Your government has tapped most of its financial reserves to subsidize several key industries, the airline industry especially."

Wu's fork tinkled into an empty cocktail glass.

"I haven't seen her in nine months," he said. "We had talked about getting married, but then the war happened."

"It's funny," Jake said, "how the rest of the world just calls it a blockade."

Wu shifted in his seat as if preparing to launch a response, but Renard wanted to diffuse the emotion.

"Diplomats will call it what they want," Renard said. "But we who fight together know the truth."

"Damn straight," Wu said.

"Today was a mighty victory, if I don't say so myself," Renard said. "But this war is far from over."

"What's next?" Jake asked.

An instinctive strategist, Renard had predicted the next several months of combat.

"We proved today that we can now punch through their blockade when needed," he said. "The blockade will still hold, but its grip is loosened. Out victory today will enable the island to last, by my calculations, an additional six to nine months on top of the six months the experts predicted it had remaining before conceding."

"Why can't we just go kick their asses?" Wu asked. "They outnumber us four or five to one, but we're better than they are all around. Our pilots, our surface combatants, and now even our submarines are better."

"Easy young man," Renard said. "Your submarines are still horribly outnumbered."

"Then why are we backing off and doing this mercenary work for Pakistan?" he asked. "Aren't they allies with the mainland anyway?"

A waitress brought their main courses. Steam rose from Renard's cut of swordfish.

"Absent the Pakistani mission, what would you have the *Hai Lang* do?" Renard asked.

"Blast every damn Chinese submarine out of the water," Wu said. "Take out some of their surface combatants, too."

"Perhaps," Renard said. "But the Chinese are already calling their submarines back to port. After losing three in one day, including two of their *Kilos*, they are going to reassess their submarine doctrine. They will analyze the defeat and realize that they have only one choice to reassert their impunity—sink the *Hai Lang*.

"We could face them head on," Renard said. "But consider that we instead deploy elsewhere. They will know we are at sea and will search local waters in vain. Their frustration in not finding us will become fear. Meanwhile, you and your comrades become more proficient in fighting the *Hai Lang* in the Pakistani-commissioned mission."

"So you might view the Pakistani mission as a real world training exercise with the benefit of fooling the mainland by our lack of presence in the Straits?" Wu asked.

Renard swallowed a mouthful of swordfish. It had been overcooked.

"Before I leave, Commander Ye will be a master in handling the *Hai Lang*," Renard said. "And you and your men will rival any wardroom and crew. As for doing the bidding of the Pakistanis, they may be allies of necessity with China, but they are the only submarine builder who will risk selling you submarines. You must look beyond this war and see your nation's future."

"It still doesn't seem right," Wu said. "We have the mainland against the ropes. We should throw more punches."

In his mind, Renard advanced his projection of the strategic scenario. If successful, a knockout punch against the Chinese submarine fleet would be premature.

"And if so, then what?" he asked. "If you decimate half of the Chinese fleet, the blockade fails."

"Nothing wrong with that," Wu said.

"Perhaps it would be victory," Renard said. "Or perhaps it would beget escalation."

"Yes," Wu said. "I've seen it on the news. Some people predict that if we last through the blockade that they'll try missile strikes to cripple our economy. Maybe even an amphibious landing of troops."

"They prefer not to damage that which they wish to reunify, but failure at sea would leave them no option."

"So there's no hope?" Wu asked.

"The future is unpredictable. A rebel province may distract Beijing, an incident may create international sympathy for your island, or the Indians may attempt to reclaim lands the Chinese stole and divert their attention. There is always hope."

Renard finished his dinner and checked that most of the others were nearing completion as he withdrew his Marlboros. He slid his gold-plated Zippo lighter underneath a cigarette, inhaled, and watched a smirk creep onto Wu's face.

"You were an American naval officer, right?" Wu asked.

"That was a long time ago," Jake asked.

"You seem to remember a lot though," Wu said, looking like he was straining to hold back an interrogation. "Some of the guys on the ship thought they recognized you. I know a couple of them are going to hit the Internet real hard tonight."

"He was assigned to the USS *Colorado*," Olivia said.

"You know," Jake said, "for ex-CIA, you sure like to blurt things out. I had to pry you away from the computer to get you to eat, and all of a sudden you're a bullhorn."

"Wait!" Wu said. "You're not one of the guys who went down with the *Colorado* in the reactor accident, are you? They said four guys died scuttling the ship."

"They didn't scuttle it," Olivia said. "It sank—"

"Quiet!" Renard said. "We'll discuss this on the *Hai Lang*. To foster trust, the crew will know the truth and be under order not to expose it. But not another word here."

Renard leaned towards Wu and whispered.

"However," he said, "since I am leading you and your countrymen into battle, I will admit that I share part of the responsibility for having sunk the *Tai Chiang*."

"The lead ship of the stealth patrol craft?" Wu asked. "They told us it was sunk by a Chinese submarine."

"Submarine, yes. Chinese, no. I'm sorry, but it was in large part our doing," Renard said. "I will tell the details to you and any shipmate who wishes to hear the story—once we are deployed."

Wu sat in an unreadable silence. Renard watched him, fearful that he may have lost his confidence.

"If this is a problem, please let me know," Renard said. "If it upsets you, it may also upset your comrades."

"I'll wait to hear the details before passing judgment," Wu said. "But some of my instructors at the Naval Academy knew the commanding officer of the *Tai Chiang*. According to them, you did the fleet a favor."

CHAPTER TWENTY-SIX

OLIVIA CREPT THROUGH A STARK corridor that reminded her of a well-kept two star hotel. The pinstriped wallpaper appeared sterile and the beige carpet drab.

She reached the door to Jake's quarters and knocked.

Jake opened the door.

"Can I come in?" she asked.

"Sure."

She entered what was the equivalent of a hotel room at the Keelung officers' quarters. She stepped to the middle of the room, thought of nothing to say, and felt stupid.

I'm being presumptuous, she thought.

She felt him creep up behind her. Like slinking pythons, his arms slid over her shoulder. He kissed her neck.

"This is complicated now, isn't it?" she asked.

"The only complicated thing is can I keep from laughing at that band aid on your head."

"I'm serious! This isn't easy."

"No sex underway," he said. "It wouldn't be fair to the rest. So we're going to have to figure it out now."

She could feel his erection push through his pants.

"It's easy for you," she said. "You just do what your penis says. I'm the one who has to think for both of us."

"Then stop thinking."

She extinguished her thoughts, faced him, and kissed him. Then she made love to him and enjoyed it.

★

The next morning, romance buzzed in her head. With the wall of secrets separating her from Jake torn down, Olivia entertained fantasies of letting herself fall in love. Then she climbed down the ladder into the *Hai Lang* and realized it would remain a fantasy.

Rickets is supporting me, she thought. *I may still be CIA, and Jake's still a fugitive from justice.*

Following her memorized path, she walked from the torpedo room to her private commanding officer's quarters. She lowered her white blouse and jeans in a drawer where she expected them to stay for weeks. She tucked her hair under a 'Hai Lang' ball cap and slid into a baggy jumpsuit.

A strange sensation crawled up her back as she realized that a confined room within a small submarine would be her home for weeks. With her focus on Hayat's dossier, the two-day exercise that defeated two *Kilos* had passed in a blink. But she wondered if she might go batty during a month-long deployment.

She heard a knock on her stateroom door. Expecting Jake, she got up, opened it and tried to sound perky.

"Hi," she said.

Cigarette smoke wafted into pipes overhead.

"May I come in?" Renard asked.

Puzzled, Olivia stepped back and slid the stateroom's visitor's chair in front of the fold out desk. He sat without asking and motioned for her to do the same.

"I don't know if you intend to arrange my arrest when this is all done," Renard said, "but your presence aboard makes me believe that you are allied with me until the *Hamza* is found—if by us or by another ship."

"The *Hamza*'s a threat to world security. You're not."

"At least for the moment, you mean," he said.

"I've gotten to know Hayat rather well," she said. "I hope that's what you're here to talk about."

He blew smoke into the overhead.

"For the record, I harbor no malcontent against you. Of course, I did at first, but you are a seductive woman who by happenstance acquired HIV and were a natural choice as a tool to manipulate Jake."

"Is everyone just a tool to you?"

"Not everyone," he said.

"But I am."

"Please don't take it personally," he said. "But you are the only one on this submarine who arrived uninvited."

"I brought Jake here, didn't I?"

"And for that, I have trusted you this far."

Unsure if she would return to the CIA even if it were possible, she lowered her gaze and tried to clear her head.

"But no further," she said.

"You are CIA in spirit, and I am wanted," he said.

"That was my past. I have a greater chance of undergoing trial for treason than returning to the CIA."

"The data the CIA sent you about Hayat suggests that they have not abandoned you," he said. "Perhaps your role in helping me track down Hayat can serve as redemption?"

The Marlboro's tip glowed amber as Renard inhaled.

"No matter," he said. "You are resourceful. I'm certain that you will navigate your future. It is our present that concerns me. Let us speak of Hamid Hayat."

"I'm only about a quarter of the way through his dossier."

"Eventually," Renard said, "I will need every clue into his command style. At the moment, however, I want your confirmation that he's going to the Indian Ocean. He has a six-day head start, and I have little leeway for error. I'll need a day to clear the blockade to the east, but after that, I must choose my direction wisely."

She played scenarios in her head, running down her mental checklist of Hayat's potential objectives. Unless she could unearth a contradiction in his dossier, the evidence pointed to India.

"I'll go through this tonight," she said.

"I would appreciate it," Renard said. "Be a good tool and study in earnest."

She scowled.

"I jest," he said. "Come now. We have several weeks together within this small cylinder. You must capitalize on every opportunity for levity."

Renard chuckled and passed through the doorway.

"But in all seriousness," he said. "While you research Hayat, I will have meals brought to you and order the crew to consider your every demand as a top priority. I will make haste for the Straits of Malacca. Before I get there, I want to know who he is, where he's going, and why. I do not jest when I say that I want to know what he ate for breakfast the day I engage him."

"You're asking a lot," she said.

"And you my dear," he said and blew smoke. "You are capable of a lot."

He reached to close the door.

"For a tool," she said.

"*Touché*," he said.

★

The *Hawaii* tilted under Commander Rodriguez. Two sailors in blue cotton jumpsuits approached, one watching the other as he carried a communiqué folder.

"Commanding officer's eyes only," a sailor said.

"I got it," Rodriguez said. "Thank you."

He accepted the folder, and opened it as the men turned away. The air became heavy as Rodriguez noticed his executive officer creeping up beside him.

"What's it say, sir?" Jones asked.

"Just give an old man a second," Rodriguez said.

He lifted reading glasses from his pocket, slid them over his nose, and read.

"Well the good news is that Taiwan has confirmed that the *Hai Lang* is nowhere near us."

"So we've been trailing the *Hamza*?" Jones asked.

"It seems that Pakistan is being tight-lipped about the location of its submarines. They stated that most of its units are deployed on naval exercises but won't give more detail."

"Nor do they have to, sir, by any agreement."

"What we do have, though," Rodriguez said, "is process of elimination. We had satellite photographs of the other Pakistani submarines leaving port in the last couple weeks. They couldn't possibly have reached this far east. It's got to be the *Hamza*."

Jones bent forward, although the motion looked more like a balloon twisting.

"That means we know who he is and where he started," Jones said while tapping a keyboard. "Starting him in Ningbo makes it look even more like he's in direct transit toward Hawaii."

"That's what I told squadron," Rodriguez said. "They know. No need to tell them twice."

"You don't seem too thrilled, sir."

Rodriguez grunted and bounced his fist on the railing surrounding the *Hawaii's* elevated conning platform.

"I'm not. Our orders are to trail him to Hawaii."

"Sounds like the cat and mouse Cold War games of the good old days, sir. And we're in total control."

"Of a game," Rodriguez said. "But what if it's not only a game?"

"Then we have to trust that someone with a little guts squeezes the truth out of some Pakistani diplomat."

"Without tipping our hand that we're trailing the *Hamza*?" Rodriguez asked. "That's tough."

"That's what those people in Washington get paid to do, sir." Jones said. "I wouldn't worry about it. We've got him dead to rights anyway."

Rodriguez sighed.

"Maybe you're right. Take us down from periscope depth, return us to a trail position on Sierra-eleven, and designate Sierra-eleven as the *Hamza*."

CHAPTER TWENTY-SEVEN

Olivia buried herself in her laptop and pieced together the history of Hamid Hayat. She hypothesized that he intended to use nuclear weapons to attack the Indian fleet with the support of a fundamentalist Islamic group that the Pakistani intelligence group, ISI, had identified as HUM, the Harkat-ul-Mujahideen.

Find a reason why he'd do it, she thought. *What does he gain by attacking? What does HUM gain?*

She started by reconstructing Hayat.

He had been born in the Northwest Frontier Province, a Pakistani province with a majority government controlled by the hard-line Islamic political party, United Action Forum. The youngest of five children, he had seen his two brothers recruited to support the Afghan freedom fighters during the Soviet invasion.

Hayat was thirteen years old when his father had sent him to live with his aunt and her husband in Karachi. Olivia's guess coincided with that of Pakistani ISI intelligence that the father, a man of frail health who had later passed away from an undocumented illness, had moved Hayat far from the soviet danger to ensure he survived.

Deeper digging into the dossier showed that Hayat had lost the younger brother in battle. The oldest brother, a devout religious man and a likely head of the house due to the ailing father, had joined the fighters and developed a following. Over the next two decades, he had risen to become a high-ranking cleric in the Harkat-ul-Mujahideen. Olivia recognized the names of Taliban and Al-Quaeda figures with whom the older brother associated.

There's the link between Hayat and HUM, she thought.

Despite the fraternal link, the dossier showed a schism between Hayat and HUM. Hayat was educated in a secular system. Growing up outside its walls, he had applied for entrance to the Pakistani Naval Academy.

Already sensing a shift in the early nineties against military leaders with ties to religion, Hayat had lied on his application and had claimed his uncle as his father. Not until the ISI investigation into the *Hamza*'s rogue status did officials uncover this lie.

His family name wasn't Hayat. Commander Hamid Hayat had taken his uncle's last name to sever ties with his family's fundamentalist roots and to seek a naval career.

That must have pissed off big brother, Olivia thought.

He entered the Pakistani Naval Academy and graduated third in his class. Earning two B's in English while catching up for the weaker schooling of his hometown, he could not catch two straight-A students, but he nonetheless displayed brilliance in his studies.

Performance grades at the academy and early fitness reports after his commissioning suggested he would make an insightful tactician and leader. He had been groomed for command since first donning the white uniform.

He had been ranked as the top junior officer during his tours of duty on a *Daphne* class submarine and an earlier *Agosta*. Before his executive officer tour on the *Khalid*, the first of the next-generation French-built *Agosta90B* submarines, reform had shaped his career.

In the late nineties, the military had made decisive moves to root out hardline Islamic influence. Officers with association to extremist groups had been retired or otherwise forced out.

While watching his government flip-flop between Bhutto and Sharif's corrupt Prime Ministries, Hayat lived during a time when the military provided the bedrock for the nation. He must have embraced secular rule as the foundation for the navy, his personal advancement within it, and his nation's stability.

As one of the military's hopefuls, he had been sent to study at the United States Naval Submarine School. Records from the school showed a curriculum of basics, but fitness reports from Hayat's executive officer tour noted he had used American principles to redefine combat tactics for the *Agosta90B* class. His tactics had become the official doctrine for the Pakistani fleet.

Already selected to command the first *Agosta90B* to be assembled in Pakistan, Hayat found a new opportunity for advancement at the end of his executive officer tour. In the post-9/11 world, Pakistan needed to nurture every diplomatic tie with the United States.

The diplomatic gesture of sending the future commander of the young nuclear state's top war machine, the pre-commission unit *Hamza*, to study public policy from America's top institution sent the message that the Pakistani military remained committed to secular control of itself and the country. President

Musharraf himself had signed the recommendation requesting Hayat's admittance to the Harvard Kennedy School of Government.

Olivia rocked back on her chair and rubbed her eyes. Someone knocked on the door.

"Come in," she said.

A tall Taiwanese sailor with minimal English skills, a junior galley mate, nodded, ducked into the room, and grabbed the dinner plate she had nibbled down to chicken bones.

When the galley mate left, Olivia stood and paced the five feet of clear space she had in her room. After her blood flow improved, she recommenced her studies.

Finding it impossible to dive into all of his work in one night, she scanned what looked like a collection of Hayat's assignments at Harvard. Two facts struck her. The first, his graduation with top honors. The second, perhaps even more impressive, President Musharraf's request to review Hayat's master's thesis. Olivia decided she would read the thesis when time permitted, but racing for a quick snapshot of his mindset, she scanned it.

The title stood out.

Protecting Legitimate Governments from Asymmetric Warfare through Naval Power

She flipped through the document Hayat had written three years earlier. Although the words 'terrorist' or 'terrorism' never appeared in the document, the thesis was Hayat's manual for a joint Pakistani-American naval effort to contain terrorists. Instead of calling them terrorists, he used an alternative word that Olivia found demeaning and arrogant as she absorbed the bitter tone of the thesis.

Those of simple fundamentalist mind.

Hayat pointed out how extremist groups could use the seas to pose threats to coastal cites, ports, and shipping. The thesis analyzed target selection, funding, planning, coordination and implementation of the attack, and post-attack propaganda to recruit new members. He viewed it as a cycle where leaders chose new targets as manifestations of jihad for the new recruits.

He concluded with a chapter on breaking that cycle. Given his slant on maritime threats, he focused on target identification and on coordination and implementation of the attack as points where naval forces could break the cycle and thwart the efforts of simple fundamentalist minds.

Simple fundamentalist mind. Olivia noted repeated use of the term and sensed by the tone of the thesis that Hayat held a grudge against the uneducated and arduous life he had escaped by moving to Karachi—the life that had ruptured his family.

Common practices he recommended for American and Pakistani navies were more small arms-trained personnel on naval and key merchant vessels. He noted that the Cold War model of big guns and cruise missiles failed to protect the modern warship against small boats swarms and swimmers. It needed rocket-propelled grenades, fifty-caliber machine guns, and even teams of armed divers while in port to make warfare less asymmetric—to fight fire with fire.

Interesting insight from a submarine officer, she thought. *But not relevant to me right now.*

As if Hayat's thesis had predicted her mental response, its next paragraph stated that a submarine falling into fundamentalist hands would pose such a significant threat to legitimate governments that the only way to counter it was to prevent it from happening.

Olivia reflected on the irony of that conclusion and flipped to his conclusions on target selection.

Hayat noted that the optimal targets for fundamentalists were those of the simplest and least ambiguous symbolism. Symbolism was more important than lives taken or detriment to an economy or military power. The World Trade Center and the Pentagon had been perfect symbols of economic and military might. The USS *Cole* had provided a symbol of unwelcome intrusion.

Olivia scanned Hayat's catalog of targets that read like a prioritized laundry list, but she read ahead to the conclusion. His ultimate choice for a target would be a combination of symbols, he had written, such as sinking a capital warship such as an aircraft carrier under the Golden Gait Bridge.

Or an Indian aircraft carrier in Mumbai, she thought.

That's what the legitimate government had to protect against, Hayat had written. He made note that a smart defensive tactic would be to create opportunities that appeared like ultimate symbolic targets and to set them as traps to flush out the attackers. Their will could be defeated through the threat of failure if attacks against the ripest targets turned out to be traps.

Blinking, she rested her eyes on a wall clock. She realized she had been studying all day. She opted for a break and stretched her legs along the small passageway outside her stateroom. Looking for a conversation to clear her head, she walked into the wardroom.

At the tiny table designed to seat six, Renard and Lieutenant Wu were playing cards.

"You guys having fun?" she asked.

"Jake and Commander Ye are on watch at the moment," Renard said. "They will operate through the night. Lieutenant Wu and I were just playing cribbage to wind down."

Wu looked at her and smiled.

"We need our beauty sleep," he said. "I'll be in the rack as soon as I teach this guy how to play this game."

Olivia noticed that his teeth were perfect. She also noticed that his pairing with Renard validated something she had consciously ignored. After Commander Ye, Lieutenant Wu was the highest-ranking military man aboard. *If he didn't have a girlfriend,* she thought. *But that's a distraction I don't need.*

"Wind down from what?" she asked.

"We submerged six hours ago and are just outside the limit of the Chinese Economic Exclusion Zone, at least as they have proclaimed it," Renard said. "We had to be on our guard during the transit, but we're now in open ocean."

She pulled out a chair and sat.

"How goes the research?" Renard asked as he dropped his cards to the table.

"Slow but steady," she said before recounting how Hayat had become a shining star in the Pakistani Navy and how he had turned his back on the extremist upbringing he had narrowly escaped.

"You say he was raised in early childhood in the Northwest Province?" Renard asked. "Could he have been faithful to their ways all along and his career a charade?"

"No way," she said. "He's smart and he knows it. There's too much real angst in his writing. He understands that his talent would have been wasted if he had followed the paths of his brothers. I'm sure he maintained an adequate face in practicing his beliefs and going through the gesture of ceremony and prayer—"

"Like many Christians of dubious piety," Renard said.

"Pretty much," she said. "But given his tone, I think he held a grudge against Islam, at least the extremists and how they had soured the core teachings."

Renard blew smoke forward in a hard stream. He appeared intense, as if wrestling for an epiphany.

"Perhaps he somehow returned to Islam," Renard said.

"That might explain his actions," she said, "but I've just barely scanned half the stuff I have on him. But if he's really turned one-eighty on his beliefs, then nuking the *Taktreet* in Mumbai would be in line with what he sees as a hard-line extremist act."

"Why?" Renard asked.

She mulled it over and recalled the thesis.

"Symbolism," she said. "The size of a carrier and its ability to extend war to the Pakistani coast. The Indians have used carrier power against them in the past."

"The group that ISI says is supporting him," Renard said, "Harkat-ul-Mujahideen. Are you familiar with them?"

"A little," she said. "From the research, but mostly from CIA history. The CIA armed the Mujahideen in Afghanistan to fight the soviets. I'm not sure what promises were made or expectations were set, but the Mujahideen felt used and abandoned when we pulled out."

"And their sympathizers and comrades in arms must certainly agree with them," Renard said. "Including the Harkat-ul-Mujahideen."

Cobwebs cluttered her mind. She needed time to assess and thought Renard was pressing her for too much too soon.

"I suppose," she said.

Renard leaned forward and his glare sharpened.

"This group, the Harkat-ul-Mujahideen, is bitter against whom?"

"America," she said. "But they've been associated with attacks on India, too. Look at the December 13 attack on the Indian parliament."

Renard leaned back, blew a cloud, and sighed.

"This is all speculative," he said. "But you have concluded that he's attacking a major warship, have you not?"

"Most likely," she said. "Maybe a city, maybe a cargo ship, but with the high probability that he's carrying nuclear weapons and the potential for fallout, the optimal attack is major warship near major city."

"Good," Renard said. "I like the logic. Land approaches to Indian harbors are well-guarded, and a submarine in extremist hands presents perhaps their only means of striking an Indian carrier. As you said, the symbolism of such an attack, especially if near a city like Mumbai, would be ideal. However, given that you found that HUM also harbors ill-will against the United States—"

"America is also a potential target," she said. "Maybe even more so."

Renard slid back his chair and stood.

"Lieutenant Wu, I concede this game. Either the cards were cursed, or you were dealing from the bottom of the deck. I'm afraid we must delay our rest. We have some estimating to do in the operations room."

Renard and Wu left the cards on the table and were half way out the door when Olivia called to them.

"What are you doing?" she asked.

"It's time for a strategic snapshot," Renard said. "We'll look at the *Hamza*'s starting point in Ningbo eight days ago, draw a circle of places it could hope to reach before running out of food and fuel, and then contact Keelung."

"Keelung?"

"Yes. They must have a good idea of where the American carriers are deployed. After our conversation, I want to see if the *Hamza* can reach any of them."

CHAPTER TWENTY-EIGHT

THE *HAI LANG* NOSED DOWNWARD AS it descended from periscope depth. An exchange with Keelung had produced the information about the American fleet that Renard needed. Half-listening to Jake give commands, Renard huddled beside Wu over the navigation chart on the operation room's starboard side.

He studied a map. From Ningbo, China, where the *Hamza* had received its supposed arsenal, a line wavered south, kinked northwest around Singapore, turned once again and tickled India's eastern coast. Also from Ningbo, a semicircle extended eleven hundred miles to the east.

"Eleven hundred miles," Wu said. "At seven knots, that's how far he could go without refueling. Do you want to see what it looks like at four knots?"

"No need," Renard said. "I'm certain he could push his fuel reserves longer, but his provisions would expire."

"What if someone's waiting to refuel him and give him fresh supplies?"

"In that unlikely event, we hope for help from a satellite," Renard said. "There's no sense in planning for such a scenario. We shall focus on what we can manage."

"Fair enough," Wu said.

"We know he can reach the Indian carriers," Renard said, "but let's assume the maximum range of eleven hundred miles and map this versus the American fleet."

"Okay," Wu said as he tapped a few keys.

With patrol radii that offered ambiguous estimates of their location, the positions of American aircraft carriers appeared. None were in reach of the semicircle.

"That's it, then," Wu said. "He can't reach any American carriers."

A sailor appeared beside Renard and handed him a teletype message.

"Thank you," Renard said as he took it.

The sailor stepped away.

"You are correct, Lieutenant Wu," Renard said, "if you ignore that carriers don't stay in one spot forever. Let's see which ones are scheduled for transit in the near future."

Renard glanced at the teletype that held the American order of battle. Most American carriers on station would remain so for at least the next two months, and all those in port would remain in port or deploy to local waters.

One carrier, however, stood out. The USS *Stennis* was performing a workup in the Pacific Ocean but was scheduled to relieve the *Reagan* in the Arabian Sea within three months. There was a port call scheduled for Pearl Harbor. Renard glanced at the map.

The *Hamza's* range extended to the Hawaiian Islands.

"The *Stennis*," he said. "It is within range at Pearl Harbor. Let's run this by Miss McDonald."

*

The *Stennis*, Olivia thought. *In Pearl Harbor.*

Renard and Wu had mentioned it as a possible target and had left her to contemplate it. As she reflected upon the carrier, it made perfect sense as an ultimate target for a group like HUM.

In addition to being a capital warship, the *Stennis* had taken part in the war on terror, invading holy lands, and it was the platform from which President Bush had declared victory.

The symbolism compounded itself if the *Hamza* attacked it in Pearl Harbor, a location of prime American emotion. Finally, nuclear weapons would threaten Honolulu, a city of three-hundred thousand Americans, with fallout and serve as de facto retaliation against the only nation to have used nuclear weapons in anger.

A perfect target, she had thought when Renard mentioned it. She had nearly shot out of her chair, but Renard had calmed her by mentioning that an attack against the *Stennis* would be suicide.

If the *Hamza* destroyed the *Stennis* in Pearl Harbor, it would be depleted of all fuel and rations while floating near the teeth of the greatest and sure-to-be angriest naval power in the world. It would be found and it would be destroyed. To attack the *Stennis*, the *Hamza* would have to be partaking in a suicidal mission, most likely jihad.

Nothing in *Hayat's* dossier hinted at suicide. His rationale for leaping from successful professional naval officer to hard-line fundamentalist radical eluded her.

Olivia sighed.

I haven't read it all yet, she thought. *There's so much. I need to narrow in on something soon.*

She heard a knock, and Renard cracked the door open and popped his head through it.

"If you're trying to pressure me to go faster," she said, "it's not going to work."

"Actually," he said, "I came to offer you a reprieve. I've calculated my speed advantage over the *Hamza*, and the worst case scenario grants me four days before I would need to turn towards *Hawaii*."

"Why so long?"

"The *Stennis* is not scheduled to arrive for forty-six more days," he said. "Averaging twelve knots, we can reach Pearl Harbor in thirty-five days. If you conclude that the *Hamza* is indeed targeting the *Stennis*, there is leeway."

"Wait," she said. "How come we can make twelve knots and the *Hamza* can only make seven?"

"Because we can arrange for underway refueling. Commander Ye assures me a ship will meet us en route. It is a difficult procedure, and it might cost us a day or even two awaiting calm waters, but replenishment at sea can be done. We will also make more noise in transit than the *Hamza* and risk being detected, but if we are discovered, diplomacy may explain our presence. The *Hamza* does not have that luxury."

"So I can be more thorough," she said. "If I do the math, I should have more than four days, though."

"Yes," he said. "We will make for the Straits of Malacca now, because our speed advantage to that point gives us less time. If we need to turn around, though, we will essentially be backtracking. So you get roughly half the time, minus an extra cushion."

She pushed her chair back and leaned forward.

"If I thought Hayat was suicidal," she said, "I'd commit to the *Stennis* right now. But you say an attack on Mumbai is not suicidal, and that tips it the other way."

"He could reach Karachi after attacking Mumbai," Renard said, "especially if the commander of a second Pakistani combatant is willing to guard his retreat."

"I have no evidence that he's suicidal. So far, all I know is that ISI believes he reconciled with his brother four or five months ago. I don't know why yet."

Renard reclined against the doorframe.

"When you determine why he returned to his brother and the HUM," he said, "I am sure you will know if he's suicidal or not."

*

Two days later, Jake felt the fatigue of submerged underway operations. No sunlight, confinement to cramped spaces, and long hours had always taxed his endurance. Jake found it particularly difficult on a submarine so small that his old stomping ground of the USS *Colorado*, a Trident Missile submarine, could have carried it as cargo.

He also disliked the frequent excursions to periscope depth to snorkel. With Renard burning the *Hai Lang's* battery to drive its main electric motors two knots faster than the recommended ten-knot transit speed, the *Hai Lang* came shallow every three days, slowed to ten knots, and sucked in air through its induction mast to run the diesel engine and recharge the battery.

Although he suspected nobody hunted the *Hai Lang*, Jake disliked the vulnerability of frequent snorkeling. He knew it would be worse if not for the MESMA system augmenting the batteries underwater.

With the reprieve of a four-section watch shared between himself, Renard, Wu, and Ye, Jake took a moment to explore the *Hai Lang*. He wanted a closer look at the technology he had studied, and he also wanted the relative privacy of the engineering spaces where less than half of the crew bothered to travel.

He passed through the after battery compartment and the after auxiliary machinery room that contained the oxygen generator and carbon dioxide scrubber.

He entered the extra hull section that extended the *Hai Lang* nine meters but permitted air-independent propulsion through the ethanol-liquid oxygen MESMA plant. The familiar hiss of steam filled the section, and Jake felt heat waft over his body as he passed through.

His jumpsuit unzipped and flopped over his waist, Claude LaFontaine exposed a sweat-marked tee-shirt. He was examining gauges on a control station as a Taiwanese sailor, also in a tee-shirt, climbed up from the lower deck and joined him. LaFontaine turned to Jake.

"*Bonjour!*" he said. "How are you?"

"Fine," Jake said. "What's up?"

Jake nodded at a tank he recognized as the ethanol storage tank.

"No problem there," LaFontaine said. "And no problems below, either."

Jake looked below and felt a chill as he noticed he stood over a cryogenically cooled tank of liquid oxygen and a seawater condenser.

"Any problems at all?" he asked.

"Not if Pierre keeps us at a steady speed," LaFontaine said. "It's the transient response to power changes that trip this thing offline. The gases discarded from the combustion chamber—now keeping that at the right mix is a delicate balance. Requires constant vigil."

"Reminds me of the evaporator we used on the *Colorado*," Jake said. "If you didn't balance the steam and water flows, the thing tripped offline."

"If you say so," LaFontaine said. "Just make sure Pierre remembers to order more ethanol and oxygen for our refueling. These are a lot harder to find than diesel fuel. I don't want him forgetting, or else we'll have to snorkel once in theater with that *Hamza*, and that would be bad, given that they have a MESMA system just like ours."

The winding groan of an underpowered turbo-generator filled the room. The Taiwanese sailor beside LaFontaine scurried away but returned in a matter of minutes as the generator fell back into its fifty-hertz harmony.

Jake wanted to know if the problem had been with the electronic governor or with the steam supply, but a distant voice filled with excitement distracted him.

He waved goodbye to LaFontaine and made it two steps when the voice cried out again. A frightening creature appeared before him.

Incandescent lighting gave Olivia's makeup-free face a yellow-ivory glow. The vessels in her eyes resembled roadmaps, and she held her eyes as open as possible as if inviting Jake to navigate by them. Frayed tufts of red hair exploded from under her ball cap.

"Slow down," Jake said. "You're babbling."

She grabbed his arm and mumbled a story of horror and excitement. Jake caught only pieces of it, but he followed her to the wardroom.

"Come on!" she said as she yanked him.

At least she ducked when she turned, he thought. *She's learning.*

In the wardroom, Renard and Wu enjoyed another game of cribbage, and the smug look on the Frenchman indicated he was earning revenge.

Jake sat while Olivia paced in the small space.

"I just figured it out," she said.

She shook her hands as if trying to rid her fingers of the tremble he had felt in them.

No one needed to ask what she had figured out, but Renard prompted her as she struggled for a beginning point.

"Where's he going?" he asked.

"The *Stennis*," she said.

"That's suicide," Renard said. "You've discovered something that suggests his willingness for jihad?"

She inhaled deeply and let out a breath.

"Damn right I did," she said. "He's dying."

CHAPTER THIRTY

RENARD CONSIDERED THE CONVERSATION TO be one of his life's most important. He had sent Lieutenant Wu to exchange places with Ye to listen to Olivia's evidence.

"Why did Khan not mention this?" he asked.

"He didn't know," she said. "Hayat was diagnosed with pancreatic cancer in New York. He was attending the wedding of a colleague he'd met at Harvard, but flight records and medical records show that he headed right to the hospital after landing. He was complaining of severe nausea and stomach pains. A day later, he gets the test results back."

"Pancreatic cancer?" Renard asked, his confidence in Olivia growing.

"One of the worst," she said. "Very painful. Six months to a year to live."

"This is information we never would have had without your presence," Renard said. "And your analyses thus far have been superb. I commend you."

"I owe one to Jerry Rickets," she said.

"But I must dig into this deeper," Renard said. "One man, a commanding officer especially, wields tremendous power over his people. But to dupe them all into a suicidal mission? That would take a combination of charisma and influence that even I do not possess."

Jake stared sideways at him.

"What?" Renard asked. "I convinced you to steal a Trident Missile submarine."

Jake shook his head as Olivia continued.

"I looked into the crew manifest," she said. "Standard bunch except for the executive officer, Faisel Raja. He was born and raised in Baluchistan, another province with deep ties to Harkat-ul-Mujahideen. His parents were rich enough to get him decent schooling, and he made it into the Pakistani Naval Academy. Problem is, there's an easy tie between him and HUM. He never went out of his way to hide it."

"And that's detrimental to a Pakistani officer's career?" Jake asked.

"Yes. A big reform almost ten years ago. They turned the whole military secular. Bad news for Faisel Raja, who started getting poor fitness reports and looked like he'd be drummed out before making lieutenant commander. Then, all of a sudden, a month after Hayat reconciles with his big brother the HUM cleric, Raja's promoted and selected as Hayat's new exec."

"Apparently the HUM holds influence with the military," Renard said.

"Through the United Action Forum party, probably," she said. "Maybe not enough influence to make flag officers, but definitely enough to make a lieutenant commander."

Renard inhaled the sweet taste of tobacco and contemplated his decision.

"We have much to arrange with Keelung and Karachi," he said. "Fuel, an extended lease agreement, perhaps additional provisions."

Ye nodded.

"The provisions and fuel can be arranged, I'm certain," he said. "But I cannot predict the lease."

"I'm confident Li and Khan will agree," Renard said. "My decision is made. If anyone wishes to countermand me, now is the time. If not, we will ascend to periscope depth immediately, contact Keelung, and make the arrangements. We will intercept the *Hamza* en route to Pearl Harbor."

*

Jake felt deflated after three weeks and no sign of the *Hamza*. Life aboard the *Hai Lang* had returned to the submarining norm—excruciatingly mundane.

He reached toward the ship's control panel and tapped Henri on the shoulder.

"How much left on the battery?" he asked.

"Thirty-nine percent," Henri said. "I wish I could say as much for the fuel."

"I know," Jake said. "We're going to have to break for our fuel rendezvous soon. Pierre wants us to turn south tonight, and I don't blame him. If we miss that refueling tanker, we're stuck out here."

Jake felt the air pressure behind him drop. He turned and noticed two Taiwanese sailors holding their breath and staring at Antoine Remy. The French sonar technician clasped his headset and reminded Jake of a toad covering its ears.

Remy stared with big eyes, and Jake knew he had found something.

Hamza, Jake thought.

In ninety seconds the operation room's population doubled. Jake took his stance over the Subtics monitors and placed the earpiece over his ear. The *Hai Lang* was at battle stations.

Renard stood behind the periscope. Jake walked to him.

"Antoine heard diesel engines," he said. "I guessed a speed of seven knots and came out with a range of nineteen miles. That's a swag, though."

"I know," Renard said, "but it's all we have. We'll assume it's the *Hamza* and drive a better solution on it."

"We're low on fuel," Jake said. "We barely have enough to get to our rendezvous ship."

"Very well," Renard said. "We'll slow to five knots and head due north. If the contact is indeed the *Hamza*, it will head east, and we will drive appreciable bearing rate to refine the solution. Let fate then decide if we have enough fuel for an approach and engagement."

*

An hour later, Jake stared over Remy's shoulders. His excitement piqued as Remy announced his findings.

"I hear their screw," he said. "It sounds just like ours! It's the *Hamza*!"

Before anyone answered, Remy blurted another report.

"Diesel engine noises have secured," he said. "I hear hull popping. I've lost the screw, too. They've dived below the surface layer."

Jake stood and locked eyes with Renard.

"They're gone, Pierre," he said. "We can probably regain them if we chase them. We have the advantage."

"But no fuel, *mon ami*," Renard said. "You said it yourself. Our reach is limited."

"One shot," Jake said. "We've got plenty of torpedoes. Let's send a slow, low-probability shot at them and see if we get lucky."

Renard blew smoke, and it wafted into the overhead.

"We might alert them to our presence."

"So what?" Jake asked. "They don't have the fuel to chase us either. By the time we reach our refueling rendezvous, we'll be long gone from wherever they hear our weapon, and I bet they won't even hear it."

"You have a good point. Do you also have a targeting solution?" Renard asked.

"Set in tube two."

"Tube two?" Renard asked.

"Yeah," Jake said. "A tube on the disengaged side. If by chance someone's listening for a torpedo, it's better to shoot from the opposite side of the submarine. That hides some of the noise."

"A tactic I had forgotten," Renard said. "Why did you not correct me when I shot the *Kilos*?"

"Because you had it right then," Jake said. "I guess that was by random luck."

Renard exhaled another lungful of smoke.

"Random luck plays a part, *mon ami*. Shoot tube two."

Minutes passed, and Jake watched the *Hai Lang's* silent torpedo vector in the *Hamza's* direction.

"Does the torpedo hear the *Hamza*?" Renard asked.

Jake shook his head.

More time passed, and the torpedo's fuel waned.

"The *Hamza* is too quiet," Jake said. "We can barely hear it, but the torpedo can't hear it at all. Do you want to go active?"

"Do you?" Renard asked.

I was afraid he'd ask, he thought.

"In a tail chase, weapon-on-stern, with uncertain range to the *Hamza*, it would announce our presence with little hope of the torpedo acquiring. They're too far away, and the torpedo's almost out of fuel."

"Too far for command detonation?"

"Damage to them would be minimal at best," Jake said. "Probably just a tap on the shoulder saying we're here."

"I agree, *mon ami*," Renard said. "Shut down the weapon, and let us make for our rendezvous."

*

Commander Rodriguez trotted to the *Hawaii's* control room. Jones stooped over a monitor with a fire control technician.

"Transients bearing one-zero-eight," Jones said.

"What sort of transients? Launch transients?"

"Could be, sir, but we can't tell. There's nothing else on that bearing. I'd say it was a merchant, except that I would have expected more noise."

Rodriguez reviewed his tactical scenario. For nearly four weeks the *Hamza* had bee-lined towards Hawaii, and refinement of the solution set its destination near the channel entrance to Pearl Harbor.

"We can break trail from the *Hamza* for a while, executive officer," he said. "It looks like he's got no surprises up his sleeve and we can catch up with him later. Let's see who made that noise."

*

Twelve hours later, the Hawaii's deck angled below Rodriguez. He watched a monitor as if watching television. The photo-optics mast portrayed a scene far more entertaining than anything he'd seen on cable.

"Are we sure that's not the *Hamza*?" he asked.

Watching the monitor, Jones stood beside him.

"Positive, sir. I think we found its alter ego."

"Can you make out the name of that tanker?"

"No, sir. But I bet if we can upload this back home, someone will be able to clean it up and match it with some port authority manifest somewhere."

Rodriguez glanced again at the monitor. A surfaced diesel submarine was mated to a tanker that dwarfed it in the moonlight. Cables ran what looked like fuel lines into the submarine's hull. A second monitor showed the scene in night vision, outlining chains that lowered boxes to the submarine's open forward hatch.

"Looks like they're loading some food, too."

"So this has got to be the *Hai Lang*, sir," Jones said. "It's chasing down the *Hamza*."

"Or racing it somewhere," Rodriguez said.

"Should we risk a secure uplink, sir?"

"Not yet," Rodriguez said. "We'll wait until they submerge before we broadcast. But until someone tells us otherwise, our focus remains the *Hamza*."

CHAPTER THIRTY

The vomiting sessions grew more frequent, and Hayat could no longer conceal his weight loss with baggy coveralls. He had asked the corpsman to explain his emaciation as an exercise program with the side effect of exhaustion. The crew either believed the lie or feigned accepting it.

Courageous, competent, and strong, he thought. *A mighty crew as a mighty gift.*

He ingested another round of codeine and bismuth fluid and headed toward the operations room. The walk seemed longer each time.

He braced himself against the hatch frame for support as he passed through. Feeling weak in the knees, he reached for Raja.

Raja had learned to accept his handshake while stabilizing him and guiding him into the captain's chair behind the periscope. He had become so good at the supporting gesture that Hayat no longer felt the men's eyes scrutinizing him as he wobbled into the seat.

He sat and recovered his strength. Raja had also learned to distract the operations room by having them refine the ship's trim or navigation until Hayat was ready to speak. Hayat watched Raja and noted that he glanced back frequently, looking for a cue.

Hayat opened his mouth, and Raja was there.

"Yes, sir," Raja said.

"At four knots, how far are we from the loiter point?"

"Fifteen days, sir."

"The battery?"

"Sixty-eight percent, sir."

"The *Stennis*? Arrival date?"

"Unchanged, sir," Raja said. "We are picking up more and more radio traffic as we approach. Many merchants are talking about the carrier's visit."

Hayat considered his options.

"We can change depth while loitering to verify the arrival of the target," he said, each word an effort. "We can proceed per plan. Snorkel to a full battery, and then submerge the ship and slow to four knots. We will run on the MESMA system thereafter. This snorkel procedure shall be the *Hamza's* last."

*

Ten weeks of chasing the *Hamza* had turned up two detections. The first had been the long-range torpedo shot that had missed. The second, three days ago, had been a snorkeling sound. Renard had followed that sound but then lost it.

Fuel, fresh vegetables, and the original detection of the *Hamza* had raised his spirits and that of the crew. The second regain had provided new hope just as the fresh vegetables ran out and the crew had to feed upon dry and frozen goods.

Renard sensed that he might never catch the *Hamza* until it was too late. As he swiped the flame of his Zippo under a Marlboro and puffed it to life, he mulled over his next steps.

As if sent by divine providence, Jake sauntered into the operations room and joined him.

"Maybe we just ought to race ahead of him and wait," Jake said. "He's probably slowed to be careful as he gets closer. We already tried to beat him in transit, but I say we just ambush him."

"I could not have said it better, *mon ami*," Renard said. "I grow weary of this difficult hunt. An ambush is exactly what we shall do."

*

Rodriguez went over a list of the *Hawaii's* supplies. He had already pushed a week beyond the expected patrol's duration. The outlook was bleak.

"Tell the supply officer to cut back rations," he said.

Jones looked at him in horror.

"Sir, do you mean to starve the men?"

"No, I mean smaller portions. Every man has the option for seconds, or thirds, or whatever, but we need to be smart about this. No more heaping bowlfuls that someone ends up throwing out because it's not as good as his wife's cooking. First rule, you take it, you eat it, or you find a shipmate who will. Second rule, dish out smaller portions so the first rule doesn't bite us."

The color returned to Jones' face.

"I'll take care of it, sir."

Rodriguez knew his crew would find a way to stretch the rations, but how long, he couldn't tell.

"The *Hamza's* still tracking at four knots?" he asked.

"Yes, sir," Jones said. "Almost for a week now. It traveled ten weeks at seven knots and then slowed to four for the last week. At that rate, he'll be at Pearl in another week. He's got to be low on supplies, too."

"That's comforting," Rodriguez said. "That might just force him to do whatever he's going to do and leave before we run out of supplies."

"I get the sense you'd shoot him now, if you could, sir."

Reminded of his quandary, Rodriguez cringed.

"Part of me is saying that's exactly what we should do, but our orders are still to trail and to not engage unless he makes a hostile move."

"Some might say a submerged approach to Pearl is a hostile move," Jones said.

"You know I do, but I hate to admit that the bureaucrats may be right on this one. We've been doing this to the free world for fifty years. Unless he does something violent, we have no rights."

"Well, sir, if the *Hai Lang* shows up, it might take care of this for us, and it may be playing by a different set of rules."

"We'll see. It's this type of game that makes me wake up in the morning."

*

Renard had sprinted ahead of his best guess of the *Hamza's* position and loitered twenty miles from Pearl Harbor. Knowing that snorkeling would put him at risk, he relied on the MESMA system to keep the *Hai Lang* running submerged and undetected.

After waiting a week with no sign of the *Hamza*, he grew concerned. The *Stennis* was scheduled to arrive the next day, and some of its battle group support ships had already docked in Pearl Harbor.

"Are you sure you don't want to try a drone?" Jake asked. "We have two."

"Letting you load the second drone was my folly," Renard said. "It is a waste. Please, do not ask me again. We will find the *Hamza* with the proper tactics."

"I hope so," Jake said. "To miss the *Hamza* now would be worse than never having tried."

CHAPTER THIRTY-ONE

Jake stood before the periscope well's railing, below Renard, who stood on the slightly elevated conning area behind the rail. Although his body placement showed deference, he struggled to keep from screaming.

"Pierre," he said, "you're stuck in the fucking past. You need to let me use the remote vehicle. You're not going to find the *Hamza* without it."

Looking weary and agitated, Renard forced a puff of smoke from his cheeks.

"How?" he asked. "A glorified shell of a torpedo is going to unravel the secrets of the *Hamza's* location? The secrets we could not find during a weeklong search?"

"Maybe," Jake said. "It can conduct an active search without compromising our position."

"No compromise?" Renard asked. "You'd geo-locate us for any listening adversary to within miles of the drone."

"The Taiwanese designed it for ten miles."

Jake looked towards the row of Subtics monitors in hopes that Ye would back him up. Ye's back had been to the conversation, but he turned and nodded.

"We employed one to ten miles during shakedown."

"Thanks," Jake said. "Ten miles is plenty of gravy. No one could target us on that, and all it does is tell the *Hamza* we're out here. Hell, I know giving up the advantage of surprise sounds stupid, but it might distract them from attacking the *Stennis*. We're no longer hunting the *Hamza* as much as we're protecting the *Stennis*."

Renard slid his Marlboro to the corner of his mouth. He extended his arms to the railing and hung his head. As his voice fell to a whisper, Jake knew he had his attention.

"In French," Renard said. "For privacy."

"*D'Accord*," Jake said.

"The ship's speed would be restricted?" Renard asked.

"Five knots, although it's just a design guess. You'd actually need to come to a stop for a couple hours."

"That would leave only a few hours before the *Stennis* approaches the harbor—less if the *Hamza* intends to attack before the carrier reaches harbor."

"You heard Olivia," Jake said. "This guy isn't interested in random destruction. He's looking to destroy a symbol within a symbol. He wants headlines that say 'the carrier upon which Bush declared victory was destroyed in Pearl Harbor'. Plus he needs to attack from upwind for the fallout to reach Honolulu."

"Fair enough if you trust Olivia's analysis," Renard said. "But she's pieced together the evidence by herself over a few weeks while pursuing our adversary. The amount of data—the exploration and rejection of scenarios—this type of thing takes teams of analysts in air conditioned rooms months to resolve."

"I trust her," Jake said. "We have to trust her."

"Agreed," Renard said, "only because there is no other choice. I still assume that the *Hamza* is close by with hostile intent. However, I'm at my wit's end to find it. Go ahead, then. Explain your plan."

Jake leaned and spoke into Renard's ear. He divulged his thoughts, and when he finished, Renard stood straight.

"Dear God, man!" Renard said. "This counters everything I have learned in my career."

"Technology is driving the new way of submarine warfare," Jake said. "Now's the time to embrace it."

*

Two hours later, the *Hai Lang* drifted and Jake sat at the forward-most Subtics dual-stacked monitor station. Staring at the adjacent monitor, a Taiwanese sailor with negligible English skills sat beside him. Ye stooped between them and translated.

"The drone is ten nautical miles ahead," Ye said.

"Yeah," Jake said. "That was patient driving."

"Conserving the drone's fuel," Ye said. "We still have seventy percent fuel remaining. "Petty Officer Zhu is ready for you to give drone orders."

"Have him turn it one full rotation," Jake said.

Ye nodded and translated. Zhu tapped buttons on his keypad.

"He really knows which keys give which commands?"

"He wrote the program that converts keystrokes into drone commands," Ye said. "He also worked closely with the engineers who built the drone."

"I guess you left the dumb ones back in Taiwan."

Reacting to Jake's tone, Zhu winked. Jake smiled, but his expression waned as he studied the monitor.

An overhead view of the drone showed it driving a tight circle, but its acoustic input showed nothing but marine life—a random waveform of static in the higher broadband frequencies. Jake put a headset over his ears to listen but heard nothing but crackling shrimp.

He yelled across the line of Subtics monitors.

"Antoine, can you listen to the drone's hydrophones?"

Antoine Remy glanced up from his monitor. He nodded, told the Taiwanese sonar operator beside him to keep listening for the *Hamza* through the *Hai Lang's* sensors, and flipped a switch on his console. He pressed his phones against his ears and closed his eyes.

"Nothing," he said. "Sorry, Jake."

Jake peeked over his shoulder and was surprised to see Renard looking at him.

"Go ahead, Jake," Renard said. "Transmit active."

Jake grabbed Ye's shoulder.

"Let's see if we can find him or at least flush him out," Jake said.

"You mean maximum power?" Ye asked.

"Yeah. There's no need to finesse this. It's time to challenge the *Hamza* to a dual."

Ye translated, and Zhu tapped the keyboard. Jake watched a wall of sound walk up his monitor.

"Turn twenty degrees to the right and try again."

Ye nodded and translated. Again no active return.

"Keep turning," Jake said. "Twenty-degree intervals."

On the sixth turn, Jake saw a fuzzy trace—a target six miles from the drone. He flipped through images on his monitor to correlate the trace with anything the *Hai Lang* itself heard and was disappointed to see that the drone's new discovery matched an inbound fishing trawler Remy had classified fifteen minutes ago.

"At least this validates that the drone works," he said. "And the range is impressive. How much power do you guys pump through that little thing?"

"With no warhead, the engineers had room for a larger active seeker," Ye said. "The greater power permitted a lower frequency, which gives greater range."

"But shitty accuracy," Jake said. "Like closing your eyes in an auditorium and trying to point at the tuba. You can't get a good bearing unless you guys embedded a mini-Cray computer in that thing for some heavy integration."

"The guidance wire sends raw data to Subtics for processing," Ye said. "It is no strain on Subtics, and the minimal onboard intelligence leaves more room for fuel and hydrophones. We plan to even install an integrated video, heat seeking, and particulate detection sensor—"

"Just tell me about the one in the water," Jake said.

A cloud of smoke rose above Jake. He turned over his shoulder, and Renard was glaring.

"Not one eighty, please," Renard said.

"Yeah," Jake said. "Almost forgot. Skip ahead to two-hundred degrees. Let's not ping ourselves."

On the final turn-and-ping interval, Jake reclined in his chair. Frustrated, he looked to Remy.

"Any activity Antoine?" Jake asked. "You have better hydrophones on the *Hai Lang*. The drone might miss what you can hear. Any chance we forced him into repositioning?"

"What do you think I've been listening for?"

Jake felt silly for having asked and shook his head. A hand slapped his shoulder.

"Don't give up," Renard said. "I'm starting to like this scenario. All sensors on our ship are optimized while we drift, and with your drone ten miles out, we've set up a corridor through which the *Hamza* must move if it wishes to attack a harbor-bound vessel. Keep at it, man."

Jake nodded and flipped a switch on his console to bring up a sound propagation display.

I've got to try something else, he thought.

On his lower monitor, wavy lines near the ocean's surface diverged, converged, and diverged again into the distance. Other lines diverged and curved into the depths, never to touch again. He grabbed Commander Ye's shoulder and pointed.

"You see here," Jake said. "All sound bends toward colder temperature. If you know your environment's temperature gradients, you can use it to your advantage. See how the sound bends?"

"I have trained to use this tactical data, but I've never had a chance to test it," Ye said.

"We dropped a bathythermograph thirty minutes ago, so this map—this environment—is pretty accurate. Let me call it up in three-dimension. It shows volumes."

Ye nudged Jake as he squinted.

"It looks like both the *Hai Lang* and the drone are too shallow to hear deeper sounds."

Jake pointed at arced lines that rose from the deep.

"But if we can take the drone deeper," he said, "we can intercept some of the deep sound as it bounces off the ocean bottom. And look here. Even with the angled slope leading up to the islands, the bottom-bounce propagation path returns shallow about twelve miles out."

"If the *Hamza* is that far out," Ye said, "it must reposition to attack. Either that, or it would have to shoot a well-timed, slow torpedo to extend its range. But then its target would have time to detect the attack and evade."

"Maybe," Jake said. "But we assume the *Hamza* is shallow and relying on periscope visual detection and extending a radio mast to listen to harbor chatter. If this guy's really good, he can ascend and descend without leaving his position. He could listen, look, and descend periodically, and with all the radio chatter, he'd have plenty of warning before the carrier comes in."

"You believe he's waiting deep, then?"

"It's worth listening," Jake said. "And the sound environment supports it."

Jake looked at the propagation paths again. He tapped his keyboard, and the shallow-water paths disappeared. Gazing at the bottom-bounce paths, he let his mind play the game of trying to position the drone in a sound channel that resembled a slanted MacDonald's restaurant arch.

"You said the drone can go to more than a thousand meters," Jake said. "That's design. Can it go deeper?"

"How deep do you need?" Ye asked.

"Sixteen hundred meters," Jake said.

Ye exchanged words with Petty Officer Zhu, the Taiwanese sailor who spoke no English but seemed to know everything about Jake's drone. Ye nodded.

More smoke appeared over Jake's head and billowed into the vents behind the stacked monitors.

"Go on, Jake," Renard said. "You cross an acoustic layer, it's a whole new world. That drone can dive far deeper than we can. Send it deep."

"You seem to be taking a lot of interest in this so-called shell of a torpedo," Jake said.

"With time running short, I'm open to its possibilities now," Renard said. "Maybe I'm no longer stuck in the fucking past, as you say."

*

His fingers rapping against his keyboard with methodical precision, Petty Officer Zhu spiraled the drone downward with patience and dexterity. On his monitor, Jake watched the drone settle deep.

Zhu rattled off a comment that Ye translated.

"We've reached the limit of the guidance wire," Ye said. "The drone is at maximum depth and distance."

Jake stood and shouted across the *Hai Lang's* operations room.

"Pierre," Jake said, "it's probably a good time for another bathythermograph. It might tell us how well this drone is placed."

Renard had been engaged in conversation over Remy's shoulder. He looked up and whispered to the Taiwanese petty officer seated beside Remy.

Jake was unsure if Renard had heard him until a temperature gradient unfolded on his monitor. The converging and diverging lines representing the sound channels reached into the depths as a newly expended bathythermograph descended below the *Hai Lang*.

Jake liked what he saw.

"Maybe some weather's moving in," he said, "or there's a tidal effect. Whatever it is, the sound channels have changed."

"The drone is at the bottom of the shallow channels and near the top of the deeper channels."

"Depending how accurate this model is, that means we might hear in both channels, or we might not hear anything. Let's give it a chance to listen full circle," Jake said.

The monitor showed the drone crawling through another tight search circle, and Jake listened as it carved its path through the depths. The drone's acoustic input showed nothing of interest. Jake looked to Remy.

"Don't ask," Remy said. "I was already listening. Just more whale food and volcanic rumbling."

"Take it active again," Jake said. "All you got."

Zhu tapped the keyboard and a wall of sound walked up Jake's monitor. Nothing. Two twenty-degree turns later, Jake nearly leapt out of his chair.

"You see that?" he asked.

"Yes," Ye said. "All of it."

Like ghosts, four fuzzy masses appeared on the monitor. Jake stood to tell Renard what he saw, but a white cuff passed in front of his face as Renard pointed at the electronic specters.

"Four traces?" Renard asked. "That's too many submarines—inconceivable."

"Two pairs of traces," Jake said. "One pair on each bearing, each bearing including a shallow direct-path acoustic return and a deep bottom-bounce acoustic return."

"Two submarines, each heard twice," Renard said.

Jake interrupted as Ye translated for Zhu.

"Is that drone capable of determining angle of elevation?" he asked.

"No," Ye said. "Just a two dimensional bearing."

"That's what I was afraid of."

Jake tapped his keyboard and a monitor revealed a two-dimensional view. The *Hai Lang*, a blue inverted triangle, was at the center, the entrance to Pearl Harbor was to the northeast, and four red inverted triangles appeared to the southwest. The drone's inverted blue triangle lay at the screen's top.

"We know the range from the drone to each of the four contacts," he said. "What we don't know is which two contacts are acoustic phantoms, and which of the other two is the *Hamza*."

"An excellent summary," Renard said. "The other submarine is probably an American vessel observing the *Hamza*. Sadly, they are too uncertain of its intent to violate it rules of engagement and to destroy it in international waters."

"That's what we're here for," Jake said. "Now all we have to do is wiggle that drone in a little closer and—"

"Helm, all ahead standard," Renard said.

Henri, seated forward of Jake at the ship's control panel, raised his eyebrow but said nothing.

"Well, my friend," Renard said. "You heard me."

Henri turned and maneuvered a joystick. A line extended from the *Hai Lang* triangle on Jake's monitor to indicate the forward motion.

"Standard?" Jake asked. "We have total tactical control. Don't barrel in there like a bull in a china shop. All we have to do is sneak the drone in there, but if you go to ahead standard they might hear us."

"I'm sorry, but we have no choice," Renard said.

Jake didn't understand but watched as Renard stepped up to Remy, nudged the sonar operator aside, and pressed a button at the monitor.

"You've been quite busy, Jake," Renard said, "and I didn't want to distract you. Take a look."

Jake glanced at a bright blue square as it materialized on his monitor.

"We've been tracking the *Stennis* on its final approach to the harbor," Renard said. "Our time is up."

CHAPTER THIRTY-TWO

A CREATURE OF HABIT, COMMANDER Rodriguez studied the raw acoustic data. A physics major from the University of Virginia, he enjoyed the dynamics. He watched a fuzzy trace careen like a waterfall down a screen that showed azimuth direction in three hundred and sixty degrees.

Flipping through similar screens, he noticed that changing the depression or elevation angle hardly altered the intensity of the signal. The chaotic multi-frequency broadband flow noise of the aircraft carrier *Stennis* pushing the seas out of its way filled the *Hawaii's* hydrophones from sail to keel.

Rodriquez flipped to a new view that showed sounds reaching the *Hawaii* in a discrete frequency band correlating to the revolutions per minute of the *Stennis'* propeller blades. Through Doppler effect, the blades rotating towards the *Hawaii* arrived at a higher frequency than the blades that were rotating away.

Too much detail, he thought. *Keep the big picture in sight. Let the sonar team verify this.*

"Chief Bartlett," he said. "How's blade rate?"

The portly man in the blue cotton jump suit seated in front of him replied over his shoulder.

"Correlates to ten knots, sir."

"Thanks, Chief," Rodriguez said.

He looked to the row of men seated at monitors running along the length of the *Hawaii's* control room. Anticipating his next question, the *Hawaii's* solitary navigation watch stander volunteered the answer.

"Ten knots was what harbor authorities told the *Stennis* to make, sir," he said.

Rodriguez acknowledged the report and turned his attention to the screen below him. He flipped to an overhead, two-dimensional view that showed the blue square of the *Stennis*. An inverted red triangle represented the nearby *Agosta* class submarine.

He thought about asking a watchstander to calculate data but reconsidered. The automation in the *Virginia* class submarine made tapping his console easier than explaining himself and having someone else do it.

He tapped an icon on his console, and lines between the *Stennis* and the *Agosta* formed. The shortest of the lines—the closest point of approach between the two ships—was fourteen nautical miles.

Knowing his executive officer—although unimpressive to look at—was a coffee-fueled real world version of a 'mentat' from Frank Herbert's *Dune* novels, Rodriguez contemplated aloud.

"CPA is fourteen miles," he said.

He let the comment sit in the air but could feel Jones' synapses firing. Confident that his executive officer would speak when ready—and then be hard to shut up—Rodriguez offered another tidbit to bring Jones inline with his chain of reasoning.

"The fastest production torpedo in the world runs at what—sixty-five, seventy knots?" he asked. "Tops?"

Still nothing but neuro-electric energy from Jones.

"Thirteen minutes time to target, if you have a torpedo with superhuman fuel reserves," Rodriguez said.

Fearing he would be caught in an eternal monologue, Rodriguez welcomed Jones' intrusion into his personal space. The rotund executive officer's stomach bounced off Rodriguez as he turned into him.

"Oh sorry, captain," Jones said and backed up a pace.

"No problem," Rodriguez said.

"I'd like to propose some theories about this *Agosta*," Jones said. "The *Hamza* can only be doing one of three things. It's gathering intelligence, rehearsing a submerged approach, or preparing to attack the *Stennis* for real. Don't you agree?"

"Can't think of any other reason they'd be here."

"But here, just outside of Pearl Harbor, the only intel the *Hamza* could be gathering is about our fleet, but for what value? I doubt the *Hamza's* here to gather data."

"Talk to me about rehearsing, then," Rodriguez said.

"Pakistan faces a constant threat of carrier attack from India. This could be a bold exercise to get the top Pakistani submarine ready to thwart its greatest seaborne threat."

"But it's not realistic," Rodriguez said. "Any carrier in a hostile theater would have aircraft swarming around it looking for subs. The *Stennis* isn't on the defensive now."

"It's realistic enough as you can get though, because the *Hamza's* deep. That makes it hard for helicopters to find it through the acoustic layers."

"Also makes it harder to attack the carrier without visual input," Rodriguez said.

"Exactly, sir. That's what the *Hamza* could be practicing here—a deep attack without periscope use so that it's not exposed to Indian aircraft. That's why the training scenario could be what they're doing. Lord knows we spent decades doing it in our submarine history."

Rodriguez agreed but let his mind progress towards the unfathomable.

"And if this is a real attack?"

"Back to your comment about closest point of approach, sir," Jones said. "Unless the *Hamza* repositions, it's a tough shot. If they shoot before the CPA, the carrier's out of range. If they shoot after, the carrier heads into the channel and drives out of range. If they want to hit it at CPA, then the torpedo has to run at slow speed to conserve fuel. If this were a real attack, I question why they don't move in closer."

"You assume standard twenty-one inch torpedo tubes."

"True. But even if they were modified with sixty-five centimeter tubes and are carrying those monster Russian anti-ship torpedoes, we'd still have thirteen minutes to take them out, surface, and warn the *Stennis*. American nuclear carriers are among the fastest ships on the planet. It would have plenty of time to evade."

"That's what I was thinking," Rodriguez said. "But the *Hamza* doesn't know we're sitting right behind it, and an attack may be plausible."

"Plausible, sir, but unlikely."

"But you've got the preparations in place?"

"Yes, sir. Weapons are ready to engage the *Hamza*."

"Good," Rodriguez said.

"And we've got two communication buoys with redundant messages stating the *Hamza's* position and that it's launched a weapon. The message will be broadcast on multiple frequencies, and the *Stennis* would get the message if the *Hamza* fires and we launch the buoys."

Although dubious, the *Hamza's* presence did not justify a preemptive attack. Rodriguez' orders were clear. He couldn't attack a neutral country's vessel in international waters. But they were also clear that he couldn't let the *Hamza* toy with the United States.

"Well, executive officer," he said. "At this point it doesn't matter what he's doing. It's time to end this game."

"You mean to drive him off now, sir?" Jones asked.

"Yup. Let's light him up and see if we can deafen its sonar operators and send them back to—"

Chief Bartlett's portly body stiffened.

"Sir, active transmission bearing zero-four-three," he said. "It doesn't correlate to any known active sonar or torpedo system."

Jones passed in front of Rodriguez with a nimbleness impossible for his size. He bumped into the chief as he joined him at his fire control consoles.

"Closest correlation?" Rodriguez asked.

"I'm getting a list now. The closest three frequencies are the old Australian *Collins* class submarine sonar, the Russian *Sovremennyy* class destroyer sonar, and the Taiwanese unmanned vehicle search sonars. They use those in their harbor protection schemes."

"Holy shit," Rodriguez said. "You think the *Hai Lang* is here—using an unmanned vehicle?"

Jones appeared almost giddy and uncaring of danger. Rodriguez thought his executive officer would be miserable anywhere but on a submarine.

"It's possible, sir," Jones said. "Given the options, that's what it must be."

Rodriguez frowned and raised his voice.

"Possible counterdetection by *Hai Lung* and by *Hamza*. All stations analyze."

"By *Hamza* too sir?" Jones asked.

"If that active ping had enough power, it might have bounced off our hull and back to the *Hamza*. If they were paying attention, they just got a sniff of us."

As the control room fell silent—each sailor analyzing the situation—Jones stooped over a console with Chief Bartlett. After a moment, Jones stood.

"Given they weren't alert and their sonar system isn't optimized for the active frequency, there's much less than a fifty-percent chance the *Hamza* heard us."

Rodriguez found the information comforting.

"And the unmanned vehicle? The *Hai Lang*?"

"Greater than fifty-percent chance," Jones said. "Even with our anechoic hull coating, I think the *Hai Lang* got a strong enough return to know where we are."

Chief Bartlett interjected an idea.

"Our active intercept receivers were able to pinpoint a bearing and range to the unmanned vehicle," he said. "Should we dedicate a torpedo to it?"

"What?" Rodriguez asked. "Waste a torpedo on an unmanned vehicle?"

"In case we're wrong, and it's another submarine."

"Fine," Rodriguez said. "Go ahead, but keep tubes one and two ready on the *Hamza*."

The somber faces in the control room reminded Rodriguez of a soccer team that had just gone down two goals to zero. The room seemed to deflate, and he needed to find a spark of energy.

He did his best acting job.

"What's everyone looking so depressed for?" he asked as he sat and let an easy grin cover his face. "I hate getting counterdetected as much as the next guy, but the *Hai Lang* just made this easy for us. Let them take care of the *Hamza*. We'll watch it happen."

*

Commander Hayat swallowed tea with a bitterness he found excruciating. The codeine mixed with it was a third of the lethal dose, but despite all his strength, he needed the narcotic to keep his pain in check.

It clouded his mind, but he no longer felt alone in guiding his ship. In addition to the omnipresent will of Allah that had guided him to within striking distance of his objective, Lieutenant Commander Raja had proven himself loyal, courageous, and a quick learner.

Hayat wondered if he'd be alive long enough for his next prayer session to thank his maker. If not, he'd have eternity to do so.

"Sir," Raja said.

The voice snapped him from his doped trance.

"Yes, Raja?" he said.

"I need your guidance," Raja said. "I fear that we've been detected."

Hayat's consciousness returned.

"By whom?"

"Unknown," Raja said. "We're analyzing, but it was an active seeker. We cannot correlate to any known sonar system, even adjusting for Doppler."

"Then we assume that it is a new American unmanned harbor protection system," Hayat said. "What is the probability of detection?"

"Quite high, sir," Raja said.

Hayat glanced at a monitor and noticed that the *Hamza* was tracking the *Stennis*' acoustic data and matching against the mighty carrier's expected trajectory.

"It is of no import," Hayat said. "The carrier is close. We will have accomplished our mission before any platform with a weapon could stop us."

Raja's mouth opened and he stared nowhere.

"Raja!" Hayat said.

"Yes, sir."

Hayat felt a jolt of nausea but swallowed it back.

"Are you afraid to die?"

"I …"

"Raja!"

"After seeing you embrace death with fearlessness, I can only hope to enter the afterworld with such courage."

"Then help me fight this ship to its end. I need you. My time is near, and our fates are one. Erase doubt and fear. Bring our destiny to fruition."

Raja's back straightened and his expression became stolid.

"Your orders?" Raja asked.

"Use the Shkval to cripple the carrier. Time the attack so that the carrier glides helplessly into the harbor, and then launch a nuclear torpedo."

"I understand the Shkval, sir, but the torpedo? Why just one?"

"I do not want torpedoes interfering with each other. However, exactly one minute after firing the first, fire the second. But with the second, third, and fourth—all of which I wish you to fire as long as we are capable—have them turn into the harbor and attack any vessel of opportunity."

"You've envisioned this all along, sir. It is brilliance. It is truly the work of Allah—"

"You and I know it is, but until we succeed, the crew must believe they are merely orders from Karachi."

CHAPTER THIRTY-THREE

"Slow to ahead one-third," Renard said.

That's better, Jake thought.

Jake saw nothing interesting materialize on his Subtics monitor, and he looked towards Remy. France's best retired sonar operator clasped headphones to his ears.

"*Oui*," Remy said. "I hear submerged contact two. I hear the hydraulics system," he said. "This is the *Hamza*."

"How sure are you, my friend?" Renard asked. "Men will die based upon your answer."

As Remy opened his mouth, a trace with impossible speed materialized on Jake's screen. He depressed buttons so that the screen accepted data from both his drone and the indigenous sensors of the *Hai Lang*.

"Pierre!" Jake said. "High-speed torpedo coming from contact two. I'm not sure it's a torpedo, but whatever it is, it's heading toward the *Stennis*. Shit! Three hundred knots? That can't be right, but it's tracking on both the drone and our bow array."

"Contact two must be the *Hamza*," Renard said, "Shoot tube two!"

The *Hai Lang* shook, and compressed air from the torpedo room filled the air. Jake's ears popped.

"You don't waste any time," Jake said. "Gutsy call."

"We can only pray that it was the right one."

*

Jake ripped headphones off his head. The Subtics display told him all he needed. The *Stennis* had accelerated into the harbor, but the weapon of inconceivable speed had caught it in less than three minutes.

The sea erupted. Jake heard its echoes dying within the *Hai Lang*, and the submarine's Subtics system presented a myriad of data testifying that the carrier had been hit.

"Damn!" he said. "The *Stennis* was just hit. Heavyweight torpedo-sized warhead."

"Keep your wits about you, man," Renard said. "It was an underwater rocket of some sort, but let's not assume that the *Hamza* is armed with unbeatable weapons. Our own weapon appears well enough placed."

Jake glanced at his monitor. The Pakistani submarine accelerated with a plethora of flow noise.

"Recommend a forty-degree steer of our torpedo to starboard," Jake said. "He's trying to evade."

Renard glanced at a screen over Remy's shoulder.

"Do it, man," he said.

Jake guided the weapon, and the *Hamza* seemed trapped.

"We got him," Jake said. "That son of a bitch is ours."

*

Hayat felt himself slipping into death's cold hands.

"Sir," Raja said, "we hit the carrier in its stern. All its screws have stopped. The shot could not have been better! It's drifting into the harbor."

"This is perfect," Hayat said. "Calculate for the carrier's drift and fire the nuclear weapon."

Hayat heard whispers in his operations room.

"Some of the men are protesting, sir," Raja said.

"This is not unexpected," Hayat said. "Do not falter."

An alarm rang in the *Hamza's* operations room.

"Read it and silence it," Hayat said.

Raja darted across the room and reached for the nearest Subtics console. The alarm died.

"American torpedo!" Raja said. "To the right of the line of sight and drawing left. Converging on us!"

"An American submarine has apparently been watching us," Hayat said. "The shot will be accurate."

"Recommend evasion, captain," Raja said.

"After you launch the weapon," Hayat said.

Protests from sailors in the operations room buzzed in Hayat's head.

"See that it is done, Raja," Hayat said. "Now!"

Raja pushed a sailor from his Subtics monitor and tapped keys. A whine and compressed air filled the room.

"Tube two is launched, sir," Raja said.

Hayat reclined, and peace overcame him.

"You may navigate the ship through torpedo evasion. I wish you luck, Faisel, and I will see you in Paradise."

His destiny fulfilled, Hamid Hayat let himself die.

*

Jake listened to the seas through the drone. He thought he heard a new torpedo but had to ignore it while deciding what to do with the *Hai Lang's* weapon.

"Contact two has accelerated," Remy said.

"Recommended steer?" Renard asked.

"I can't tell from passive bearings yet," Remy said. "Jake, do you have anything from the drone?"

"From the drone—contact two has accelerated and turned towards our torpedo. No steer required, but I recommend slowing it and letting it begin its search."

Renard gave the command, and the torpedo slowed. It picked up the *Hamza* on its first ping.

"Excellent," Renard said. "But why would they run towards our weapon? It's illogical. Is it suicide?"

A woman's voice carried the answer.

"No," Olivia said. "It's not suicide—not yet. From your best guess of the situation, he's hit the carrier at its screws, but that's not enough. That's just a setup for the real thing."

"How long have you been here?" Renard asked.

"I came in when I heard the explosion," she said. "I just wanted to see—"

"If you insist on staying," Renard said, "just keep out of the way."

Jake caught glimpses of her slinky curves through baggy coveralls and understood why Renard had asked her to stay clear of the control room. Even while silent, she was distracting.

She crouched beside him.

"What do you have?" she asked.

Jake pointed at the monitor.

"I just figured out why he's running at our weapon. The other submarine shot at him. The drone hears their torpedo, but the *Hamza's* countermeasures have blanketed the sector and we can't hear it from here. The active seeker is an American frequency."

A puff of smoke appeared over Jake's head.

"You've identified which contact is the American, then?" Renard asked.

"Yeah," Jake said. "And their torpedo's on target, too. The *Hamza* doesn't have a chance."

"But it can still strike," Renard said. "Any sign of counterfire?"

"Still looking," Jake said. "There's a lot of noise."

"No need to wait. I will evade toward the harbor in case they shoot back down the bearing of our weapon," Renard said and stepped behind the periscope. "Henri, all ahead standard."

"All ahead standard, aye, sir," Henri said. "We have only thirty minutes left on the battery at that rate."

"That's enough," Renard said.

Expecting a torpedo from the *Hamza* to appear, Jake stared at his monitor, but the drone heard nothing.

Then an inverted triangle appeared.

"What's that?" Olivia asked.

In his earphones, Jake heard high-speed screws.

"Torpedo in the water!" he said. "There's no active seeker. Just screws and flow noise. Antoine, back me up."

Remy pressed the phones to his head and nodded.

"High speed screws," Remy said. "It's a torpedo. It seems to be running slow."

"Forty knots," Jake said. "I just got some active return on it. Probably to extend the range. It's headed toward the carrier."

"It's nuclear," Olivia said. "It's got to be. That's his final blow. This is his ultimate act of symbolism."

Olivia leaned into Jake but said nothing. He felt her slip away and dart out of the operations room.

"All ahead flank!" Renard said.

Jake watched Henri nudge his throttle joystick forward as the control room fell silent.

"Pierre?" Jake asked. "What are you doing?"

"Plot a course to intercept the torpedo," Renard said.

Jake turned to his monitor. The speed leaders from the *Hamza's* torpedo reached out to that of the *Hai Lung*."

His adrenaline spiking, Jake stepped to Renard.

Appearing resigned to his fate, Renard exhaled smoke and gave a cavalier grin.

"What, Jake?" he asked. "What else can we do? We fail if that weapon hits the carrier. Thousands will die instantly. Tens, perhaps hundreds of thousands will die in the fallout. We have no choice."

A shock wave passed through the *Hai Lang*'s hull, followed by a deep rumble. Remy announced the obvious.

"Explosion and hull rupture. That was the *Hamza*," he said. "It's sinking."

"And now we are all that stand between the destruction of that carrier and all of Pearl Harbor," Renard said.

"Do you intend to just sacrifice us? There are other options," Jake said.

"You've known me too long to think I will go down without a fight," Renard said. "I have an idea, but tell me, just to be thorough, what is on your mind?"

*

In the minutes required for the *Hai Lang* to cut across the *Hamza*'s torpedo's path, Renard outlined a plan with Jake. His eyes followed Jake as he marched back and forth behind the men seated at the Subtics monitors. His friend appeared fearless and in control.

My finest recruit, Renard thought. *By far.*

When he glanced at his monitor, he noticed the feed from the drone was gone. Flank speed had strained and snapped its guidance wire, but the drone had done its job with the *Hamza* and its weapons.

Four miles from the crippled carrier, the torpedo ran at its constant speed. The overhead view showed the *Hai Lang* a mile and a half ahead of the torpedo. Renard decided to turn his tail to the weapon and let it catch him.

"Henri," he said. "Right ten degrees rudder. Steer course zero-four-zero."

The ship heeled over and steadied on course.

"We can't hear anything," Jake said. "We have to trust that we've resolved the torpedo's course and speed."

"I know," Renard said, "but I don't dare slow down. The weapon could overtake us. We must be between it and the carrier when its seeker activates."

Renard watched the calculated distances shrink. Pointed at the carrier, his ship closed to within three miles of it. The *Hamza*'s torpedo was a mile behind him.

An electronic chime sounded. Although it signaled what he had hoped to discover, a pit formed in his stomach.

Jake reached but the Taiwanese sailor seated before him had already silenced the alarm. The sailor, Ye, and Jake exchanged quick words.

"Active torpedo seeker," Jake said. "Russian design. Probably from the Chinese arsenal."

"*Mon Dieu*, Miss McDonald was correct. It is nuclear-tipped," Renard said.

"Pierre? The turn?" Jake asked.

"Yes, of course," Renard said. "Henri, right ten degrees rudder, steady course three-four-five."

The ship rolled and steadied, but the torpedo ran straight.

"Torpedo has failed to acquire," Jake said.

"Left ten degrees rudder, steer course zero-two-five," Renard said. "We shall cross back in front of it."

On a monitor near the captain's chair, Renard saw the torpedo ignore the *Hai Lang* again.

"Recommend we come shallow," Jake said.

"We are shallow," Renard said. "Any more shallow and we'd need wings."

"Surface the ship," Jake said. "It's an upward seeking weapon. It's looking for a keel above itself."

"We'd lose speed," Renard said. "Our evasion will be at risk."

Although having protested, he knew Jake was right. A mile and a half from the carrier, almost in the harbor himself, Renard made up his mind.

"Drive us to the surface, Henri" he said.

Renard held the polished rail that encircled the *Hai Lang's* periscope as the ship angled upward. The submarine started to bob as it broached, and the angle leveled off. Restrained by the water's surface tension, the ship's speed fell from thirty-one knots to twenty-two.

The torpedo closed to within half a mile.

"Any closer," Renard said, "and it won't matter which ship takes the torpedo. Both will be lost. The deception maneuver must work now, or it shall never work. Henri, right full rudder."

Without a submerged sail to counterbalance it, the ship rolled hard to the left. Renard staggered towards the Subtics monitors but caught himself.

"I cannot hold the surface long," Henri said. "We are too heavy and losing speed in the turn."

"Very well," Renard said. "Either the torpedo has acquired us or it has not."

"Terminal homing!" Jake said. "Torpedo has acquired and is range-gaiting."

"Henri," Renard said, "make your depth thirty meters."

The ship dived and accelerated. Renard felt Jake brush by and swoop towards Remy's ear. After rapid-fire banter, Jake appeared before Renard.

"It's accelerating towards sixty-five knots," Jake said. "Conservative guess—it's eight hundred yards behind us. Speed advantage thirty-five knots. Forty-one seconds to impact."

"But at least it's following us and headed to sea," Renard said. "No matter what, our mission is accomplished."

"Our evasion," Jake said. "We can still do it."

For a moment, Renard envisioned himself carrying his son on his shoulders and walking with Marie up the slopes of *Mont Saint Victoire*. He wanted to return home.

"And so we shall," he said. "Launch countermeasures."

Jake stormed to Commander Ye and conveyed the command. Canisters of compressed gas popped on either side of the *Hai Lang's* hull as they spat countermeasures into the water. A hiss echoed throughout the operations room and slipped into the ocean's submerged recesses as the *Hai Lang* raced away.

"Right ten degrees rudder," Renard said. "And dive, Henri! Drive us to the bottom as fast as she will go!"

*

The Russian ET-80 torpedo sent a signal down the wire streaming from its stabilizer fin requesting a confirmation of its position. There was no response, and the torpedo's algorithms had to accept the onboard gyroscopic positions as truth. It turned on its seeker and noticed a target where it should have been—on the surface and heading into the harbor.

With minimal battery charge remaining, the weapon accelerated with intent to fulfill its destiny. Poised to detonate its twenty-kiloton plutonium fission warhead, the torpedo noticed that the target had accelerated and turned erratically, and it raced after its prey.

A wetness sensor on the plastic skin indicated the intermittent presence of gas. The gyroscopes sensed a small plummet in depth as bubbles displaced water, and the seeker could not capture a return.

The torpedo drove through the countermeasures and pinged where the target should have been but heard nothing. It aimed its acoustic energy to the left and heard no return. It aimed to the right, and reacquired its prey.

Its battery charge dying, the torpedo squeezed life from itself and bore down on its target. Sensing it was close enough to detonate, it sought a final series of pings and then—the final signal to unleash its fury—the interruption of its self-generated magnetic field. It created the field above its shell and closed in.

It pounded the target with sound, but the return was stronger from the depths. Seeking to slide its magnetic field under a surface ship's keel, the weapon angled downward. It dived deeper until it hit the depth limit set by the protocols of attacking a surfaced vessel.

As it headed towards the ocean floor, the nuclear torpedo reacted to prevent itself from attacking the submarine that had launched it, turned from the target, and set a new course to search again for the target where it was supposed to have been—in the harbor.

The weapon slowed and swam toward the carrier, but a program warned the torpedo that battery cells were inverting, the stronger cells recharging the depleted ones. The torpedo accelerated, shortened its ping interval, but exhausted its final watt of power. It unleashed its suicide protocol, opened valves that inundated a small ballast tank, and sank.

CHAPTER THIRTY-FOUR

RENARD CLENCHED A STAINLESS STEEL rail and held his breath. He wanted to believe he would live.

"Do you hear anything, Antoine?" he asked.

Remy shook his head.

"We're going too fast to tell," he said, "and we're blind in our stern sector due to our countermeasures."

"We'll keep running just a few more minutes then," Renard said. "How far are we from our countermeasures?"

Jake glanced over Ye's shoulder.

"One mile," Jake said.

"That's far enough," Renard said. "Launch another pair of countermeasures."

Canisters of compressed gas popped on either side of the hull as they spat hissing countermeasures.

"Right ten degrees rudder, Henri," Renard said.

As the ship reeled, Jake appeared before Renard.

"We're going to make it," he said.

"I agree," Renard said. "The torpedo must have exhausted itself by now."

"Yeah," Jake said. "It's over. We did it."

"Henri, steady on depth and slow to five knots," Renard said. "No need to invert our battery cells."

As the tension in his muscles waned, Renard assessed his victory. Sailors certainly had given their lives on the *Stennis*, but the toll would be a tiny fraction of the tally had the nuclear torpedo detonated. As for the harbor and surrounding cities, including Honolulu, he had spared them from shock waves and fallout.

He also realized that he had sent more than thirty dutiful Pakistani sailors to their death. Their greatest mistake had been following orders of a charismatic commanding officer who was seeking personal peace in a violent way.

He inhaled cool tobacco flavor and decided to delay his lamentations for the dead.

There was still business he needed to finish.

"Henri," he said. "Belay my last ordered depth. Surface the ship."

*

The *Hai Lang* rolled with the calm surface waves. With a ball cap pulled low, a jacket lapel pulled high over his neck, and sunglasses to conceal his identify from any onlooker, Renard accompanied Lieutenant Wu in the bridge atop the sail.

While Wu raised the Taiwanese flag to make obvious the submarine's nationality, Renard called Admiral Khan. The conversation was brief and bittersweet as Renard declared victory at the expense of a Pakistani submarine and dozens of Pakistani lives.

As Renard ended the call, he sensed that Khan had held hope that the *Hamza's* run could have been thwarted without violence. But as the admiral had accepted the results, he agreed to work with Defense Minister Li to manage the diplomatic fallout, and he conceded that Renard could position the Taiwanese submarine atop the Pakistani wreckage for salvage rights.

Khan also agreed to pay Renard his twenty-five million euro bounty upon verification of the *Hamza's* demise through diplomatic channels.

Renard scurried down the ladder and explained his conversation with Khan to Ye and Jake. Then he gave his final command on the *Hai Lang*.

"Henri, station us above the wreckage of the *Hamza*," he said. "Ten knots, course two-six-zero."

"That's fast, given our low battery and fuel."

"I know," Renard said, "but we must make haste."

"I will need to make a call to Keelung," Ye said. "We must hasten the departure of an underwater salvage team."

"And you will need to contact the defense minister," Renard said. "He and Admiral Khan will jointly be facing a hefty amount of diplomatic damage control."

"I will call him," Ye said as he pulled a global account phone from a cubby under a Subtics monitor.

Renard went to his chair, sat, and inhaled from his Marlboro.

"I would bet my bounty on the *Hamza* that there is at least one more nuclear weapon on the seafloor near or within the *Hamza's* hull," he said. "There still may be opportunity to transform your nation into a nuclear power."

Ye raised a thumb as he climbed the ladder, but Jake turned from Henri and glared.

"Your bounty on the what?" he asked.

Renard reclined and blew smoke.

"Don't worry, *mon ami*," he said. "I'll be sharing it liberally with all present …"

Heads in the operations room turned towards Renard.

"… provided we all agree that our weapon hit the *Hamza* before that of the American submarine," he said.

*

Ten hours later, as the anchored Taiwanese submarine drifted over the wreck of the *Hamza*, Jake stood beside the ladder leading to the tiny bridge atop the *Hai Lang's* sail. The sun's rays poking through the access trunk had turned red as the sun set overhead.

"You can't show yourself outside this hull," Renard said. "No need to confirm our presence on video camera. Had I not needed to speak to Khan, I would not have risked it myself."

"We've been inside this thimble for two months. I forgot how much being underwater made me miss the sun."

Jake walked to the railing, pasted his eye to the periscope, and saw the superstructure of the *Stennis*. The smoke billowing from its stern had subsided, but from the radio chatter Jake surmised that a swarm of coast guard and naval vessels provided security, medical, and damage control assistance to the *Stennis*.

Radio chatter also indicated that twenty-eight sailors had died in the engine rooms of the *Stennis*. Jake reminded himself that they would have died—along with tens of thousands more—if he had not helped.

Looking closer, he watched the bizarre mélange of ships forming a welcoming party that now encircled the *Hai Lang*. To the north, a *Perry* class frigate cut slow ovals in the water. Jake was certain he had seen the barrel of its amidships three-inch Otto-Malera gun rise and fall as if ranging the *Hai Lang*.

To the west, a *Hamilton* class coast guard cutter mimicked the frigate by standing guard over the Taiwanese submarine with its three-inch cannon. Smaller coast guard patrol vessels armed with machine guns and men in bright orange vests carrying rifles floated within shouting range but had used only bullhorns to harass the Taiwanese sailors who ventured topside.

Despite a Notice to Mariners declaring the area around the *Hai Lang* off limits, dozens of leisure craft dotted the waters, aiming video cameras back at Jake. The coast guard vessels tried to drive them back, but the numbers of civilian craft approaching the area mounted beyond the coast guard's capacity to engage them.

"Plenty of people are going to have interesting videos to show their friends and family," Jake said.

"It is no mistake," Renard said. "Defense Minister Li asked Taiwanese expatriots in Hawaii to make sure the media knew about our little situation. The navy or coast guard will make no move against us in international waters while on video. Look above."

Jake swiveled the optics overhead. It took him several minutes to find them all, but he saw five helicopters—one coast guard, one navy, and three from local television station affiliates. Small aircraft also encircled the submarine, most likely taking personal video from above.

"Can we watch ourselves on television?" Jake asked.

"Petty Officer Zhu is trying to arrange the wiring," Renard said. "The ship is not designed for it, but I have a sense that he may figure something out."

From Jake's perspective, most of the day since sinking the *Hamza* in the morning had passed as an uncomfortable mélange of American vessels taking station on the *Hai Lang* and offers of assistance, orders to dock in Pearl Harbor, and threats to be boarded.

As Ye, the legitimate commanding officer of the *Hai Lang*, had refused all assistance and orders to leave his position over the *Hamza's* wreckage, the threats had grown more severe and the ships with the three-inch guns had arrived. But as the civilian craft had appeared, the threats had tapered.

A high-speed motor whizzed up to the hull. Jake swiveled the scope aft and looked down. A small boat had raced by the *Hai Lang*. Four men of college age wore khaki cargo pants, golf shirts, and sunglasses. They raised their thumbs as they passed. One lifted a beer and whipped his tongue across his face. Two bent over and mooned the coast guard craft that pursued them.

Jake laughed it off as a college prank until he noticed one of the men hurling coiled rope into the water. Following the rope to one end, Jake saw that it was tied to a bobbing fuel drum. The rope's other end was tied to a smaller rope which, in turn, held a softball that had been hurled over the back of the submarine.

Classic underway replenishment maneuver, Jake thought.

On the *Hai Lang's* back, sailors pulled the small rope until the larger rope emerged on the deck. Then they heaved the rope and drum aboard.

"Hey, Pierre," Jake said. "I think the word's out that we're low on fuel."

A clamor rang from the ladder as Ye descended from the bridge. His boots hit the deck.

"You wouldn't believe what just happened," he said.

"I saw it," Jake said. "It was sweet."

"Every gallon helps," Ye said. "And if one boat can help us, more will surely follow. Minister Li has made it known that we are in need."

"You don't look too happy, though," Jake said.

"I just received a new threat from the American Navy," Ye said. "They claim they want to launch a search and rescue operation for possible survivors on the *Hamza*. The deep submergence rescue vehicle is airborne from San Diego and already halfway here. It will be here and ready to search tomorrow morning."

"Twenty-four hours—anywhere in the world," Jake said. "That's their advertising motto. I guess it's true."

"We've been listening," Renard said. "If there were survivors, they would be banging metal and calling for help. We have heard nothing. A submarine this small hit by an F-17 torpedo—perhaps a few men on either extreme of the ship, but I fear the silence confirms their demise."

"The Americans will still insist on inspecting the wreckage," Ye said.

"The Taiwanese deep salvage dive team?" Renard asked. "They are en route, are they not?"

"Yes," Ye said. "They will arrive in the night."

"Then perhaps a joint search and rescue effort would be a proper gesture," Renard said. "Followed shortly or even conducted simultaneously with a salvage operation."

"I will ask Minister Li to arrange that," Ye said.

"A delicate negotiation for which Li is skilled," Renard said.

CHAPTER THIRTY-SIX

With the help of four more renegade fuel drops, the *Hai Lang* was able to run its diesel engine to power its minimal electrical loads. It survived the night anchored over the wreckage of the *Hamza*.

Jake had awoken with a view similar to that of the prior day. During breakfast, the call they had been waiting for came over the radio.

Unarmed, the Chief of Staff, Seventh Fleet and his aide would board the *Hai Lang* accompanied by a high-ranking CIA officer. Commander Ye had agreed to the boarding.

With this knowledge fresh in his mind, Jake stood over Olivia in the commanding officer's stateroom. She knelt with her knees under her chin on the fold-out rack.

"I was afraid yesterday, Jake," she said.

He wanted to hug her, but she seemed content wrapped within herself.

"It's time," he said. "We're letting a small group aboard the ship this morning. One of them is a CIA bigwig. They're coming. They'll be here within an hour."

"I was afraid," she said. "I wanted to hug someone when it was over, and you were the only one in my entire stinking life I could think of that I wanted to hug me back. But you were busy."

"We're okay now," he said.

She looked up.

"You mean we're safe," she said. "I sure as hell don't know if I'm okay. You know what I mean?"

He sat beside her and put a tentative arm over her shoulder. She leaned into him.

"You hardly talked to me for two months," she said.

"I didn't know what to say. I kept it superficial, I guess. This was no time or place for romance."

"Well how about simple manners? I know we started under a ton of lies, but can't we at least be friends now?"

"I'd like to be," he said. "But for all I know, I'm facing a Court Martial. There aren't enough well-wishers to give us enough fuel to make it back to Taiwan. I suppose Taiwan could commission another tanker, but that's a lot easier for the coast guard to stop than water skiing boats."

"I don't know if I want to go back," she said. "I don't know if I can."

"You know," Jake said. "My father was CIA. I lost him on a blown intel drop in China."

"You haven't had good luck with the CIA, I guess."

"Shitty," he said. "But according to my mom, my dad was gung-ho. He would have found his way into danger, no matter what. He loved what he did. It's hard to blame the CIA for it."

"You're saying I should get over it, too?" she asked.

"It's all you can do," he said.

Jake heard clinking above him that indicated a small boat had mated to the *Hai Lang*.

"And our guests are here," he said. "You know who the CIA bigwig is?"

"Rickets," she said. "Give him twelve hours' notice and he's halfway across the globe."

*

Olivia popped her head through the forward hatch and felt like a mole afraid of sunlight. She raised her hand to her brow and squinted. A couple of Taiwanese sailors knelt by a cleat while Commander Ye and Lieutenant Wu, in their dress whites, faced a skiff that was being mated to the *Hai Lang*.

A senior enlisted Taiwanese sailor stood beside Ye and Wu in his dress whites, and to his side were two topside sentries in their best uniforms.

Olivia inspected her faded jeans and white blouse and feared she had underestimated the formality of the boarding. She glanced at the skiff where a full bird captain accompanied an admiral dressed in American khaki.

At least they're in a working uniform, she thought.

A wide silhouette in a three-piece suit stared at her. She tried to focus on the man, but her eye was drawn to several men in dark windbreakers huddled over assault rifles that dangled at their sides.

The senior enlisted sailor raised a silver whistle to his lips and blew. As the high-pitched whine carried over the deck, all sailors, even those who had worked mooring lines over cleats, saluted. One of the sentries barked in accented English.

"Chief of Staff, United States Seventh Fleet, Arriving!"

Olivia didn't know how to react and decided it was best to just stay still.

The tall, lean admiral returned the salute. When he dropped it, the whistling died, and Ye stepped forward with his hand extended.

"Vice Admiral Jenkins," he said. "I am Commander Danzhao Ye, commanding officer, Republic of China vessel *Hai Lang*. I welcome you aboard."

Admiral Jenkins accepted the handshake but scowled.

"Commander Ye," he said. "From the testimony of assets I had in the area, I understand you did my nation a service yesterday. But we've got ourselves an international situation, and the world is breathing down my neck for a resolution."

"Of course," Ye said. "Please come below, but I must insist that my engineering spaces remain off limits."

As Ye and Wu led the admiral and his aide into the torpedo room, the man in the suit stepped forward. Olivia recognized him as Rickets.

"McDonald?" Rickets said.

He looked fatigued. Olivia guessed he had been traveling and receiving briefs for the last twenty-four hours.

"Jerry? What sort of jurisdiction do you have here?"

"You," he said. "I told the admiral a CIA operative was serving as an intelligence specialist aboard."

"So I'm not facing charges?"

He blushed and flashed a rare smile.

"I know what happened," he said. "And I'm pretty damn sure you made it possible. I still want you back, but no matter what you decide, I've covered your trail. You're no criminal."

He extended his hand.

"Are we okay?"

She turned her head and let the rising sun's reflection mesmerize her. Then she shrieked and whipped her palm across his face. The impact cracked so loudly that one of the sentries had to grab the other to keep him from falling over. Rickets reeled with the impact but managed to stay standing.

He blinked and raised his hand to his mouth. As he wiggled his jaw around and realized nothing had been broken, his face softened.

"Damn, woman," he said. "You've got some power."

"You deserved it," she said. "And you're lucky that's all you get before I forgive you."

"Then you forgive me?"

"I guess I just did."

They shook hands.

"Even if you don't come back to the CIA, at least I'll be able to sleep better now."

Olivia felt like a weight had been lifted off her shoulders.

"You didn't come here just to talk to me, did you?"

"No," he said. "We have a lot to assess, you and me, but I also want to see Slate and Renard."

"You're not going to force me to play stupid, are you?" she asked.

"I'm sure they're hidden somewhere on this ship hoping to hitch a ride back to Keelung," he said.

"And if they were?" she asked.

"If you'll come clean and verify their roles in this," he said, "I would tell them it's not necessary for them to hide. What's going on here is messy enough without anyone having to find out that there are two fugitives and a handful of French submarine veterans aboard. I've got a plan."

CHAPTER THIRTY-SEVEN

Jake placed his feet on the main electric motor. While conserving fuel, the *Hai Lang* would need only the smaller cruising motors tucked deeper toward the stern where the ship tapered. His legs stiffened as he crouched on the motor with his back against the *Hai Lang's* hull.

"How long do you think we're going to have to hide back here?" he asked.

"I have no idea," Renard said. "The boarding party will leave when it leaves."

The French contingency was sprawled with Jake and Renard between the inline electric motors and other crannies in the rear of the engine room.

"This should help pass the time, though," Renard said.

He pulled a bottle of cognac from his jumpsuit. A round of cheers followed.

"Where'd you hide that?" Remy asked.

"In the executive officer's stateroom, of course."

"I didn't even see it," Jake said.

"No doubt, *mon ami*," Renard said. "I am far more familiar with this class of ship than you, and that includes hiding spaces."

When the bottle reached him, Jake took a huge swallow. It bit the back of his throat and warmed his stomach. As he extended the bottle towards LaFontaine, the door from the diesel compartment opened, and two unexpected people appeared. Followed by a large black man in a pinstriped suit, Olivia walked towards Jake. The banter of the Frenchmen died, and Jake's heart sank.

"Gentlemen," Olivia said. "I present you CIA Director Gerald Rickets. No need to play games with who's who here. Just listen to what he has to say."

"I know what you guys did," Rickets said, "and it was some serious, gutsy stuff. You saved countless American lives yesterday."

Rickets tugged at his suit lapels and cleared his throat.

"Yes?" Renard asked after blowing a cloud of smoke. "We are acutely aware of our contributions. Did you come here to thank us, or perhaps to explain why we, at least Jake and I, will rot in American federal jail cells?"

Rickets grunted.

"Cocky to the end," he said.

"If you wish to judge me," Renard said, "then be aware that I have only ever tried to protect your nation and its democratic allies. Do not be so quick to label me a criminal."

Rickets' glare hardened.

"If you'd seal your mouth, you'd realize that I've come here to offer a deal."

Jake's spirits rose.

"A deal?" Renard asked as he slipped off the main motor. "Why didn't you say that? I live for negotiation."

"Negotiation?" Rickets asked. "I doubt it. I think you'll be thankful enough for what I have for you."

Renard stepped to Rickets and extended a hand.

"Okay then," he said. "I am Pierre Renard, and these are men loyal to me. I'm sure you know them all, by dossier at least. If you can offer each man a destiny commensurate with what they have earned, we will do whatever bidding you wish."

Rickets accepted Renard's hand.

"Let's start with the easy ones," he said. "Those guys, everyone except you and Slate, have committed no crimes and are free to go. I'll arrange military transport for each back to Marseille, but they must travel in secrecy, starting with the moment they pop their heads outside this submarine."

Renard glanced at his countrymen. Per Renard's payment for their efforts, France's five newest millionaires nodded and raised thumbs.

"Agreed," he said.

"Much as I know you were behind the theft and loss of the *Colorado*, I don't have enough evidence to make it stick," Rickets said.

"Pity," Renard said.

"But I can make your life hell," he said. "I can have you watched—and that includes your family. I can turn every trip across a national border into a strip search, I can make commercial air flight nearly impossible, and I can keep your chartered flights grounded. You don't want me as an enemy."

Renard puffed smoke into a ventilation intake.

"What would you have me do, then?" he asked.

"I am confident there are nuclear weapons within the *Hamza's* hull, and there's one lying on the ocean bottom in American waters. The one you evaded, I mean."

"It is all quite possible," Renard said.

"I want you to make sure that each one finds its way to Taiwan without American intervention."

"Dear god, man!" Renard said. "This is exactly what I had intended."

"This is a gift," Rickets said. "It's the cleanest chance to arm Taiwan with nukes. Even if Beijing finds out where the weapons came from and wants to accuse Washington of helping Taiwan salvage the warheads, they'd have a tough time explaining how they wound up here in the first place."

"Indeed," Renard said. "Purchasing Russian warheads and reselling them to a Pakistani rogue submarine for an attack against America. I see your logic. I like it."

Jake felt that his fate was the next subject of conversation. He glanced at Olivia, but she cast her eyes to the deck.

"And what of Jake?" Renard asked.

"Lieutenant Jacob Slate, United States Navy," Rickets said, "is a traitor and subject to a Court Martial."

Jake's spirits fell.

"However," Rickets said, "given his service to his country yesterday, I can make a concession."

"I'm free? I'm pardoned?" Jake asked.

"Never," Rickets said. "There will never be a pardon for you. That would require admitting you survived in the first place. No, you instead revert back to that Jacob Savin pseudonym Renard set up for you and return to France. Your life becomes that living hell Renard gets if he doesn't cooperate. I mean you don't so much as go to the Swiss border and inhale their air without one of my agents knowing about it."

A fantastic joy overcame Jake.

I am free—enough, he thought.

"Consider it witness protection under parole where you're confined to France indefinitely. You'll be checking in with one of my men every day until I get tired hearing from you. And believe me, that will be decades."

"Can I ever return to the states?" Jake asked.

"We'll talk about it when you're old enough that no one would recognize you. Don't push for more. I always have the option of arranging a top-secret Court Martial. You better just agree while I'm in a good mood."

Renard glared at Jake, his expression demanding him to shut up.

"I would hate to see you in a bad mood," Renard said. "We accept your terms, all around. What is the protocol?"

"All of you," Rickets said. "You dress up like you did when you made that phone call on the bridge today."

"You saw that?" Renard asked. "Impressive."

"Yeah. Candid camera. Don't ask. Anyway, you guys dress up so that you can't be recognized, and at nine o'clock tonight, you all board a coast guard vessel that'll be mating with the *Hai Lang*. From there to the coast guard base, to a waiting van, then to a C-130. This will be serious cloak and dagger stuff, but as long as you guys get out of here without the media asking about the white guys who popped out of the Taiwanese submarine, we have a deal."

Renard blew another cloud into the ventilation.

"And the weapons?" he asked. "You would have Taiwanese divers clear out the vessel first under the guise of looking for survivors. When they stumble upon the nuclear weapons and confirm their presence, then what?"

"That's for you to coach Commander Ye about before your departure," Rickets said. "But I will grant you this. The first place the rescue submersible is going to stop is over that weapon you evaded. It sank itself in American waters, but the world doesn't need to know that. It'll be the first weapon returned to this submarine, and you officially found it on the *Hamza* in international waters."

"Then you'll refuel the *Hai Lang*?" Renard asked.

"Yes," Rickets said. "Admiral Jenkins will bend over backwards to get your guys out of here. Your comrades will have food, fuel, whatever they want before they leave, just as long as they leave with the *Hamza*'s nuclear weapons."

Jake felt a rush of emotions, and he realized that with his freedom resolved, they highlighted his loneliness.

"What about her?" he asked.

"She has a bright future in the CIA," Rickets said. "She has decided to return. But no more high-risk stuff for a while. She's been through enough on her last two field assignments, and she did some great work figuring out where Hayat was taking the *Hamza*. She'll make a fantastic analyst."

Olivia raised her eyes.

"Look, Jake," she said. "I—"

Jake hopped off the main motor and went to her. He extended a hand, and she accepted it.

"CIA Officer Olivia McDonald," he said. "It has a nice ring to it. I'd say to keep yourself safe, but it looks like you've figured that out already."

She pulled him into a hug.

"I get vacations, you know," she said.

"You know where to find me," he said.

CHAPTER THIRTY-EIGHT

His Avignon apartment had at first been a place to slink and hide from the law. Now it was his real home. Sensing late autumn's encroaching chill, Jake turned up the heat. Four weeks had passed since sinking the *Hamza*.

Settling into a kitchen chair in front of a laptop, he waited for his coffee maker to finish its filtration. He grabbed a cup and sat down again.

Reading the CNN homepage, he noticed a headline that startled him. He sipped coffee and glanced at a clock on his wall. It was just after eight in the morning, but he decided it was late enough to call his friend. With a two-year old son and a pregnant wife, Renard had probably been rousted at six.

He picked up the phone and dialed. He knew his conversation was being recorded but didn't care.

"*Allo*," Renard said.

"Have you read the headlines?" Jake asked in French. The language had become like his maternal tongue. It sounded beautiful and sweet.

"Yes," Renard said. "Our friend made history today."

"Not surprised," Jake said. "We trained him well."

Translating into French, Jake read the headline and sub-headline aloud.

"Battle-bruised Taiwan, nearing internal collapse, successfully tests nuclear weapon at sea. The submarine *Hai Lang*, or 'Sea Wolf', sank an aging Taiwanese *Guppy* class submarine yesterday with a heavyweight nuclear-tipped torpedo, bringing the supposed renegade Chinese province into the nuclear age."

"Captain Ye and Lieutenant Commander Wu have much to be proud of," Renard said.

"Captain and Lieutenant Commander?"

"The deeds of the men aboard the *Hai Lang* have not passed unnoticed," Renard said. "They are Taiwan's finest sons and are being rewarded for their skill and heroism. There were a total of twelve promotions on that ship."

Jake reflected that the *Hai Lang's* crew deserved its reward. They had been brave.

"Shit, Pierre. What happens now? I mean to Taiwan."

"China has the might to overtake Taiwan based upon sheer numbers, but they must walk the delicate balance of preserving Taiwan's value as a financial and economic center. If they destroy Taiwan while taking it back, then they have failed."

Jake finished his coffee and held the phone to his ear while pouring another cup.

"We did what we could, right, Pierre?" he asked.

"Of course, *mon ami*."

"But did we do the right thing from the beginning?" Jake asked. "You used me at first, with the *Colorado*, but I joined you out of spite. It wasn't until later that I saw your grander vision. You really think we can make a difference. A difference for peace, don't you?"

"I never would have approached you had I not. That is my ultimate purpose. I have armed our comrades—correction—we have armed our comrades in Taiwan to protect their own destiny, and it is at this point that we must back out of their affairs."

"I hope they survive."

"As do I, my friend."

Jake listened and thought he heard a man calling out in Italian in the background.

"Where are you?" he asked.

"Oh," Renard said. "You must have heard the postman. Marie is with him at the door. We are vacationing in Tuscany. I thought I had told you, but I might have told little Jacques instead. I talk to him so much, you know."

"Are you at safe haven? I mean the old one you had prepared for us?"

"It is no longer safe haven," Renard said. "It is just haven. We are already safe. Your lady friend, she is arriving today?"

"Yeah. Just before lunch," he said. "Thanks for reminding me. I've got to clean this place up. Give my love to Marie and Jacques."

"It will be done. Give the same to Olivia."

*

The doorbell rang. Jake literally jumped down the stairs, dodged the corner of his pool table and reached for his apartment's lower door. As he opened it, the sun shone behind the loveliest creature he had known.

Olivia held a box of chocolates and a red teddy bear.

"You going to let me in?" she asked.

"After what I went through cleaning this place this morning," Jake said, "you're going to inspect every inch."

She extended her gifts. Jake tossed them onto the pool table and drew her to him.

"It's good to see you, Olivia."

"Let's start this over again," she said.

"It'll be nice having the secrets behind us."

"I think so, too," she said and squeezed him in with a strength he had considered beyond her.

She sniffed, arched her back, and raised her voice.

"You wore Drakkar Noir," she said.

"You said you were ready to try it. It's part of starting over."

"No," she said. "It's no problem. I don't feel sick at all.

She laid her head on his shoulder and clutched his shirt.

"In fact," she said, "I think Drakkar Noir might be my favorite. As long as it's on you."

THE END

978-0-595-47203-1
0-595-47203-6